GRANTA

TRAVEL WRITING

10

Editor: Bill Buford
Assistant Editor: Diane Speakman
Managing Editor: Tracy Shaw
Subscription Promotion: Graham Coster
Executive Editor: Pete de Bolla
Design: Chris Hyde
Editorial Assistants: Michael Comeau, Margaret Costa, Michael Hofmann, Todd McEwen, Teresa Whitfield
Editorial Board: Malcolm Bradbury, Elaine Feinstein, Ian Hamilton, Leonard Michaels
US Editor: Jonathan Levi, 242 West 104th St, New York, New York 10025

Editorial and Subscription Correspondence: Granta, 44a Hobson Street, Cambridge CB1 1NL. (0223) 315290.
All manuscripts are welcome but must be accompanied by a stamped, self-addressed envelope or they cannot be returned.

Subscriptions: £10.00 for four issues.

Back issues: £2.50 for issue 3; £3.50 for issues 5 to 9; issues 1, 2, and 4 are no longer available. All prices include postage.

Granta is set by Lindonprint Typesetters, Cambridge.
Printed in Great Britain.

Granta is published by Granta Publications Ltd and distributed by Penguin Books Ltd, Harmondsworth, Middlesex, England; Penguin Books Australia Ltd, Ringwood, Victoria, Australia; Penguin Books Canada Ltd, 2801 John Street, Markham, Ontario, Canada L3R 1B4; Penguin Books (NZ) Ltd, 182–90 Wairau Road, Auckland 10, New Zealand. This selection copyright © 1984 by Granta Publications Ltd. Each work published in Granta is copyright of the author.

Cover by Chris Hyde

ISSN 0017-3231
ISBN 014-00-7052-4

Published with the assistance of the Eastern Arts Association

Granta 10 reprinted 1984 (three times)

CONTENTS

Observations

Gabriel García Márquez Watching the Rain in Galicia   10

Todd McEwen They tell me you are Big   13

Russell Hoban An Octopus at Paxos   16

Jonathan Raban Sea-Room   19

James Fenton Road to Cambodia   35

Redmond O'Hanlon Into the Heart of Borneo   59

Colin Thubron Night in Vietnam   83

Martha Gellhorn White into Black   93

Bruce Chatwin A Coup   107

Richard Holmes In Stevenson's Footsteps   129

Norman Lewis Village of Cats   153

Saul Bellow Old Paris   163

Patrick Marnham Holy Week   175

Jan Morris Interstate 281   191

Paul Theroux Subterranean Gothic   211

Hugh Brody Jim's Journey   231

Notes from Abroad

William Weaver Italy   247

Notes on Contributors   255

Editorial   5

THE HOGARTH PRESS
A New Life for a Great Name

The new list will be launched
on 29 February
and will include

—— The Best in Travel Writing ——

V.S. PRITCHETT
The Spanish Temper
with a new introduction by the Author

ROBERT LOUIS STEVENSON
The Amateur Emigrant
with an introduction by Jonathan Raban

———— and The Best in ————

Autobiography	Humour
Belles Lettres	Fiction
Biography	Literary Criticism
Crime	Poetry

Editorial

World War Two marked the end of the great age of travel. And it is easy to see why. Not only did the war make travel difficult, but the world that emerged after it—a monoculture of mass consumerism, package-holidays and the extraordinary imperialism of the American hamburger—left little room for the sensibility characteristic of so many of the writers of the twenties and thirties. The books of Robert Byron, say, or Waugh, Auden and Priestley are virtually Edwardian in temperament: they hark back to an earlier time. They wrote, as Paul Fussell has pointed out in *Abroad,* to celebrate a 'Golden Age': the corners of the world uncontaminated by the manifestations of modernity. 'One travelled,' Fussell says, 'to discover the past.'

It is a bit more difficult to account for why, so long after World War Two, there should suddenly be a revival in travel writing—evident not only in the busy reprinting of the travel classics but in the staggering number of new travel writers emerging. In many respects these writers—and the publishers who are retrieving the earlier ones—still address the past, although they now seem to address the past not to discover but to preserve it. Later this year Penguin will re-issue Kevin Andrews's *Athens,* and in his preface to the new edition, Andrews justifies the new interest in old books by his belief that they serve as laments for places now lost to us 'for the simple reason that—without recognizably barbarian invasions—bulldozers have lifted towns and landscapes off the surface of the planet, and cement has been poured into the resulting void.' Andrews's reasoning is evident especially in James Fenton's contribution to this issue. In explaining why he felt the need to write about Cambodia, Fenton says that he wanted to represent, before it disappeared, an old Cambodia, and he

5

cites Norman Lewis, whose *A Dragon Apparent* offers the last view of an old China before it was submerged by the twentieth century. But I am slightly suspicious of Fenton's remarks—they seem incomplete—and they don't account fully for why his piece is so extraordinary and so exciting to read.

Certainly the most obvious attraction of travel writing is in what it represents: escape. And this itch for escape, this need to keep moving, is evident not only in the writing collected here—for Jonathan Raban and Hugh Brody, for instance, it's an obsession—but also in the lives of the authors themselves. They seem—every single one of them—to have some kind of disease; a fever, certainly. This collection is by no means comprehensive, in part because it is extremely difficult commissioning work from travel writers: it is their occupational hazard that they are never home. There are many, for instance, whom I simply never reached. I am convinced that Gavin Young and William Least Heat Moon, author of the successful *Blue Highways,* have never been in one place for longer than the time it takes to eat a meal. In pursuit of Patrick Leigh Fermor, I had a very curious conversation—it must have lasted for about five minutes—in which I spoke a slow, clear English to a woman who, understanding nothing, replied in what I assume to have been a slow, clear Greek. I did gather two pieces of information, however: 'Fermor' and something that sounded very much like 'Spain'.

It wasn't much easier with the authors I did reach. It took me weeks to discover just where on the globe I might find Paul Theroux, and when I did (he was rowing around Long Island) it took me another fifteen days before I ever got him on the phone. After reports that Bruce Chatwin, who seems to be congenitally absent, was momentarily in Wales, then Australia and finally Greece, I heard a rumour that his rucksack had arrived, mysteriously, at a friend's flat. Expecting that the man himself would follow, I immediately started writing letters, none of which were ever answered: inveterately mobile, Chatwin merely arrived one afternoon in the office. As we go to press, there are—of the seventeen contributors to this issue—only five still in the country.

I n a time of unemployment and economic restraint, it is of course tempting to see a relationship between the escape these authors offer and our own plight. Their tales of the exotic could be seen to bear the same value as that of books and film, say, during the depression: they provide arm-chair emancipation. And emancipation of this sort is certainly available in the writings collected here. But they are also achieving something else.

When I recall these pieces, I do not immediately think of descriptions of place. James Fenton was in Southeast Asia for two years; he did stay in a Buddhist monastery; he did eat a bowl of live ants. Redmond O'Hanlon can indeed identify virtually every bird flying in the Borneo jungle. Martha Gellhorn was stoned by blacks. Colin Thubron did sleep in a cemetery in Saigon and was, in fact, surrounded throughout the night by howling dogs. Bruce Chatwin was caught in a coup in Benin and, in going over the proofs with me, he kept consulting his notebook to recall the exact phrases used by the corporal who claimed that Chatwin's pen was not a pen but a gun. But these pieces succeed not by virtue of the details they report—exotic as they are—but by the contrivance of their reporting. They are all informed by the sheer glee of story-telling, a narrative eloquence that situates them, with wonderful ambiguity, somewhere between fiction and fact.

There is of course nothing new in this kind of ambiguity, although travel writing seems to be its purest expression—purer even than the New Journalism of the sixties and seventies to which it bears more than a few similarities. But if there is a revival in travel writing, this ambiguity—this generic androgeny—is partly reponsible for it. Travel writing is the beggar of literary forms: it borrows from the memoir, reportage and, most important, the novel. It is, however, pre-eminently a narrative told in the first person, authenticated by lived experience. It satisfies a need. A need for a fiction answerable, somehow, to the world. Or perhaps I've got it wrong. Perhaps it's a need for a world answerable to our fictions.

Bill Buford

OBSERVATIONS

Watching the Rain in Galicia
Gabriel García Márquez

My old friend, the painter, poet and novelist, Héctor Rojas Herazo—whom I hadn't seen for a long time—must have felt a tremor of compassion when he saw me in Madrid in a crush of photographers and journalists, for he came up to me and whispered: 'Remember that from time to time you should be nice to yourself.' In fact, it had been months—perhaps years—since I had given myself a well-deserved present. So I decided to give myself what was, in reality, one of my dreams: a visit to Galicia.

No one who enjoys eating can think of Galicia without first thinking of the pleasures of its cuisine. 'Homesickness starts with food,' said Che Guevara, pining perhaps for the vast roasts of his native Argentina while they, men alone in the night in Sierra Maestra, spoke of war. For me, too, homesickness for Galicia had started with food even before I had been there. The fact is that my grandmother, in the big house at Aracataca, where I got to know my first ghosts, had the delightful role of baker and she carried on even when she was already old and nearly blind, until the river flooded, ruined the oven and no one in the house felt like rebuilding it. But my grandmother's vocation was so strong that when she could no longer make bread, she made hams. Delicious hams, though we children did not like them—children never like the novelties of adults—even though the flavour of that first taste has remained recorded for ever on the memory of my palate. I never found it again in any of the many and various hams I ate later in any of my good or my bad years until, by chance, I tasted—forty years later, in Barcelona—an innocent slice of shoulder of pork. All the joy, all the uncertainties, and all the solitude of childhood suddenly came back to me with that, the unmistakable flavour of the hams my grandmother made.

From that experience grew my interest in tracing the ancestry of this flavour, and, in looking for it, I found my own among the frenetic greens of May, the sea and the fertile rains and eternal winds of the Galician countryside. Only then did I understand where my grandmother had got that credulity which allowed her to live in a supernatural world in which everything was possible and where rational explanations were totally lacking in validity. And I understood from where her passion for preparing food for hypothetical visitors came and her habit of singing all day. 'You have to make a meat and a fish dish because you never know what people will want when they come to lunch,' she would say, when she heard the train whistle. She died very old and blind and with her sense of reality completely unhinged, to the point where she would talk about her oldest memories as if they were happening at that moment, and she held conversations with the dead she had known alive in her remote youth. I was telling a Galician friend about this last week in Santiago de Compostela and he said: 'Then your grandmother must have been Galician, no doubt about it, because she was crazy.' In fact all the Galicians I know, and those whom I met without having time to get to know them, seem to have been born under the sign of Pisces.

I don't know where the shame of being a tourist comes from. I've heard many friends in full touristic swing say that they don't want to mix with tourists, not realizing that even though they don't mix with them, they are just as much tourists as the others. When I visit a place and haven't enough time to get to know it more than superficially, I unashamedly assume my role as tourist. I like to join those lightning tours in which the guides explain everything you see out of the window—'On your right and left, ladies and gentlemen...'—one of the reasons being that then I know once and for all everything I needn't bother to see when I go out later to explore the place on my own.

Anyway, Santiago de Compostela doesn't leave time for such details: the city imposes itself immediately, complete and timeless, as if one had been born there. I had always believed, and continue to believe, really, that there is no more beautiful square in the world than the one in Siena. The only place that made me doubt its authority as the most beautiful square is the one in Santiago de Compostela. Its poise and its youthful air prohibit you from even thinking about its venerable age; instead, it looks as if it had been built the day before by someone who had lost their sense of time. Perhaps this impression does not come from the square itself but from its being—like every corner of the city—steeped to its soul in everyday life. It is a lively city, swept along by a crowd of happy, boisterous students who don't give it a chance to grow old. On the walls that remain intact, plant life makes its way through the cracks in an implacable struggle to outlive oblivion, and at every step, as if it were the most natural thing in the world, one is confronted by the miracle of stones in full bloom.

It rained for three days, not inclemently, but with unseasonable spells of radiant sun. Nevertheless, my Galician friends did not seem to see these golden intervals and apologized for the rain all the time. Perhaps not even they were aware that Galicia without rain would have been a disappointment, because theirs is a mythical country—far more than the Galicians themselves realize—and in mythical lands the sun never comes out. 'If you'd come last week you'd have had lovely weather,' they told us, shamefaced. 'It's very unusual weather for the time of year,' they insisted, forgetting about Valle-Inclán, Rosalia de Castro and every Galician poet who ever lived, in whose books it rains from the beginning of creation, and through which an interminable wind blows, perhaps the very same that sows the lunatic seed which makes so many Galicians delightfully different.

It rained in the city, it rained in the vivid fields, it rained in the lacustrine paradise of the Arosa and the Vigo estuaries; and, over the bridge, it rained in the undaunted and almost unreal Plaza de Cambados; and it even rained on the island of La Toja, where there's a hotel from another world and time, which seems to be waiting for the rain to stop, the wind to cease and the sun to shine in order to start living. We walked through this rain as if through a state of grace, eating shellfish galore, the only live shellfish left in this devastated world; eating fish which, on the plate, still looked like fish; and salads that continued to grow on the table. And we knew that all this was by virtue of the rain which never stops falling.

It's now many years since, in a Barcelona restaurant, I heard the writer, Álvaro Cunqueiros, talk about Galician food and his descriptions were so dazzling that I took them for the ravings of a Galician. As far back as I can remember I've heard Galician emigrants talk of Galicia and I always thought their memories were coloured by nostalgic illusions. Today I recall my seventy-two hours in Galicia and I wonder if they were all true or if I myself have begun to fall victim to the same delirium as my grandmother. Among Galicians—as we all know—you never can tell.

Translated from the Spanish by Margaret Costa

They Tell Me You Are Big
Todd McEwen

*T*he technological parade of welcome: I was already dead with fatigue. Thank you for flying with us today, here is your ticket, change planes in Chicago, you'll have to change planes in Chicago, change in Chicago. They said it so often I began to get the idea I should change planes in Chicago. *Change planes*: the phrase began to lose any reference to travel; it acquired a dread phenomenological taint. But I did not change those sorts of planes in Chicago. Rather, in Chicago I *changed size.* For when I deplaned (more tech-talk) I walked into Big People Land.

I was obliged to go a short distance through a glass tube, the story of a life, from one gate to another. I then had an hour, a whole, giant hour to myself. In Big People Land. And there they were. They were all about me: large surely-moving salesmen and mammoth middle managers, corn-fed beef-fed farm-bred monuments to metabolism. Flying from dairy states to beef capitals to commodities centres. From Fon-du-Lac to Dubuque, their huge briefcases *stuffed with meat.* Clinching beefy deals with muscular handshakes. Their faces were florid Mt Rushmores with aviator spectacles and sideburns uniformly metallic; their eyes, bovine, the size of Dutch plates, reflected their Low Country ancestries. Their hands were steam-shovels, their shoes big as our tiny neurotic New York family car. I'm not talking fat, although flesh is essential in Chicago. I'm talking big-boned, as the apologists say. I, a tiny under-nourished New York worrier, had been injected into the enlarged heart of America.

Airports like abattoirs are white. All this moving meat, these great bodies laughing, phoning, making valuable contacts, astonished me. I was overwhelmed by the size of everything and everybody, their *huge bigness*! I had to sit down. But where? Everything I sat in dwarfed, *engulfed* me. I was a baby opossum, writhing in a tablespoon in a Golden Nature Guide. I felt fear, tininess and hunger. I decided the only way to become as big as the Big People was to begin eating.

In the infinite coffee shop, my eyes struggled to take in the polyptych menu and its thousand offerings. Eggs with legs, friendly forks and spoons marched across it. GOOD MORNING! *Barnyard Suggestions...* What! I thought. Wanna meet this chicken in the hayloft in half an hour, fella? But these were not that kind of barnyard suggestion. Here in Big People Land, land-o-lotsa wholesomeness, they were suggesting I eat the following: **(1)** 3 strips of bacon, 2 pancakes, 2 eggs (any style), 2 sausages, juice, toast and coffee; **(2)** 6 strips of bacon, 5 pancakes, 4 eggs (any style), 3 sausages, juice, toast and coffee; or **(3)** 12 strips of bacon, 9 pancakes, 7 eggs (any style), 1 ½ gallons of juice, 3 lbs of toast and a 'Bottomless Pit' (which I took to be a typographical error for 'Pot') of coffee. Thus emptying any barnyard I could imagine of all life. Again I was lost. I felt I was visiting Karnak. I pleaded for half an order of toast, eight pieces.

Outside the window, far away, Chicago was dawning. Obsidian towers, an art deco pipe-organ sprouting from the gold prairie, Lake Michigan still dark beyond. A brachycephalic woman was seated opposite me, biting big things. Her teeth were the size of horse teeth. She said we could see into the next state. She was eating such big things and so quickly a wind was blowing at our table. I turned from this and peered out through the clear air, into the next state. In the far distance I saw great shapes which I knew weren't mountains but my giant Mid-western relatives I am too small ever to visit.

Now I was filled with huge toast. I crawled, miniscule, back through the tubes to the gate. I bought a newspaper and my money looked puny and foreign in the vendor's big paw. In the chairs of Big People Land, my feet never touched the floor. I began to open the *Sun-Times*. But. It was big. Here it wasn't even Sunday and I was suddenly engaged in a desperate battle with what seemed to be a colossal duvet, a *mural* made of incredibly stiff paper. It unfolded and unfolded. It was a whale passing by, it covered me and all my possessions. It surged over the pillar ashtray and began to creep like fog over the gentleman next to me. Help I said. Scuse me, watch your paper there he said. *His tongue was the size of my dog.*

I was exhausted. I could do nothing but wait for my plane to be announced. I watched the Big People. What is it like to move about the world, to travel, free of the fears of the tiny: the fear of being crushed by all the big things Big People make and use? Not just newspapers and barnyard suggestions and airplanes but their Big Companies and their Eternal Truths and the endless statistics of baseball.

The airport was hugely hot with Big-People warmth. Warmth from the roaring heaters of their big roaring cars, from the blazing camp-fires of their substantial vacations. And I thought perhaps a few of these Big People were glowing not only from tremendous breakfasts and the excitement and reward of business but from their still-warm still-tousled beds of large love.

One Less Octopus at Paxos
Russell Hoban

We were at our regular swimming-place which is partly pebbly beach and partly big flat rocks when there came along in the shallows among the rocks by the shore a stocky young woman in a hooded wet-suit top with a diving mask and a snorkel and flippers and a speargun and a big sheath-knife strapped to her right leg. She was nosing among the underwater rocks in an ardent and serious way like a dog at a rabbit hole. She fired the speargun, then held up the spear with an octopus writhing on it. It was a mottled pinky-brown and its head was about as big as two clasped hands.

She slid it off the spear, grabbed it by a couple of tentacles, and beat it again and again on a flat rock, spattering briny drops each time. The octopus clung to the rock with its free tentacles; they came away with sounds like kisses as she peeled it off the rock and put it into a plastic bag.

She had pushed up her mask and pushed back her hood. She had a dark face, a serious look and a heavy frown. She had short dark curling hair. She had a squeeze-bottle of detergent; a bystander explained that she'd squirted it into the octopus's hiding-place in the rocks to make it come out (not being able to breathe) and be speared by her.

Later I found myself imagining that young woman's preparations for her trip to Paxos. I saw her at the windows of travel agents, I saw her turning the pages of brochures, I saw her looking at octopus pictures in books. I saw her marking off days on a calendar. I saw her at the supermarket, picking up bottles of detergent and reading their labels. I saw her packing her wet-suit, her mask and snorkel, her flippers, her speargun, her knife, her bottle of detergent. I saw her in the underground, sitting up straight with a serious face, going to Victoria. Her luggage was a rucksack and a diver's bag made of heavy

PVC. I saw her on the train to Gatwick. I saw her checking in at the airline counter. I saw her on the plane to Corfu eating breakfast with a serious face, perhaps reading a diving magazine.

I saw her on the boat from Corfu to Paxos looking steadfastly at the sun-points on the water and watching for the shape of the island.

I saw her in her room unpacking the wet-suit, the mask and snorkel, the flippers, the speargun, the knife, the bottle of detergent. I saw her sitting on the bed looking down at her naked feet.

Distant View of a Minaret

AND OTHER STORIES

ALIFA RIFAAT
Translated by DENYS JOHNSON-DAVIES

More convincingly than any other woman writing in Arabic today, Alifa Rifaat, an Egyptian in her early fifties, lifts the veil on what it means to be a woman living within a traditional Muslim society.

Her writing articulates a subtle revolt against, and a sympathetic insight into, the place of women in the essentially male-dominated Islamic environment. Change, development, understanding are called for, but the invocation is couched within a strictly religious, even orthodox Qur'anic framework.

'Her stories…have a frankness and a power that makes them of immediate relevance to the West' *Guardian*

£6.95   Hardback

Quartet Books Limited
A member of the Namara Group
27/29 Goodge Street
London W1P 1FD

JONATHAN RABAN

SEA-ROOM

Whenever I find myself growing grim about the mouth; whenever it is damp, drizzly November in my soul; whenever I find myself involuntarily pausing before coffin warehouses, and bringing up the rear of every funeral I meet; and especially whenever my hypos get such an upper hand of me, that it requires a strong moral principle to prevent me from deliberately stepping into the street, and methodically knocking people's hats off—then, I account it high time to get to sea as soon as I can. This is my substitute for pistol and ball. With a philosophical flourish Cato throws himself upon his sword; I quietly take to the ship.

Herman Melville, *Moby Dick*

It was the classic last resort. I wanted to run away to sea.

It started as a nervous itch, like an attack of eczema. All spring and summer I scratched at it, and the more I scratched the more the affliction spread. There was no getting rid of the thing. Lodged in my head was an image, in suspiciously heightened colour, of a very small ship at sea.

It was more ark than boat. It contained the entire life of one man, and it floated serenely offshore: half in, half out of the world. The face of its solitary navigator was as dark as demerara. He wasn't flying a flag. His boat was a private empire, a sovereign state in miniature, a tight little, right little liberal regime. He was a world away from where I stood. Lucky man. He'd slung his hook, and upped and gone. Afloat, abroad, following his compass-needle as it trembled in its dish of paraffin, he was a figure of pure liberty. He had the world just where he wanted it. When he looked back at the land from which he'd sailed, it was arranged for him in brilliant perspective, its outlines clean, like the cut-out scenery of a toy theatre.

I was plagued by this character. Each time I gave him notice to quit my private territorial waters, he sailed mockingly past. Smoke from his pipe rose in a fine column of question-marks over my horizon. His laughter was loud and derisive. He wouldn't go away.

I was landlocked and fidgety. I paced the deck of an urban flat and dreamed of sea-room, with the uncomfortable feeling that I'd picked up a dream which didn't belong to me, as if I'd tuned in my mental radio to the wrong station.

L ots of people would claim the dream as their own. The idea of taking ship and heading off into the blue is, after all, a central part of the mythology of being English. Elias Canetti writes that the 'famous individualism' of the Englishman stems directly from his habit of thinking of himself as a lone mariner; a perception endorsed by whole libraries of bad Victorian novels.

In the books, the English are always running away to sea. The ocean is the natural refuge of every bankrupt, every young man crossed in love, every compromised second son. The Peregrines and Septimuses of the world behave like lemmings: their authors seem powerless to stop them from racing for the nearest quayside at the first sign of trouble.

They do it with such stylish finality too. The bag is secretly packed in the small hours, the farewell letter left like a suicide note beside the ormolu clock on the hall table. Goodbye, family! Goodbye, friends! Goodbye, England!

They close the front door behind them as gently as if they were dismantling a bomb. They tiptoe across the drive, careful not to wake the dogs, their faces grave at the audacity of what they've done. They pass the misty church, the doctor's house behind its cliff of pines, the bulky shadows of Home Farm. By sunrise, they're on the open road, their past already out of sight.

When next heard of, they are up on deck with a full gale blowing out of the Sou'west. The ship is falling away from under their feet in a mountainous swell. They cling to the shrouds, their hands bloody from hauling on ropes and scrubbing decks with holystone. They are changed men.

The sea voyage is more than an adventure; it is a rite of passage, as decisive as a wedding. It marks the end of the old self and the birth of the new. It is a great purifying ordeal. Storms and saltwater cleanse the ne'er-do-well and turn him into a hero. In the last chapter he will get the girl, the vicar's blessing and the family fortune.

I knew that I was pushing my luck, and running against the clock.

Peregrine and Septimus aren't usually men of forty with dental problems and mortgages to pay. I wasn't a scapegrace young tough. I wasn't made for the outdoors. My experience of the sea was confined to paddling in it with the bottoms of my trousers rolled up, collecting coloured pebbles, and lolling on the edge of the ocean in a stripey deckchair until the peeling skin on my nose made me head back to the more manageable world of the hotel bar.

My kinship with the runaways was of a different kind. What I envied in them was the writing of their letters of farewell.

Dear Father,

By the time you read this, I shall be...

Magic words. I was excited by their gunpowdery whiff of action and decision. Both were in pretty short supply where I was sitting. Moping at my worktable, I decided to change a comma to a semi-colon. Framed in the window under a bleary sky, the huge grey tub of the Kensal Green gasometer sank lugubriously downwards as West London cooked its Sunday lunch.

...far away on the high seas. Please tell Mother...

Well, I had fallen out with the family, too. I couldn't put a date on the quarrel: there'd been no firelit showdown in the library, no sign of the riding whip, not even any duns at the front door. It had been a long unloving wrangle, full of edgy silences, niggling resentments and strained efforts at politeness. One day I woke to realize that there was nowhere I felt less at home than home.

Perhaps it was simply that I'd turned into an old fogey a bit earlier in life than most people. At any rate, my own country suddenly seemed foreign—with all the power that a foreign land has to make the lonely visitor sweat with fury at his inability to understand the obvious. *Je ne comprends pas! Min fadlak! Non parlo Italiano! Sprechen Sie English—please!*

I'd started to forget things, as the senile do. Wanting a small brown loaf, I strolled down to the bakery on the corner. I should have remembered. It didn't sell bread any more. It sold battery-powered vibrators, blow-up rubber dolls and videotapes of naked men and women doing ingenious things to each other's bodies. The African Asian who now rented this flesh shop was noisily barricading his windows with sheets of corrugated iron.

He seemed calm enough; a man competently at home on his own patch. He expected a race riot at the weekend.

'The police come and tell us to do it. Saturday, we have trouble here. Too many Rastas—' he waved, in a vague easterly direction, at the dark continent of Portobello, and placidly banged in another nail.

He made me feel like a tourist; and like a tourist I goggled obediently at the local colour of this odd world at my doorstep. Four doors down from the bakery there'd been an ailing chemist's full of stoppered bottles and painted drawers with Latin names. Someone had pulled it out of the block like a rotten wisdom tooth and left a winking cave of galactic war machines. All day long they chattered, bleeped and yodelled, as the local kids zapped hell out of the Aliens. The kids themselves looked pretty alien to me: angry boys, bald as turnips, in army boots and grandfathers' braces; dozy punks with erect quiffs of rainbow hair, like a troupe of Apaches.

Our only patch of civic green space had been taken over by joggers in tracksuits. They wore yellow latex earmuffs clamped round their skulls with coronas of silver wire. They were filling their heads with something: Vivaldi? The Sex Pistols? No. Both would be equally old hat. They quartered the oily turf, blank faced, as exclusive and remote as astronauts.

The streets themselves looked as they'd always done; imperially snug and solid. On a sunny morning, you could easily believe that nothing essential had changed among these avenues of plane trees and tall, white stucco mansions. Even now, there were nannies to be seen—solemn Filipino women, who pushed their pramloads as if they were guarding a reliquary of holy bones in a religious procession. Vans from Harrods still stopped at brass-plated tradesmen's entrances. From a high open window there still came the sound of a child practising scales on the family piano. *Doh, reh, me, fa, ploink. Fa, fa, soh, lah, tee, ploink, doh.*

But there were misplaced notes on the streets, too. At every hour there were too many men about—men of my own age with the truant look of schoolboys out bird-nesting. They huddled outside the betting shops. Alone, they studied the handful of cards in the window of the government Job Centre. The vacancies were for Girl Fridays, linotype operators, book-keepers—nothing for them.

Nor for me, it seemed. I felt supernumerary here. Letting myself in to the whitewashed, partitioned box where I lived, I was met by the wifely grumble of the heating system. It wasn't much of a welcome, and I returned it with a stare of husbandly rancour at the litter of unread books, unwashed dishes and unwritten pages that told me I was home.

I wasn't proud of the way I lived, lodged here contingently like a piece of grit in a crevice. There was something shameful in being so lightly attached to the surrounding world. I wasn't married. I was childless. I didn't even have a proper job.

When I had to give the name of my employer on official forms, I wrote: 'SELF'. This Self, though, was a strange and temperamental boss. He would make me redundant for weeks on end. He sent me on sick leave and sabbaticals, summoned me back for a few days' worth of overtime, then handed me my papers again.

'What am I supposed to do now?'

'Get on your bike,' said Self, not bothering to look up from the crossword in *The Times*.

I'd grown tired of my dealings with Self. He struck me as a textbook example of what was wrong with British industry. He was bad management personified: lazy, indifferent, smugly wedded to his old-fashioned vices. Self loved the two-bottle business lunch. He collected invitations to drinks at six-to-eight. His telephone bills were huge. He poisoned the air with tobacco smoke. It was a miracle that under Self's directorship the company hadn't yet gone bust.

I told him about the Right to Work.

'We'd better lunch on that,' said Self.

By the brandy stage, Self and I were reconciled. We merged back into each other.

I was fogbound and drifting. One morning I breathed on the windowpane and played noughts and crosses against myself. I waited for the telephone to peal. It didn't. In the afternoon I went to the public library and looked up my name in the catalogue to check that I existed. At night I listened to the breaking surf of traffic in the streets, and the city seemed as cold and strange as Murmansk.

An hour of so before the house began to shudder to the cannonball passage of the underground trains, before the early-morning rattle of milk bottles on steps, I was woken by the bell of the convent down the road. It was ringing for Prime and sounded thin and squeaky like a wheezing lung. The sun never rises on North Kensington with any marked enthusiasm, and the light that had begun to smear the walls of the room looked dingy and secondhand. I didn't much care for the appearance of this new day, and took flight into a deep sea-dream.

In novels, when the black sheep of the family takes ship, his running away is really a means of coming home. His voyage restores him to his relations and to society. I had the same end in view. I wanted to go home; and the most direct, most exhilarating route back there lay by sea. Afloat with charts and compass, I'd find my bearings again. I saw myself inching along the coast, navigating my way around my own country and my own past, taking sights and soundings until I had the place's measure. It was to be an escape, an apprenticeship and a homecoming.

It was a consoling fantasy. I sustained it by going off at weekends and looking at real boats. As a minor consequence of the recession, every harbour in England was crowded with boats for sale: hulks under tarpaulins, rich men's toy motor cruisers, abandoned racing yachts, converted lifeboats and ships' tenders. Their prices were drifting steadily downwards, like the pound; and their brokers had the air of distressed gentlefolk eking out the last of the family capital. They made a feeble play of busyness and spotted me at once as another optimist trying to rid himself of his unaffordable boat. *No dice*, their eyes said, as they shuffled the paper on their desks.

'I'm looking for a boat to sail round Britain in,' I said, trying the words out on the air to see if they had the ring of true idiocy.

'Ah. *Are* you now—' The broker's face was rearranging itself fast, but it looked as if he'd forgotten the expression of avuncular confidence that he was now trying to achieve. All his features stopped in mid-shift: they registered simple disbelief.

He showed me a wreck with a sprung plank. 'She's just the job, old boy. It's what she was built for.'

A sheet of flapping polythene had been pinned down over the foredeck to stop leaks. The glass was missing from a wheelhouse window. It was easy to see oneself going down to the bottom in a boat like that. It had the strong aura of emergency flares, Mayday calls and strings of big bubbles.

'Know what she was up for when she first came in? Ten grand. And that was over four years ago—think what inflation must have done to that by now.' The broker consulted the sky piously, as if the heavens were in the charge of a white-bearded wrathful old economist. 'At two-five, old boy…two-five…she's a steal.'

Lowering myself down slippery dockside ladders to inspect these unloved and unlovable craft, I felt safe enough. The voyage stayed securely in the realm of daydream. I liked the pretence involved in my seaside shopping expeditions, and from each broker I learned a new trick or two. I copied the way they dug their thumbnails into baulks of timber and the knowledgeable sniff with which they tasted the trapped air of the saloon. I picked up enough snippets of shoptalk to be able to speak menacingly of rubbing-strakes and keel-bolts; and soon the daydream itself began to be fleshed out in glibly realistic detail.

As I came to put names to all its parts, the boat in my head grew more substantial and particular by the day. Built to sail out of the confused seas of Ladbroke Grove and Notting Hill, it had to be tubby and trawler-like. It would be broad in the beam, high in the bow, and framed in oak. It would ride out dirty weather with the buoyancy of a puffin; inside, it would be as snug as a low-ceilinged tudor cottage. It was perfectly designed to go on imaginary voyages and make dream-landfalls.

Then I bought a sextant, and the whole business suddenly stopped being a fantasy.

The sextant was old. I found it stacked up with a collection of gramophones and ladies' workboxes in a junkshop. Its brass frame was mottled green-and-black, the silvering on its mirrors had started to blister and peel off. It came in a wooden casket full of accessory telescopes and lenses bedded down in compartments of soft baize.

It had been made for J.H.C. Minter RN, whose name was engraved in scrolled letters on the arc by J.H. Steward, 457 West Strand, London. A certificate vouching for its accuracy had been issued by the National Physical Observatory, Richmond, in July 1907. Its pedigree made it irresistible. I had no very sure idea as to how a sextant actually worked, but this tarnished instrument looked like a prize and an omen.

For the first few days of ownership, I contented myself with rubbing away at it with Brasso until a few of its more exposed parts gleamed misty gold out of the surrounding verdigris. I loosened its hinged horizon- and sun--glasses with sewing--machine oil. I brushed the dust out of the baize and polished the oak case. Midshipman Minter's (*was* he a midshipman?) sextant was restored to a pretty and intricate ornament for a drawing--room.

Next I went to a shop in the Minories and came away with a chart of the Thames estuary, a pair of compasses, a protractor, a nautical almanac and a book on celestial navigation. At last I was in business again with a real vocation to follow. For months I had stumbled along at my old journeywork of writing reviews of other people's books and giving voice to strong opinions that I didn't altogether feel. Now I was returned to being a freshman student, with the art of finding one's own way round the globe as my major subject. I holed up with the sextant and the book on navigation, ready to stay awake all night if that was what was needed to master the basic principles of the discipline.

I read on page one:

> We navigate by means of the Sun, the Moon, the planets and the stars. Forget the Earth spinning round the Sun with the motionless stars infinite distances away, and imagine that the Earth is the centre of the universe and that all the heavenly bodies circle slowly round us, the stars keeping their relative positions while the Sun, Moon and planets change their positions in relation to each other and to the stars. This pre--Copernican outlook comes easily as we watch the heavenly bodies rise and set, and is a help in practical navigation.

Obediently I saw the earth as the still centre of things, with the sun and the stars as its satellites. I was happy to forget Copernicus: my own private cosmology had always been closet-Ptolemaic. This geo--centric, ego--centric view of the world was infinitely preferable to the icy abstractions and gigantic mileages of the physicists. Of course the sun revolved around the earth, rising in the east and setting in the west; of course we were the focus of creation, the pivot around which the universe turns. To have one's gut-instincts so squarely confirmed by a book with a title like *Celestial Navigation* was more than I could possibly have bargained for. I became an instant convert. I saw Sirius and Arcturus tracking slowly round us like protective outriders; I watched Polaris wobbling, a little insecurely, high over the North Pole.

For the essence of celestial navigation turned out, as I read, to consist in a sort of universal egoism. The heavenly bodies had been pinned up in the sky to provide an enormous web of convenient lines and triangles. Wherever he was, the navigator was always the crux of the arrangement, measuring the solar system to discover himself on his ship, bang at the heart of the matter.

Here is how you find out where you are. You are standing somewhere on the curved surface of a globe in space. Imagine a line extending from the dead-centre of the Earth, through your body, and going on up into the distant sky. The spot where it joins the heavens over your head is your zenith, and it is as uniquely personal to you as your thumbprint.

Now: your latitude is the angle formed at the Earth's centre between the equator and your zenith-line. You are a precise number of degrees and minutes north or south of the equator. Check it out in an atlas. The latitude of my North Kensington flat is 51°31′ North.

The sun, remember, revolves around the earth. Imagine now that it is noon on one of those rare days—at the time of the spring or autumn equinox—when the sun is exactly over the equator. Get your sextant ready.

Focus the telescope, twiddle the knobs and set the mirrors to work. Excellent. You have now measured the angle formed between your horizon and the sun over the equator. If you happen to be standing in my flat, I can tell you that the figure you have just read off from your sextant is 38°29′.

And what use, pray, is that? inquires Poor Yorick.

It is a great deal of use. Take it away from 90° and what do you get?

51°31′. Our latitude.

Precisely.

I don't understand why.

Think. Your zenith-line cuts your horizon at right-angles. If the sun is over the equator, then the angle formed on the earth's surface between the sun and your zenith-line is the same as the angle formed at the earth's centre between your zenith-line and the equator.

I never did understand spherical geometry.

Nor did I, but the calculation works, and you can play exactly the same game with the Pole Star as you can with the sun. Find the angle between it and your horizon, and you can quickly work out your latitude in degrees north or south.

51°31′ North is not a position: it is a line several thousand miles long encircling the Earth. To find North Kensington on that line, you must time the sun with a chronometer and so discover your longitude.

Longitude—your personal angle east or west of the zero meridian—is measured from Greenwich. 'Noon' is not a time on the clock: it is the instant when the sun is highest overhead above your particular meridian. In North Kensington, which is West of Greenwich, noon comes later than it does to the Royal Observatory, for the sun goes round the earth from east to west at a reliable speed of fifteen degrees of longitude in an hour, or 360° in a day.

Pick up the sextant again and clock the angles of the sun around noon. It rises...rises...rises, and now it starts to dip. What was the exact moment when it peaked? Just forty-eight seconds after noon by Greenwich Mean Time? Please don't argue. Let's agree that it was forty-eight and not a second more or less.

Forty-eight seconds, at a minute of longitude for every four seconds of time, is twelve minutes of longitude. You are precisely twelve minutes West of Greenwich, or 0°12′ W.

So there is home: 51°31′ N, 0°12′ W. St Quintin Avenue, London W10, England, the World, the Celestial Sphere. How easily is the lost sheep found, at least at noon on the vernal equinox, with the aid of Midshipman Minter's sextant. No matter how twisty the lane, or how many back alleys must be broached to reach him, the navigator dwells in the intersection between two angles. His position is absolute and verified in heaven. It all makes a great deal more sense than house numbers and postal codes.

That is the theory. But nautical astronomy is founded on a nice conceit, a useful lie about the way the universe works. It's muddied by the unruly behaviour of the sun and stars as they whizz round us on the celestial sphere. The sun, unfortunately, is a vagrant and unpunctual bird. Only twice in the year is it actually over the equator at noon. Between March and September it strays North, lying at a slightly different angle every day; between September and March it goes south. Solar noon never quite corresponds with noon by Greenwich Mean Time. It can be late or early, according to the clock, by as much as twenty minutes.

It would have been pleasant to go abroad, Crusoe-fashion, with just a sextant and a good clock. In practice, apparently, both were useless without a book of tables called an *Ephemeris*—tables that are meant to keep one posted on what all the heavenly bodies are up to at any particular moment.

It was time to take my first noon sight. I unfolded the sextant from its wrapping of dusters, feeling that I was handling an instrument of natural magic. From the *Ephemeris*, I'd found that today, because the sun was now down south over Africa, nineteen degrees beyond the equator, it was running three minutes late.

I stood at the kitchen window and squinted through the telescope at the jam of cars and trucks moving slowly past on the elevated motorway like targets in a shooting-gallery, and made my first significant and disconcerting discovery: London has no horizon.

This was serious. Without a horizon, you don't know where you are. Unless you can measure the angle between yourself, the sun and the plane surface of the earth, you might as well be underground. London presented an impenetrable face of concrete, clotted stuccowork, bare trees, billboards, glass, steel, tarmac and no horizon anywhere. No wonder it was famous for getting lost in.

I had to guess at where the city's notional horizon might be, and found a window-ful of typists four floors up in a nearby office block. I focused the eyepiece on the girls and gently lowered the reflected image of the sun to join them in their typing pool. It was three minutes past noon. The girls had a peaky, distracted, time-for-lunch look; the sun, clarified through blue smoked glass, was rubicund and warty. The girls worked on, oblivious to the presence of this uninvited guest, as I twiddled the micrometer-screw with my thumb and laid the sun neatly between the filing cabinet and the Pirelli calendar.

With the swivelling magnifier on the arm of the sextant I read the sun's altitude on the inlaid-silver scale, took away the nineteen-degree declination of the sun, subtracted the total from ninety, and found my latitude—45°30′ N.

Had I only been in Milan or Portland, Oregon, it would have been spot-on. As it was, it did at least put a precise figure on the complaint from which I'd been suffering for the last few months: I was just six degrees and one minute out of kilter with where I was supposed to be.

The details were wonky but the exercise opened a shutter on a tantalizing chink of air and space. It seemed to me that the navigator with his sextant had a unique and privileged view of the world and his place in it. He stood happily outside its social and political arrangements, conducting himself in strict relation to the tides, the moon, the sun and stars. He was an exemplary symbol of solitude and independence. His access to a body of arcane and priestly knowledge made him a Magus in a world where Magi were in deplorably short supply; and I was bitten by pangs of romantic envy every time I thought of him. The fact that he was probably also soaked to the skin, parking his breakfast over the rail, with his circulation failing in fingers and toes, didn't then strike me as being either likely or relevant. This was North Kensington, after all, where the sea-beyond-the-city was always unruffled, bright and cobalt-blue.

I tacked up a quotation from *Purchas His Pilgrims* over my desk:

The services of the Sea, they are innumerable: it yields…to studious and religious minds a Map of Knowledge, Mystery of Temperance, Exercise of Continence, Schoole of Prayer, Meditation, Devotion and Sobrietie…. It hath on it Tempests and Calmes to chastise the Sinnes, to exercise the faith of Sea-men; manifold affections in it self, to affect and stupefie the subtilest Philosopher…. The Sea yeelds Action to the bodie, Meditation to the Minde, the World to the World, all parts thereof to each part, by this Art of Arts, Navigation.

In the seventeeth century the navigator really had been the hero of the moment: John Donne, for instance, could define passionate love in terms of the movement of a pair of navigator's compasses on a chart, and Purchas's seductive litany had in it all the intellectual excitement of seagoing in the English Renaissance. There was something worthwhile to aim at. It would, I thought, be wonderful to be able to salvage just a small fraction of that sense of the philosophical bounty of the sea.

Leaning out of the window to shoot the sun, the sextant clamped to my eye, I attracted the attention of a good many upturned faces in the street below. Even in North Kensington it's rare to see such an unabashed voyeur in action in the middle of the day, and I came in for a fine selection of sniggers, jeers and whistles. The passers-by were quite correct in their assessment of my case: I was a peeping-Tom. I felt aroused and elated by what I was watching through the telescope—the teasing prospect of another life, a new way of being in the world, coming slowly into sharp-focus.

As soon as I saw it, I recognized the boat as the same craft that I'd been designing in my head for weeks. The tide had left it stranded on a gleaming mudbank up a Cornish estuary. It stood alone, in ungainly silhouette; a cross between Noah's abandoned ark and the official residence of the old woman who lived in a shoe.

The local boatyard had given me the keys and a warrant to view. I slithered across the mud in city clothes, past knots of bait-diggers forking worms into buckets. There wasn't much romance in the discovery of the boat. Each new footstep released another bubble of bad-egg air. The trees on the foreshore, speckled a dirty white with china clay dust from the docks across the river, looked as if they had dandruff. The surface of the mud itself was webbed and veined with tiny rivulets of black oil.

The boat had been lying here untenanted for three years. It was trussed with ropes and chains on which had grown eccentric vegetable beards of dried weed and slime. Its masts and rigging were gone, its blue paintwork bleached and cracked. My shadow scared a sunbathing family of fiddler-crabs in the muddy pool that the boat had dug for itself as it grounded with the tide. They shuffled away across the pool-floor and hid in the dark under the bilges.

No one would have said the thing was beautiful. What it had was a quality of friendly bulk, as solid and reassuring as an old coat. I liked its name: *Gosfield Maid* sounded like a description of some frumpish, dog-breeding country aunt. I've always had a superstitious belief in anagrams. Rearranged, the letters came out as *Die, dismal fog.* Not bad, under the circumstances.

I found a boarding ladder under a dusty tree, climbed nine feet up on to the deck and became a temporary captain lording it over a small and smelly ocean of mud. I inspected my ship with ignorant approval. The deck was littered with pieces of substantial ironmongery that I didn't know the names of or uses for, but I trusted the look of their weathered brass and cast steel. Up front, two anchors lashed down in wooden cradles were big enough to hold a freighter. There was nothing toylike or sportive about this boat: it was the real thing—a working Scottish trawler refurbished for foul-weather cruising.

The wheelhouse stuck up at the back like a sentry box. It was snug and sunny inside, a good eyrie to study the world from. Leaning on the brassbound wheel, I followed the sweeping upward curve of the deck as it rose ahead to the bows. From here, the boat looked suddenly as graceful and efficient as a porpoise. It had been built to take steep seas bang on the nose, and its whole character was governed by its massive front end. Given pugnacious bows like that, you could go slamming into the waves and ride the tallest breakers, with the rest of the boat tagging quietly along behind.

The compass above the wheel was sturdy and shiplike, too. It showed our heading as West-North-West, on course across the wooded hills for Devon, Somerset and Wiltshire. I rocked the bowl in its hinged frame and watched the card settle back into position as the lodestone homed in on the pole; a small satisfying piece of magic...one more bit of the marvellous jigsaw of ideas and inventions by which captains find their way around the world.

Four steps down from the wheelhouse the boat turned into a warren of little panelled rooms: a kitchen just about big enough to boil an egg in, a lavatory in a cupboard, an oak-beamed parlour, a triangular attic bedroom in the bows. The scale of the place was elfin, but its mahogany walls and hanging oil-lamps suggested a rather grand Victorian bachelor elf. Its atmosphere was at once cosy and spartan, like an old-fashioned men's club.

I opened a porthole to freshen the pickled air in the saloon. It was possible now to make out a fine seam down on the far edge of the flats where shining mud was joined to shining water as the tide inched upriver from the sea. I sprawled on the settee, lit a pipe, and generally wallowed in my captaincy. This wasn't just a boat that was on offer; it was a whole estate. Whoever bought it would have a house to live in, a verandah to sit out on, a fine teak deck to pace, acres of water to survey, and a suit of sails and a diesel engine to keep him on the move through life. Who could ask for more of Home?

JAMES FENTON
ROAD TO CAMBODIA

Norman Lewis describes how in 1949 China, which had been open to the West for barely fifty years, closed down again 'for a change of scene': 'If you had wanted to go to China it was too late. You would have to content yourself with reading books about it, and that was as much of the old, unregenerate China as you would know. At this moment the scene shifters were busy and they might be a long time over their job. When the curtain went up again it would be upon something as unrecognizable to an old China hand as to Marco Polo.'

Lewis asked himself which country would be the next to suffer in this way, and he decided that it was high time to visit Indochina. *A Dragon Apparent* was the result which, like *The Quiet American*, is highly revered by the English and American correspondents who worked in the area.* After Dien Bien Phu, however, nobody was able to repeat Lewis's journey throughout the peninsula, unless, like the late Wilfred Burchett, they did so as guests of the Communists: North Vietnam was invented, and closed down. But the remainder of the area stayed open to the traveller for a decade and a half, until 1970. By that time the North Vietnamese had taken over the Cambodian countryside, Laos had become gradually impossible to explore, and South Vietnam was simply too dangerous.

Things improved, from the traveller's point of view, after the Paris Peace Agreement in 1973. Theoretically, western journalists were able to visit any of the 'liberated areas' of the south, and some of us profited from the opportunity. After the fall of Saigon in 1975, there was about a week in which travel was suddenly even easier, because nobody had yet been told to stop us from having a look around. Then we were confined to the capital and starved of news. The curtain descended well and truly over the whole peninsula for what turned out to be the most thorough, and drastic, change of scene.

I had wanted to write some kind of sequel to Norman Lewis's *A Dragon Apparent*, but although much of my book was finished, I could never bring myself to complete the account of the last months of the Phnom Penh regime. As I tried to write about it, I found that nothing but horror could be gained from the experience in Cambodia, and it was impossible to think back to what, for me, had been happier times. There is something hedonistic about travel writing, something egocentric. The masters of the art (Lewis, Greene, Naipaul) may rise above this vice, but, for my own part, it was impossible to complete a travel book about such a catastrophe.

I abandoned the book, but, before doing so, I wrote the piece that follows. It describes a smuggling town to which I believe I was the only Western visitor, and it looks at the Cambodian areas of South Vietnam.

There may also be some contemporary relevance. The Mekong Delta had once belonged to Cambodia, but the Cambodian Empire was in danger of disappearing altogether when, in the nineteenth century, the French established their protectorate in Indochina. In subsequent years, it was not the French, however, but the Thais and the Vietnamese who were always considered *the* historical threat to Cambodia's existence. It was in the face of this threat that Khmer Rouge nationalism developed, but it was the Khmers Rouges themselves, ironically, who ended up destroying their own country and who made it vulnerable to Vietnamese hegemonism. In the Mekong Delta (Kampuchea Krom), the towns are now Vietnamese, but the countryside retains pockets of Cambodian life. But I am afraid that in Cambodia itself the same process will be repeated: Cambodia will be incorporated into a land-hungry empire. Those who oppose this are obliged to answer an impossible question: Are you really prepared to reinstate the Khmers Rouges? Are you really prepared to subject the country to another war?

Towards the end of 1974 I made two trips to the Mekong Delta, where I narrowly avoided meeting the Khmers Rouges (to my great relief) and the Vietcong (to my regret). I enlisted the help of a Vietnamese student as interpreter, and we set off by bus from Saigon to Cantho. At the terminal just outside Saigon, there were vast crowds of screaming touts, who rushed at you and tried to seize your baggage. Little girls were most insistent that you would need sunglasses for the journey. Every form of food and refreshment was pressed into your hand.

The first leg of the journey was by mini-bus, non-stop to Cantho. We fell in with a couple of Vietnamese who were on their way to Ha

Tien, the sea-port by the Cambodian border. You must go to Ha Tien, they said, because of the market. Everything is so cheap: cloth, drink, cigarettes, you could buy whatever you wanted at a fraction of the price in Saigon.

It was impossible to go with our two Vietnamese friends at first, because we were researching into the Cambodian communities of the delta. However, after a couple of days in Ba Xuyen province, where for some reason all the Cambodians appeared to be getting married (it was, I suppose, the Khmer equivalent of Whitsun), we decided to return to Cantho and rejoin them on their journey. As it happened, our friends were nowhere to be found, so we set off on our own to Ha Tien on one of the large, ancient, bone-shaking buses which served the route. The trick with these buses was not to sit at the back, because it would be full of chickens, ducks and catfish, and not to sit in the middle, because there was no room for your legs, and not to sit at the front, because it was absolutely terrifying. For the first part of the journey we sat at the back, and every time the bus hit a bump—that is to say every five minutes—I would hit the roof. Later I sat at the front, and watched a series of near misses. There were two boys on the bus employed to collect the fares and, as we made our rapid progress on the clearer stretches, to hang from the doors screaming at anyone near the road to get out of the way.

Two things held us up. First, there was a series of refreshment stops as vendors climbed aboard and screamed 'Boiled crab!' or 'Shrimp pancake!' in your ear, or proffered chunks of sugar cane. Some of these stops had been arranged with the driver. Others had been ingeniously devised—a sort of commercial ambush. One woman had placed her baby in the path of the bus as if to say: 'Either you buy my rather indifferent madeira cake or you kill my baby. The choice is yours.' The second reason for hold-ups was the activity of the Vietcong frogmen, who had blown up several bridges along the way. This also added to the expense of the trip, since although Thieu's army had plenty of equipment to meet such emergencies, they considered that they should be paid for their efforts. At one point, as we waited for the bus to be precariously loaded on to the pontoon ferry, I went and talked to the small group of soldiers beside the destroyed bridge. They pointed to a clump of bushes about a hundred and fifty yards away and said that the Vietcong were there. I wasn't sure whether they were telling the truth. It seemed ridiculous that the situation could be tolerated. But it was typical of the delta in those times; typical indeed of large areas of Vietnam at that time. The *amour propre* of the Saigon government, and the tolerance of the Vietcong, kept roads open through areas that did not belong to Saigon in any way.

By this time it was getting towards evening, and a woman on the bus advised us that it would be better to sit away from the front seats since it was quite likely that we would be stopped either by Vietcong or by bandits. I remembered the golden rule of travel in Indochina: never be on the roads after dusk. Still, there was nothing to be done, and I was not at all worried about the prospect of meeting the Vietcong. As it became dark, barricades were put up on the roads at either end of every village. We would stop; the two boys would rush to the barricades, parley with the guards and wave us through. The excitement and the hurry mounted. We met more and more Vietnamese Cambodians. One leapt on to the bus and met his mother-in-law. He slapped her so hard on the back that she shrieked. Then he started talking to her with such speed and amusement, holding his head first on one side, then on the other, like some kind of garrulous bird, that he had soon put her into a good mood. The happiness of these two was infectious. My interpreter, who had never travelled in this area, was completely beguiled. He told me that he had never, never seen such a happy group of people in Vietnam before as on this bus.

But at the last village before Ha Tien another bridge had been blown up, and this time it was impossible to get through before dawn. We descended from the bus and went to the village café, where the arrival of a white face at such a time of night caused a great stir. The village was poor and there was nothing much to eat, but in a short while the local police and military chiefs had arrived, and we began talking and drinking together. It was a sad conversation, and much of it consisted of questions posed to me: What did I think of Thieu? What would the Americans do if there was another offensive? Could Saigon last? I tried to answer these questions, in the way I always tried, with tact and about two-thirds honesty. People imagine that the officers of the Thieu regime were corrupt and vicious to a man. In my experience, many of them were no better and no worse than anybody

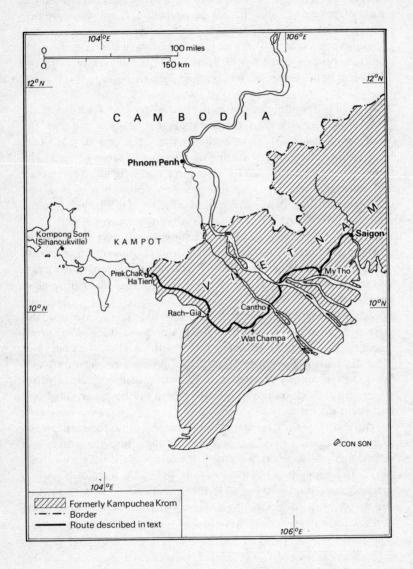

else in the world. But, of course, I only knew them when their fortunes were on the wane, and they had every reason to be reflective about the merits of their own side. In this conversation, there was only one point at which my interpreter refused to translate what I was saying; this was when I pointed out that Con Son island was one of the most notorious prisons in the world, and one of the chief reasons why the Thieu regime was disliked by so many foreigners.

By about midnight, the other travellers had found a place to sleep, either in the huts of the village or under the coach itself. We were invited to stay the next day in order to go fishing: there was a rare and highly-prized species of crab to be found nearby. We accepted the invitation, and were given camp beds and mosquito nets in the military compound. There was a gun nearby, an artillery piece, which fired off at regular intervals into the night, and the guards would occasionally fire shots into the river, to ward off any frogmen. I slept well enough, and woke in an area of most unusual beauty. A dramatic limestone crag lay on the other side of the river, which gave into a calm sea dotted with steep white islands and rocks. We said goodbye to the bus, and climbed into a fibre-glass military dinghy to go fishing.

Of course, said our friends as we prepared to set out, we could use grenades, but it's so wasteful of stock, don't you think? We agreed solemnly, but I noticed we had no tackle with us. There were only two blocks of *plastique* (explosive), one hand-grenade and a landing-net. We sped out among the beautiful islands, passing one on which a white cross stood, marking the cave where the Emperor Gia Long had spent his exile.

Once at the fishing-grounds, we stuck fuses into the *plastique*, lit them with cigarette ends, threw the *plastique* into the water, and retired to a safe distance. With the first explosion, the sea gave a slight heave and brought up a total of one fish. The second, however, succeeded in stunning about sixty sprats and one or two larger items. We decided not to use the grenade, rather to my relief, since I was mortally afraid of it. We never found the highly-prized species of crab.

*Published in 1951 and recently reissued by Eland Books.

On our return, we found that the village was being visited by two senior police officers, who were very keen to discuss the problems of Vietnam. When I told them I worked for the *Washington Post*, they were somewhat disenchanted.

'*Washington Post*,' they said, 'the paper that finished President Nixon.'

So I told them that I also worked for the *New Statesman*, which as far as I knew never finished anybody.

'When the Americans were here,' they said, indicating the twisted spans of the bridge, 'this bridge would have been rebuilt in one day. Now...' They shrugged. They said that it was impossible to continue the battle against the Vietcong without more supplies.

I questioned this, pointing out that the soldiers had been firing all the previous night against an apparently non-existent enemy, so they could hardly be that short of ammunition.

They said it was very difficult to combat the Vietcong, because they used such crude methods.

'Crude?' I asked.

'Yes, crude.' The word was spoken with a dreadful scowl.

'What do you mean, crude?'

One of the officers explained. It was these frogmen. They didn't use proper equipment. They just put a clip on their nose, tied round their head a bit of rubber hose to breathe through, attached stones to their feet, and walked along the bottom of the river. They had found from intelligence sources that that was how they had blown up all these bridges. It was impossible to see them coming. It was all very crude.

I had to agree with the officer. It did sound pretty crude. But why didn't they do the same thing in return? Why didn't the Saigon troops go walking around on the bottom of the rivers attacking Vietcong positions?

The officer looked at me with utter contempt. 'That would be quite impossible,' he said flatly.

By this time, another bus had arrived and had been ferried across the river, so we continued on our way, along a palm-fringed coast, towards Ha Tien and the Cambodian border. We could see the Elephant Mountains and the region of Kampot.

Ha Tien itself was an old town, built in the Chinese-French-Portuguese commercial style, with charming, decorated, crumbling stucco houses, and the filthiest market I had seen so far in Vietnam. Was this what we had come for? After a revolting lunch, during which my spirits sank, we asked about the big market. It turned out that we needed a honda cart to take us there. The market was not in Ha Tien. It was in a village called Prek Chak ('Poke Village'), and Prek Chak was in Cambodia.

I must have been a little thick that day: it was already about two-thirty, and not the best of times to be crossing borders. However, we set out along the road, passing rows of Cambodian refugee settlements on the way. About a hundred yards before the border post on the main road we turned left into a small village and came to a pagoda complex, where our driver left us. There was a constant stream of people passing to and fro, their bicycles laden with goods. We walked through the village and, without our asking, people showed us to the unofficial crossing-point. There was a double fence of barbed wire, newly erected, and a Vietnamese soldier stood beside it.

No, he said, it was impossible to go through. Look at the barbed wire.

Yes, I said, it has been cut; all you have to do is roll it back.

No, he said, it was only cut because the Vietcong had cut it the night before. It wasn't really supposed to be cut.

This was obviously a lie, but there were so many people around that I didn't like to try bribing the men in public. Finally I produced my military travel documents, and with ill grace the man let us through.

We walked across a field towards a collection of straw huts. There was nothing remarkable about them from a distance, but when we came closer we realized the place was very odd indeed. The huts, which were clustered around a shallow muddy creek, were crammed full of merchandise of every kind. There were cartons of cigarettes from Singapore, bales of cloth from Thailand, crates of whisky, sacks of cement; there were boxes of Chinese razor-blades and bottles of Chinese wine. Everything was in bulk. The place was a hypermarket of contraband.

As we entered the village, people looked up—not in the normal astonished way to which I had grown used in some of the remoter parts of Cambodia, but in a manner which indicated absolute blank incomprehension. They laughed—the Cambodians among them, not the Chinese—but they laughed in a different way. They seemed embarrassed. They seemed as if they had just been caught out doing something improper. And well they might seem embarrassed. For they were all gambling. Absolutely everybody was gambling. It was like—I suddenly thought—coming into some allegorical town, say in *Pilgrim's Progress*. In the muddy alleys between the huts, the children were gambling with rubber bands, squatting on their haunches and shrieking as they lost or won. In the smaller huts they were gambling with cards, dice, shells. On the other side of the creek, there were larger huts containing full-scale casinos where the really serious stuff was going on. This was run by the Chinese. Numbers or characters were drawn out of a box, and held up to shouts and groans. A vast litter of Vietnamese and Cambodian notes was raked across the tables.

Sitting in one of the many cafés, I got into conversation with some Cambodians who explained part of the history of Prek Chak. It had begun earlier in the year when the Khmers Rouges had attacked Kampot and had destroyed its usefulness as a centre for smuggling. The Cambodian navy had co-operated with the Chinese, and the South Vietnamese had not objected. So the village had grown at an enormous rate, and was still growing. As I walked round, I began to attract a crowd of children, who followed cheering and imitating my every gesture. I wanted to see if, in addition to the Saigon soldiers and police who were walking around, there were any Cambodian military. Yes there were, said somebody, down by the sea. We set off to look for them.

At this point, the children suddenly melted away. I was glad at first, but then I suddenly noticed that nobody was talking to us any longer. We became uneasy, and again we asked the way. This time a Vietnamese woman came up to us and hurriedly explained that if we didn't get out at once we would be killed. It was four o'clock, she said, and at this time the Khmers Rouges came into town. Any foreigners would be killed—one stranger had been killed the day before on the very spot where we were standing. She herself, as a newcomer, had been in terrible trouble. We must get out at once. But how? The route by which we had come in had now been shut up for the night. If we went out along the main road, via the official customs post, we would be arrested. There was one other way.

The woman led us through the village, and as she did so, people stared at us in a new way. Suddenly I realized why they had been quite so surprised when we arrived there in the first place. As the woman explained, Prek Chak belonged to Phnom Penh and Saigon by day. By night it belonged to the Khmers Rouges. Every evening they came in, sometimes trading things, but very often simply stealing them. The Vietcong and NVA [North Vietnamese Army] came in as well, from time to time, but they always paid for their purchases. Prek Chak by day was a paradise for draft dodgers, smugglers and gamblers. By night it was quite a different kettle of fish.

As we made our way through the fields, we met a line of people coming back from Ha Tien to their homes in Prek Chak. As they passed us, they told my interpreter: 'Don't be afraid. Just walk very quickly.' But soon we saw that the route by which they were coming involved at least another mile before the border. Then, we were told, there was a creek, but the ferryman at the creek did not have any authorization, and the previous night his boat had been shot at by the Khmers Rouges. Just at this time, as well.

There was nothing for it but to go back to the official border post and argue our way through the guards. By now I was really frightened, more frightened than I had ever been before. The prospect of arrest by the South Vietnamese seemed nothing compared with the prospect of meeting the Khmers Rouges. We hurried back to the border post, and were obligingly arrested. While this was happening, the South Vietnamese began for some reason to fire shells over our heads into Cambodia, and in Prek Chak the sound of automatic rifle fire began.

The trouble with being arrested was that nobody knew what to do with us. We protested that it had all been a terrible mistake—we had assumed that Prek Chak was in Vietnam, and anyway there were thousands of others crossing the border all the time. The soldiers were sympathetic, but by now they had reported our case, so it was too late to let us go. In Ha Tien we were passed from office to office. Statements were taken, and then the men who took the statements were roundly abused by their seniors for not taking more detailed statements. More detailed statements were taken. The police chief was not around. I was exhausted and irritated and by the end of three hours began to get annoyed. The police station was apparently open to the whole public, and a small crowd of children had gathered to watch the fun.

I turned to my interpreter: 'Will you please tell the officer,' I said in wounded tones, 'that in England it is customary to offer people chairs.'

From the depths of the ancient French building, a chair was brought.

We were approaching the final, most dangerous point, the status of my interpreter. 'Why doesn't he have a press card?' they asked.

I lied through my clenched teeth: 'Because in Saigon, press cards are *never, never* issued to interpreters.'

'Then how do we know he *is* your interpreter?'

'Look,' I said, 'if you want proof, I'll write you out a letter of introduction for him.' I was getting somewhat hysterical. An impressive anger began to sweep through my frame. 'In fact,' I said, 'I'll *type* you a letter for him, and sign it, *with my own signature,* in the name of the *Washington Post!*'

'All right,' they said—much to my surprise.

'Well, where's the typewriter?!!'

They led me into the building. The children milled round.

I sat down in the manner of a man who was about to blow the lid off the Pentagon. 'I'LL NEED SOME PAPER AS WELL, YOU KNOW!'

They hurried off and found a piece of paper. By now the interest was tremendous.

I put the paper in the machine. I did it beautifully. I've since seen Robert Redford do this bit on film, but he was pathetic in comparison. I really gave that paper hell. My fingers poised over the keys. I looked down. It was a Vietnamese typewriter, of course, and all the keys were in the wrong position. Pathetically, I began to look for the *W*. There didn't seem to be a *W*. The children started to snigger. It was perfectly obvious that I didn't know how to type. 'Will you please get these children out of here?' I said, furiously. Then, key by key, I composed the worst-typed letter of introduction ever.

And yet, for some reason, we were let off, and we went and indulged in a celebratory supper. When we got back to our hotel, the manager told us in lugubrious tones that the chief of police had called, and would be back in the morning. We went upstairs with heavy hearts. In the room next to ours, a Chinese merchant had laid out his purchases from Prek Chak, and had erected a small altar, with candles, joss-sticks and offerings of fruit. He was praying, he said, for three things: finance, property and protection from the Khmers Rouges. Soon, there was a knock at the door. It was the police chief, with a couple of his friends. He was profusely apologetic. He had been away all day, otherwise we would never have had all that trouble. His junior officers had not known what to do. How could he make amends? Would we come to breakfast with him the next day? He would take us for the finest Chinese soup in town. At 6.30? Good. The trouble was, he said, that we had been taken through by the military. The military did not know what they were doing. It was very dangerous for a foreigner in Prek Chak. We could have been killed. He was responsible for us. If anything had happened to us, he would personally have been very upset. He considered us, you know, he considered us to be his own sons....

After soup the next morning, the police chief put us on the bus for Saigon, instructing the driver not to charge us for the trip. After we left Ha Tien we persuaded the driver, although with some difficulty, to let us pay half fare. As we went towards Saigon, I noted from time to time that bundles of notes were produced and handed over at the military check-points. This was the protection money on which the racketeers of the Mekong Delta made their fortunes. What I did not realize until some weeks later, when it was independently confirmed, was that Prek Chak's main function was gun-running. Corrupt officials in Kompong Som, together with the Khmer Navy, brought American weapons and ammunition to be sold there to the Khmers Rouges. Later still, I was talking about Prek Chak to a soldier in Kompong Som, and he told me that the place had just been attacked by the Khmers Rouges and burned to the ground. Many of the inhabitants had been killed, the others had fled to South Vietnam where they were continuing their trade. Clearly, the place had outlived its usefulness, and had fallen under the righteous wrath of the insurgents. It certainly had stood for everything they despised.

I said to the solder: 'They were selling arms to the enemy, weren't they?' The soldier looked alarmed. I lowered my voice: 'It was well-known. The FANK [Forces Armées Nationales Khmers] officers were selling their own weapons to the Khmers Rouges.'

'Yes,' said the soldier ruefully, 'they *were* selling arms to the enemy. It is true. But they were only *small* arms.'

While in Ba Xuyen province on this trip, I had found a Cambodian monastery where we had been received very well, and which I wanted to investigate more carefully. The trouble (and the attraction) was that it was in a contested area—the Vietcong-controlled villages were only a couple of miles away. I thought that if I stayed there I might be able to cross over to a PRG [Provisional Revolutionary Government] zone, but it was obviously unfair to try to do so in the company of my interpreter.

A few days later, I therefore set out by myself, on the same sort of minibus, in the direction of Cantho. The driver was fairly careful, but the traffic was heavy. At one point a young girl stepped out from behind a car, and was hit by the bus. We drew to an abrupt halt, and the child was thrown several yards down the road. Then a large proportion of the luggage on the roof-rack slipped off and fell into the road in front of us. The child lay twitching in the road, and the driver, in terrible distress, got out, hailed a honda cart, and took the girl off to hospital. At once, all the passengers on the bus dispersed. Somebody took me gently by the arm, and indicated a large, red, ancient American car, into which we piled. We left the minibus where it had stopped, in the middle of the road.

The miserable aspect of Cantho, with its drug addicts and cripples, has been well described before (for instance, by Richard West in *Victory in Vietnam*). I shall mention just one thing I saw that night. It was a group of legless heroin addicts, sitting in wheelchairs and drinking together on the waterfront. When the time came to pay the bill, an argument broke out among them. Soon the argument developed into a fight—and a vicious fight it was. The purpose of the fight was to pull each other out of the wheelchair. I did not stay to see the result.

49

The next morning I was dropped from the local bus not far from Wat Champa. As I approached the monastery, walking through the fields, I greeted one of the peasants in Cambodian. At once, he called out to another peasant on the other side of the field, saying that I spoke Khmer. And then I heard the message passed on further, to the adjoining paddies. A sudden surge of happiness came over me, to be walking alone in the countryside, and to be walking into what was, after all, a tiny pocket of Cambodia. The morning was sunny, the occasion propitious. I had never really seen Cambodian village life functioning before, at least not since my trip through Battambang province the year before.

The monastery was set in a spacious grove of tall, umbrageous trees, and the main temple was a work of fantastic imagination. At each corner stood concrete statues of animals, brilliantly painted. The other buildings were more modest, some of them made of wood. The abbot was pleased to see me, and asked after my interpreter. Over a cup of tea, I explained that my purpose was to study a little more of the customs of the monks and to learn a little of the Cambodian language. If possible, I should like to spend a few days at the monastery.

'Aren't you afraid of the Vietcong?' they said.

'No,' I replied, 'the Vietcong always behaved well towards foreigners; I was only afraid of the Khmers Rouges.'

The monks explained that the Vietcong were visiting the village every night to collect taxes, but that they never came into the monastery. The abbot would give me some lessons in Khmer if I gave him some lessons in English. Everything seemed fine.

The monks lived what they were perfectly prepared to admit was a very lazy life. They joined the monastery as young men, at their family's request, and they would leave it when it became necessary for them to work at home. Of course, in wartime the temptation to stay on in the monastery was great. They ate two meals a day, breakfast and lunch. After that they survived on tea and cigarettes, although for senior monks there might be special treats. I once found the abbot chewing sugar-cane, which he said counted as drinking, since one always spat out the fibrous interior. One evening we ate a dish called 'fried milk', which consisted of 'Longevity Brand' condensed milk, mixed with coconut and reduced by heat until it reached the consistency of treacle toffee. The monks' day was spent in lessons—Pali and English—trips to the local villages to beg for alms, attendance at religious ceremonies, and the rest of the time sitting by the monastery pool, feeding the two enormous pet turtles—the monks' stomachs rumbling as evening came on.

The buildings were full of surprises. In one, surrounded by winking lights, the last abbot was lying in his coffin. He had died a year before, and it would be another two years before he was cremated. The present abbot's house was stuffed with souvenirs and junk. It looked like the bedroom of some sentimental bit-part actress. There were photographs, ornaments and knick-knacks, and in a loft above our heads there were piles of embroidered cushions and umbrellas stacked away. But this was nothing to the house occupied by the oldest monk in the establishment, to which we were invited one evening in order to watch the television.

This was a great occasion. There was the strangest altar I have ever seen. On the top level, there was a row of assorted Buddhas—as one might expect. Below these, and partly obscuring them, were a television set and three bottles of pop, flanked by two model Christmas trees with fairy lights, and an illuminated Star of Bethlehem. On the next level there was a row of ancient biscuit barrels and a wholesale tin of Maxwell House instant coffee. At the base there was a coffee table cluttered with china frogs, candlesticks, fluffy animals, alarm clocks and glasses full of old cutlery, all covered with dust.

The old monk also showed me his cupboards, which were full of souvenirs from the seaside, old swords and daggers, and yet more alarm clocks. He had a passion for clocks. He took out one and placed it, with great ceremony, in my hands; it was a travelling alarm, with a cunning, slatted shutter that could be pulled across the clock face.

'Are you—um—giving this to me?' I asked, embarrassed.

'No!' he said quickly, and snatched it away.

Instead, I was given something to eat. By now, the room had filled up with children and adults from the village, the generator had been turned on, the fairy lights and the Star of Bethlehem were blinking away, and I was the centre of attention for about fifty people. As it was evening, the monks were, of course, not eating, so I was going to be the only one.

I looked into the bowl that they put in my hands. It contained crushed rice, coconut and about three hundred ants, swarming all over it. There was nothing to be done. I spooned up the ants, and wolfed them down with appropriate expressions—Mmmm! Lovely! Delicious! But I didn't finish them all. I was absolutely terrified that if I did, they would produce another dish. Finally, when I had done what I considered justice to the bowl, I set it down, and the children eagerly consumed the rest.

But still—no television. The cover had been left on it, and nobody seemed interested in plugging it in. I had noticed vaguely, while eating the ants, that people had been coming in and going out, after whispered consultations with the abbot. Now there were distinctly embarrassed looks. I couldn't understand it, until a little later the abbot explained. The problem was that the Vietcong objected to the monks giving television shows, and had threatened that if they persisted the Vietcong would come into the monastery itself and take away the sets. As it happened, the Vietcong had arrived earlier than usual that night, and were now in the village. They knew perfectly well what was going on, and had sent a message that there was to be no television.

The abbot was desperately worried about losing his televisions. He spoke about them often. He had two, but the one with the twenty-five-inch screen, of which he was particularly fond, was kept in the central pagoda itself, along with the cine-projector, which was also a favourite possession. The abbot used to take siestas there in the afternoon, watching the television and wondering whether he dared turn it on. One night, when the coast seemed clear, a group of young monks did turn it on for me. We watched the local Cantho channel, which was pretty grim: a long programme of excruciating Vietnamese pop music, sung by hideous stars. I quite saw what the Vietcong objected to. However, we lounged at the foot of the great statue of the Buddha and smoked Capstans through the evening.

I went with the abbot and the oldest monk to a funeral ceremony for an old man who had died in a village not far away. We walked along the narrow paths between the houses and the fields, and every time we met someone coming in the opposite direction the oldest monk hit him over the head with his umbrella. I was not sure whether this was custom or mere eccentricity. When people called out from the fields, the abbot told them that I was from Phnom Penh—I was an upland Khmer. This caused great mirth since the upland Khmers (Khmer Loeu) were considered savages, wild tribesmen.

When we arrived in the village, the monks went into the house of the dead man, and soon settled down to a large meal that had been prepared for them. I sat outside with the villagers drinking *soum-soum*, the local rice spirit. We talked about the Vietnamese, whom they despised. There was nothing political about this. They just hated their guts. After all, the Cambodians of the delta, the Khmer Krom, still considered the whole rich area to be theirs. Saigon itself was nothing more than an old Cambodian village called Prey Nokor. The very watches of the villagers and the clocks of the monastery, were set to Phnom Penh time. (Saigon time was an invention of Diem: the North Vietnamese, the Vietcong and the Cambodians were all synchronized.) And although this area paid taxes both to Saigon and to the Vietcong, although the yellow and red Saigon flag was painted on their gates, the allegiance was to Cambodia.

But to a Cambodia with a difference. True, there had been very little interbreeding with the Vietnamese. The people retained their dark skins, which they disliked, their square chins and strong features. If you looked at their ears and lips in profile, the resemblance to the sculptures of the Angkor period was striking. And yet proximity to the Vietnamese, subjugation indeed, had forced them to accommodate to Vietnamese customs to a certain extent. Their dress was similar to the Vietnamese and they were all monogamous—'unfortunately', as one old man put it. Politically and socially they were misfits. A tradition of right-wing nationalist politics had survived there, but only in a degenerate form. I met nobody who had a good word to say for Sihanouk—whereas in Phnom Penh it was hard to find anybody who did not look back on his rule with nostalgia. The hero of the Khmer Krom was Son Ngoc Thanh, but he, after a period with the Lon Nol government, had returned to Saigon, where he was reputed to be too old and sick for any political activity.

Son Ngoc Thanh's memory was still kept very much alive by the Khmers Rouges, who referred to him regularly in their broadcasts as a member of the 'traitorous clique'. He was specially hated by Sihanouk, whose book, *My War with the CIA,* laid special blame on him for the overthrow of the royal government. The Khmer Krom had been trained by the CIA in Mike Force (*Mike*, the letter *M*, stands for 'mercenary'). In the summer of 1970, when the Lon Nol regime was struggling for survival, Mike Force troops were sent to Phnom Penh in large numbers. However, the reception they got from the Cambodians there was lukewarm at best. They were thought to be more Vietnamese than Khmer. Their superior attitude, their military sophistication and their ruthlessness were resented. They were used as cannon-fodder in a series of disastrous campaigns. Eventually, they were almost wiped out. You could still find a few of them in Phnom Penh. They were the gung-ho officers with the perfect command of GI slang. But the experience of fighting for the mother country had not been a success. They had found out, although they would not admit this, that they were not Cambodians after all. And if they were not Cambodians, and not Vietnamese, what the hell were they?

In these villages, the Khmer Krom had adapted themselves to their situation as best they could. Several of the peasants travelled to work in the PRG-controlled areas during the day. For those who lived under the nominal control of the Saigon regime, the PRG taxes were higher than for those in the liberated zones, and in addition they had to pay taxes to Saigon. I asked a large number of them whether there were many Cambodian troops among the Vietcong. Apparently the percentage was not high; this seemed to reflect the alienation of the Khmer Krom from Vietnamese politics. The only respected authority in the region was that of the monks.

To become a monk, to shave your head and eyebrows, to give up women and drink and all forms of games might not be everybody's idea of a good life. But it was a way of saying that you were a Cambodian, a way of avoiding the draft and remaining safe, for the moment at least. Beyond the monastery gates, the pleasant grove, the turtles and the pond, the chances of dying were high. There was gunfire daily as the peasants crossed the lines to and from work, and that afternoon the gunfire was nearer and louder than before. I asked the abbot what was happening. He explained that one of the territorial soldiers was about to be cremated. I went out to the crematorium ground, and watched the ceremony.

The women sat apart, wailing together in a manner which, as it gathered force, turned into what sounded like a ritual chant. The men lit the pyre with bits of old rubber tyres, which gave off a foul black smoke. As the fire began, they hacked at the coffin with axes, in order to make sure that the flames got through to the body. It was a sad and shabby occasion. The men were mostly drunk on *soum-soum*, which they passed around. A young soldier, I think he was about sixteen, was supposed to fire a salute. But he managed to jam his rifle. So the old men took the gun from him and fired the magazines off themselves. Every time they fired, there was an answering volley which came, I think, from the house where the dead soldier had lived. I reflected that the old men had fought for the French, their sons had fought for the Americans, and their grandsons were fighting for the Vietnamese.

By now the coffin was beginning to disintegrate. I wanted to stay and see the whole process to the bitter end. But one of the monks came up to me, pointed at the pyre and screwed up his nose. He told me not to wait around any longer.

Why not? I asked.

Bad dreams, he said, and besides, they were waiting in the monastery for me to give an English lesson.

I walked with him to one of the classrooms, where a group of eager, eyebrowless faces sat patiently. The teacher put a copy of *Understanding English* into my hands, and I began to read out loud. It was a book designed for the type of summer language school that exists on the south coast of England. The main characters in the stories were European students, each with his or her engaging little characteristics. It was full of bad puns and coy little jokes, and as I read the stories out, in a clear, slow, solemn voice, I could hear my own voice ringing round the classroom. No doubt I could be heard as far as the cremation ground, and they would think that the monks were furthering their religious education. By the end of the chapter, I realized that nobody—neither the teacher nor the pupils—had been able to follow a single word.

Every evening I would put on a loincloth and go to the wash-house where my ablutions were an object of great interest and mirth. One thing puzzled the monks. Why did I never relieve my bowels? Was I ill? Was I different in some curious respect? Since I had never had a moment of privacy from the time of my arrival, it was clear that something was wrong. On the third day, therefore, I announced that the time had come. Consternation!

'No have Kiss Me,' said a monk.

This remark might have been disconcerting, had I not been aware that 'Kiss Me' was a brand of toilet-paper. I don't know whether the monks had ever heard the song *Kiss Me Quick*, but one could imagine that they would have well appreciated its urgent rhythms. I took my little can of water down the path, which led past a pleasant stream luxuriant with lotus blossom, beside which the secluded closets stood. A great wave of sympathy and pleasure spread through the monastery.

I used to eat not with the monks—that was forbidden—but with the various lay personnel of the establishment. One evening, as I was sitting with the abbot and a few of the monks, the cook brought in his baby daughter to show me. The child was paralysed from the waist down, and he did not have enough money to get her proper medical attention. In the quietest, most modest way, he asked if I would give him some money, which I was glad to do, since—apart from anything else—I was enjoying the hospitality of the monastery. I gave him as much as I could spare. The man thanked me and left. I overheard the abbot ask the monks how much I had given. It was something like twenty dollars. 'A lot,' said the abbot, rather as if I had overstepped the mark. A few moments later, the cook came back, this time with his wife and the child. They knelt at my feet and placed the baby in my arms. Then they said that they would like to give me the child, since they would never be able to look after it properly. This may sound as if they were deficient in love for the baby, but in fact it was quite the opposite, and I hated having to refuse them.

On the last night, I had bought a gift of coffee for the monks and we sat up till the early hours, talking about politics, laughing and joking. I was very pleased with the way the trip had gone, and even though my Cambodian was only rudimentary and there were few English or French speakers, I had learned a lot in the way that I preferred—not using a notebook more than was absolutely necessary, and allowing events to take their own course. I had missed out on the PRG, but you couldn't have everything, and by now my presence in the area was so well known that it would be impossible to slip across the lines without incurring the wrath of the Saigon authorities. Besides, I doubted very much if it was wise to go from this dotty little pocket of reaction across to the liberated areas.

There was one monk who was much shrewder than the rest. Suddenly he said: 'Of course, we know why you have been staying with us all this time.'

I thought he was going to mention the Vietcong, and indeed he did: 'You're from the CIA, aren't you?'

I laughed. 'If I were from the CIA, I would be afraid to stay here. Besides, I'm not American.'

'That's what you say. But how do we know? This is an interesting area for you. You want to get information about the Vietcong.'

'I'm a journalist,' I said, 'and I hate the CIA.'

'But of course you'd *say* you hated the CIA.'

He was quite serious, and what he said destroyed, at a stroke, all the pleasure of the last days. Of course that's what they'd think. Why else would a foreigner come and spend such a long time with them? What was worst of all was—they didn't *mind*. They seemed almost to be used to it. I was an American spy doing my job; they were Cambodian monks, doing theirs. That was the world as they understood it, and it wasn't until I had thrown what amounted almost to a tantrum that they took the allegation back, and we patched up our friendship.

REDMOND
O'HANLON
INTO THE HEART OF
BORNEO

The situation in Sarawak as seen by Haddon in 1888 is still much the same today. He found a series of racial strata moving downwards in society and backwards in time as he moved inwards on the island.

C.D. Darlington
The Evolution of Man and Society, 1969

As a former academic and a natural history book reviewer, I was astonished to discover, on being threatened with a two-month exile to the primary jungles of Borneo, just how fast a man can read.

Powerful as your scholarly instincts may be, there is no matching the strength of that irrational desire to find a means of keeping your head upon your shoulders; of retaining your frontal appendage in its accustomed place; of barring 1,700 different species of parasitic worm from your bloodstream and Wagler's pit viper from just about anywhere; of removing small, black, wild-boar ticks from your crotch with minimum discomfort (you do it with sellotape); of declining to wear a globulating necklace of leeches all day long; of sidestepping amoebic and bacillary dysentery, yellow and blackwater and dengue fever, malaria, cholera, typhoid, rabies, hepatitis, tuberculosis and the crocodile (thumbs in its eyes, if you have time, they say).

A rubber suit, with a pair of steel-waders, was the most obvious form of protection, I thought. But then the temperature runs to one hundred and twenty degrees in the shade, and the humidity is ninety-eight per cent. Hose and McDougall's great two-volume masterpiece *The Pagan Tribes of Borneo* (published in 1912), Alfred Russel Wallace's *The Malay Archipelago: the Land of the Orang-Utan and the Bird of Paradise* (1869), Odoardo Beccari's *Wanderings in the Great Forests of Borneo* (1904), Hose's *The Field-book of a Jungle-Wallah* (1929) and Robert Shelford's *A Naturalist in Borneo* (1916) offered no immediate solution. And then meek, dead, outwardly unimpressive, be-suited and bowler-hatted Uncle Eggy came to my rescue. Uncle Eggy was in the war against the Japanese in Borneo, and a member of the Special Operations Executive—the SOE. So armed with my newly-remembered ancestor, I decided—before venturing into Borneo untutored—to seek help from the SOE's intellectual descendants, the SAS.

The training area of 22nd SAS near Hereford is the best place on earth from which to begin a journey up-river into the heart of the jungle. The nearest I had ever come to a tropical rainforest, after all, was in the Bodleian Library, via the pages of the great nineteenth-century traveller-naturalists, Humboldt, Darwin, Wallace, Bates, Thomas Belt—and, in practice, a childhood spent rabbiting in the Wiltshire woods. My companion, James Fenton, however, whose idea the venture was, enigmatic, balding, an ex-correspondent of the war in Vietnam and Cambodia, a jungle in himself, was a wise old man in these matters.

Still, as the gates swung open from a remote control point in the guardroom and our camouflaged Landrover climbed the small track across the fields, even James was unnerved by the view. Booby-trapped lorries and burned-out vehicles littered the landscape; displaced lines of turf disclosed wires running in all directions; from Neolithic-seeming fortressed earthworks, there came the muffled hammering of silenced small-arms fire; impossibly burly hippies in Levi jeans and trendy sweaters piled out of a truck and disappeared into the grass; mock-up streets and shuttered embassies went past, and then, as we drove round a fold in the hill, an airliner appeared, sitting neatly in a field of wheat.

We drew up by a fearsome assault-course and made our way into the local SAS jungle. Apart from the high-wire perimeter fence, the frequency with which Landrovers drove past beyond it, the number of helicopters overhead and the speed with which persons unknown were discharging revolvers from a place whose exact position it was impossible to ascertain, it might have been a wood in England.

'What a pity,' said Malcolm, our SAS instructor and guide, 'that you can't come to Brunei with us for a week. We could really sort you out and set you up over there.'

'What a pity,' I agreed, moistening with sweat at the very thought.

'Now,' said Malcolm, taking a small green package out of the newly-designed Bergen back-pack, 'it's all very simple. You find two trees eight feet apart where there's no evidence of any silt on the ground—the rivers can rise eighteen feet overnight and you don't want to drown in a wet dream, do you? Check the tree trunks for termites. Termites mean dead branches and dead branches, sooner or later, mean dead men. We lost a lot of men like that, in storms at night. Tie these cords round the trees, put these metal stiffeners across each end like this, and there's your hammock. Now—here's your mossie net, and you just tie it over your hammock and peg it out by these strings to the surrounding bushes until it forms a good tight box like that—and you really want to watch it, because malaria pills only give you thirty per cent protection. Here's your top cover and that's it. There's your genuine basha.'

A long green tube had materialized above the brambles in front of us, seemingly in a minute or two.

'Stop around three or four in the afternoon,' said Malcolm, 'give yourself plenty of time. Light one of these blocks that makes no smoke and boil up a cup of tea. And just sit by your tree until dark if the enemy are about.'

Back at the quartermaster's stores we signed for our new kit. One silver and one prismatic compass (black and tight and heavy as a little bomb in its canvas belt-case); two *parangs*— thick knives eighteen inches long which had chopped and slashed their way through the Indonesian confrontation from 1962 to 1966; torches, belts, pouches, powders, insect repellents, parachute cord, water bottles, water purifying tablets, stoves, fuel blocks, mess tins, the complete basha equipment and rations enough (Menu C) for three patrols moving in groups of four for three weeks.

We were in the company of a soft-spoken major. A veteran of Special Forces campaigns in Occupied Europe in the Second World War, of the war in Malaya, of Jebel Akhdar, Aden, Borneo and Dhofar, he was huge. It was vastly reassuring to think that so much muscle could actually squeeze itself into a jungle and come out again undiminished. And his office, hung with battle honours, SAS shields emblazoned with the regiment's motto, *Qui ose gagne*; with a mass of wall charts documenting the progress of his latest candidates; with cartoons of all the wrong ways to resist interrogation; and libraried with strictly practical works of natural history—on edible fungi, on traps and tracking and poaching, on different recipes for the cooking of rats and instructions on the peeling of cockroaches—was an impressive place.

'You'll find the high spot of your day,' said the major, 'is cleaning your teeth. The only bit of you you can keep clean. Don't shave in the jungle, because the slightest nick turns septic at once. And don't take more than one change of clothes, because you must keep your Bergen weight well down below sixty pounds. And don't expect your Iban trackers to carry it for you, either, because they have enough to do transporting their own food. So keep one set of dry kit in a sealed bag in your pack. Get into that each night after you've eaten. Powder yourself all over, too, with zinc talc—don't feel sissy about it—you'll halve the rashes and the rot and the skin fungus. Then sleep. Then get up at 5.30 and into your wet kit. It's uncomfortable at first, but don't weaken—ever; if you do, there'll be two sets of wet kit in no time, you'll lose sleep and lose strength and then there'll be a disaster. But take as many dry socks as you can. Stuff them into all the crannies in your pack. And, in the morning, soak the pairs you are going to wear in autan insect repellent, to keep the leeches out of your boots. Stick it on your arms and round your waist and neck and in your hair, too, while you're about it, but not on your forehead because the sweat carries it into your eyes and it stings. Cover yourself at night, too, against the mosquitoes. Take them seriously, because malaria is a terrible thing and it's easy to get, pills or no.

'Get some jungle boots, good thick trousers and strong shirts. You won't want to nancy about in shorts once the first leech has had a go at you, believe me. Acclimatize slowly. The tropics takes people in different ways. Fit young men here just collapse in Brunei. You'll think it's the end of the world. You can't breathe. You can't move. And then after two weeks you'll be used to it. And once in the jungle proper you'll never want to come out.

'It's a beautiful country and the Iban are a fine people. I was on the River Baram myself, but to go up the Rajang and the Baleh will be better for your purposes. That's a good plan. The Baleh is very seldom visited, if at all, up-river, and the Tiban mountains should be very wild indeed. They look small on a map, those mountains, but they're tough going. One steep hill after another. And you have to be good with a compass. Any questions? No. Good. Well done, lads, Goodbye and good luck.'

James and I drove out past the guardroom and the police post, in a stunned silence, the back of the car bristling with serious dark-green and camouflage-brown equipment; and we fell into the King's Arms. But we were on our way. It was too late to stay at home.

It was midday. Waving goodbye to the thirty or forty children and the thirty or forty dogs which had gathered on the bank, we climbed into our dugout canoe and set off up-river towards the interior, where none of our newly-hired Iban trackers—neither Dana, or Leon, or Inghai (our youngest and our bow look-out)—had ever been. For us, the unknown had begun the moment we arrived in Borneo, at the delta of the great River Rajang; for them, the unknown began now.

After about ten miles hill-*padi* fields gave way to well-established forest. And then the primeval jungle began. The river seemed to close in on us. The two-hundred-foot-high trees crowded down the slopes of the hills almost to the water's edge—an apparently endless chaos of different species of tree, every kind of green; parasitic growths sprouted everywhere; ferns fanned out from every angle in the branches; and creepers, as thick as legs, gripped each other.

The river itself began to turn and twist, too. The banks behind us appeared to merge together into one vast and impenetrable thicket, shutting us in from behind, just as the trees ahead stepped aside a meagre pace or two to let the river swirl down ahead. The outboard motor, manned by Leon and set on a special wooden frame at the stern of the canoe, pushed us past foaming little tributaries, islets, shingle banks strewn with huge rounded boulders, half-hidden coves scooped round by whirlpools. We really were, too, voyaging up-river—at first I thought it an optical illusion, but no, the canoe was actually climbing up a volume of water great enough to sustain an almost constant angle of descent, even between the jagged steps of the rapids.

Spits of land had formed wherever smaller streams joined the main flow, and here driftwood was piled, stacks of hardwood planed smooth by the rush of floodwater, flung together, bleached grey by the sun. We stopped by one such pile to hide a drum of petrol, in case we returned. A monitor lizard, reared up on its front legs, watched us for a moment with its dinosauric eyes and then scuttled away between the broken branches. A Brahminy Kite, flying low enough for us to hear the rush of air through the primary feathers of its wings, circled overhead, its flecked-brown belly white in the sun; watching us, too, before it soared away, mewing its shrill call like a buzzard.

Further up, the rapids began to become more numerous and more turbulent. At each one, as Leon drove the canoe for the central cascade of the current at full power while Dana and Inghai, their back muscles bunched, poled the bow to the left or the right of each oncoming rock, heavy waves of water would crash over us. James, sitting opposite me on the duck-boards in the centre of the canoe, facing upstream, our equipment lashed down under tarpaulins to front and rear of us, was reading his way through Pat Rogers's new edition of the complete poems of Swift. A straw boater on his bald head, his white shirt buttoned at the neck and at the wrists, his trousers no less and no more disgraceful than the ones he wore in Oxford (being the same pair), he would be, I thought, a formidable figure for the jungle to conquer. But he would need, no less certainly, a little discreet assistance against the vagaries of nature.

'Some of this juvenilia is pretty feeble,' James would mutter, displeased.

'Quite so. But–er–James?'

'Yes?'

'Rapid 583/2, Green-Heave Strength six-out-of-ten, is approaching.'

With a second or two to spare, James would shut his book, mark his place in it with a twig, slip it neatly under an edge of the tarpaulin, place his left buttock upon it, shut his eyes, get drenched, open his eyes, squeeze the water from his beard with his right hand, retrieve his book and carry on reading.

Every five hundred yards or so, a lesser Fish-eagle would regard us with its yellow eye, unmoving at first, its grey feet clamped to a favourite branch overhanging the edge of the river, flying off only as we drew almost level, flapping gently just ahead of the canoe to the limit of its territory, and then doubling back. It was odd to be journeying like this, preceded by eagles.

James, his huge head laid back on the hump of our kit under the tarpaulin, had begun one of his five-minute snoozes. The vein on his right temple was distended with blood, a sure sign that his cerebellum was awash with extra dissolved oxygen, and that some piece of programming, vital to the production of a future poem, was in progress.

'James!'

An eye opened. 'What is it?'

'Just this—if you *do* see a log floating *up-river,* let me know.'

'Crocodiles?'

'Well, not the estuarine one that really goes for you. Not up here. But authors Tweedie and Harrisson think we might see the freshwater Gharial. The fifteen-foot one with the five-foot snout and all those teeth.'

'Really, Redmond,' said James, raising himself up on an elbow and looking about, 'you're absurd. You live in the nineteenth century. Everything's changed, although you don't appear to notice. Nowadays you will have no difficulty whatever in recognizing a crocodile. Everyone knows—they come with an outboard motor at the back and a Kenwood mixer at the front.'

I sat back in the boat. When the temperature is one hundred and ten degrees and the humidity ninety-eight per cent, when you're soaking wet and rotting a bit in the crutch, then even weak jokes like that, in the worst possible taste, seem extraordinarily funny.

At four o'clock in the afternoon we entered a wider stretch of river where a tributary joined the main stream and a low ridge of shingle had formed down the centre of the water course. Dana decided to make camp.

'Good fishing. Very good,' said Leon, looking at the swirling white water, the fallen trees and the eddies by the far bank.

We pulled the canoe well out of the water and tied its bow-rope high up the trunk of a tree, in case of floods in the night, and then stretched out on the sand for a rest. Butterflies began to gather. Hundreds of butterflies, flying at different heights and speeds, floating, flapping awkwardly in small bursts, gliding, fluttering like bats, winnowing, some flying fast and direct like wrens in trouble—they made their way towards us and settled on our boots and trousers, clustered on our shirts, sucked the sweat from our arms. There were Whites, Yellows and Blues; Swallow-tails, black, banded or spotted with blue-green; and, just outside the clustering circle of small butterflies, the magnificent species which Alfred Russel Wallace named after James Brooke, *Troides brookiana,* the Rajah Brooke's Birdwing.

Sucking our clothes and skin with their thread-like probosces at one end, the butterflies exuded a white goo over us from their anal vents at the other. Getting up, brushing them off as gently as possible, I walked away from my companions the mandatory few yards and took a pee myself. While my patch of urine was still steaming slightly on the muddy sand, the males of Rajah Brooke's Birdwing (the females, being fully employed laying eggs in the jungle trees) flew over and crowded down on it, elbowing each other with the joints on their legs, pushing and shoving to get at the liquid, the brilliant green feather-shaped marks on their black wings trembling slightly as they fed. I began, prematurely, to feel a part of things.

In fact, having run to the canoe to fetch the shock-proof, water-proof, more-or-less-everything-proof heavy-duty Fuji cameras, I began to feel, as I crawled on my stomach towards the pullulating insects, very much more than a passing pride in the obvious quality of my own offering. It was while photographing this butterfly (with a fixed wide-angle lens which I knew would produce a hopeless picture), a butterfly which later proved to be very common all the way up the Baleh to its source, that I felt the excitement that Alfred Russel Wallace himself describes, on capturing its close cousin *Ornithoptera croesus*: 'The beauty and brilliancy of this insect are indescribable, and none but a naturalist can understand the intense excitement I experienced when I at length captured it.... My heart began to beat violently, the blood rushed to my head, and I felt much more like fainting than I have done when in apprehension of immediate death. I had a headache the rest of the day, so great was the excitement produced by what will appear to most people a very inadequate cause.'

I, too, had a headache for the rest of the day, but then perhaps it was the sun, or the mere thought of our fishing equipment. For after a burning swig all round from the arak rice-brandy five-gallon converted petrol-can, Dana, Leon and Inghai, drawing their *parangs* from their carved wooden scabbards, set off to cut down the saplings for our pole-beds; and I decided it was time that James and I taught them how to fish to maximum effect, like Englishmen. But first a little practice would be necessary.

Withdrawing quietly behind a massive jumble of boulders, well out of sight, I unpacked our precious cargo. Two new extendable rods, the toughest in town. A hundred yards of heavy line. A heavy bag of assorted lead weights. A termite's nest of swivels. A thornbush of hooks. Fifty different spinners, their spoons flashing in the sun, all shapes and all sizes for every kind of fish in every sort of inland water.

'The trouble is,' said James, flicking a rod-handle and watching the sections telescope out into the blue beyond, 'my elder brother was the fisherman. That was his thing, you see, he filled that role. So I had to pretend it was a bore; and I never learned.'

'What? You never fished?'

'No. Never. What about you?'

'Well, *my* elder brother went fishing.'

'So you can't either?'

'Not exactly. Not with a rod. I mean I used to go mackerel-fishing with a line. All over the place.'

'Mackerel-fishing! Now you tell me!' said James, looking really quite agitated and frightening a bright orange damsel-fly off his hat. 'Still,' he said, calming down, 'if *they* could do it, it can't be that diffy, can it?'

'Of course not—you just stick the spinner and swivels and weights on that end and swing it through the air.'

It was horribly annoying. The heat was unbearable. The fiddling was insupportable. The gut got tangled; the hooks stuck in our fingers; the knot diagram would have given Baden-Powell a blood clot in the brain. We did it all and forgot the nasty little weights. But eventually we were ready to kill fish.

'The SAS say it's simpler to stick in a hand-grenade.'

'They're right,' said James.

'But the major said all you had to do was hang your dick in the river and pull it out with fish on it.'

'Why don't you stick your dick in the river?' said James.

Standing firm and straight, James cast the spinner into the river. It landed in the water straight down at the end of the rod. Clunk. James pulled. The line snapped. We went through the whole nasty rigmarole again, with fresh swivels, weights and spinner.

'Try again. Throw it a little further.'

James reached right back and then swung the rod forwards and sideways as if he were axing a tree.

At that very moment, it seemed, the Borneo Banded Hornet, *Vesta tropica,* sank its sting into my right buttock.

'Jesus!' I said.

It was huge and jointed, this hornet, flashing red and silver in the sun.

'You are hooked up,' said James, matter-of-factly, 'you have a spinner in your arse.'

There was a weird, gurgling, jungle-sound behind us. Dana, Leon and Inghai were leaning against the boulders. The Iban, when they decide that something is really funny, and know that they are going to laugh for a long time, lie down first.

Dana, Leon and Inghai lay down.

'You should try it with harpoon!' shrieked Leon, helpless.

With great ceremony we presented our rods to Dana and Leon and a compensatory extra helping of weights and spinners to little Inghai. And with equal aplomb, the Iban took the useless gifts into care, wrapped them in cloth, and placed them in the bottom of the canoe.

Dana, meanwhile, was building a little house. Six-foot tall, two-feet square, with a conventional triangular roof and a small platform half-way up; its use was not apparent. For the spirits? For heads that might saunter by?

'For fish,' said Leon, 'for smoking fish. Now we show you how to fish like the Iban.'

Taking their wooden harpoons from the canoe, Leon and Inghai dived into the river; and disappeared completely, like a pair of Great Crested Grebe. A full forty seconds later they bobbed up again, right over on the far bank. Leon stood up and held an enormous fish above his head, harpooned through the flank. Inghai, as befitted his size, held up a tiddler. Much yelling in Iban took place. Dana, evidently stung into action, took a large weighted net out of the canoe, a *jala*, and made his way upstream to the shingle bank. Swinging it back and forth in both hands, swaying slightly, he cast it out; a slowly spinning circle of white mesh settled on the water, and sank. Jumping in, scrabbling about to collect the bottom ends of the net, Dana finally scooped it all up again, together with three catfish. They looked at us lugubriously, immensely long whiskers, their feelers, drooping down from either side of their mouths. Dana detached them with the greatest care, avoiding their dorsal and pectoral spines which, presumably, were poisonous, and tossed them up the shingle.

Leon and Inghai returned with six fish, all of the same species, *Sebarau,* handsome, streamlined, and, unlike the smooth and mucus-covered catfish, armoured with large silver scales and adorned with a bold black bar down either side.

Inghai collected driftwood and made two fires, one on the beach and the other at the base of the smoking-house. Leon gutted the fish, cut them into sections, placed some in a salting tin, some on the smoking-rack, and some in a water-filled cooking pot. Two ancient cauldrons, slung from a high wooden frame, bubbled over the fire: one full of fish pieces and one full of sticky rice. Dana returned for supper, having set a larger net part-across the current, supported by ropes to an overhanging branch and by white polystyrene floats.

Dusk came suddenly and, equally suddenly, Eared Nightjars appeared, hawking insects, stooping and turning in their haphazard, bat-like way, but always along the tops of the trees above the river banks, seeming half-transparent and weightless in their ghostly agility.

After about ten minutes, they vanished. Which was just as well, because it had dawned on me that the fish and the rice in my mess tin would need all the attention I could give it. The *Sebarau* was tasteless, which did not matter, and full of bones, which did. It was like a hair-brush caked in lard. James had made the same discovery.

'Redmond, don't worry,' he whispered, 'if you need a tracheotomy I have a biro-tube in my baggage.'

It was time to go to bed. We washed our mess tins in the river, kicked out the fire on the beach, and stoked up the smoking-house fire with more wet logs. Slinging my soaking clothes from a tree with parachute cord, I rubbed myself down with a wet towel and, naked, opened my Bergen pack to pull out my set of dry kit for the night. Every nook and cranny in the bag was alive with inch-long ants. Deciding that anything so huge must be the Elephant Ant, and not the Fire ant, which packs a sting like a wasp, I brushed the first wave off my Y-fronts. Glancing up, I was astonished to see my wet clothes swarming with ants, too; a procession of dark ants poured down one side of the rope and up the other; and, all over my wet trousers, hundreds of different moths were feeding. I rummaged quickly in the outside Bergen pocket for my army torch. As my fingers closed on it, everyone else's little fingers seemed to close on my arm. I drew it out fast and switched on: Elephant Ants, this time with massive pincers, were suspended from hand to elbow. The soldiers had arrived. I flicked them off, gratified to hear yelps from James's basha as I did so. It was good to know they also went for poets.

Slipping under the mosquito net, I fastened myself into the dark-green camouflage SAS tube. It seemed luxuriously comfortable. You had to sleep straight out like a rifle; but the ants, swarming along the poles, rearing up on their back legs to look for an entry, and the mosquitoes, whining and singing outside the various tunes of their species in black shifting clouds, could not get in.

'*Eeeeeee—ai—yack yack yack yack yack!*' Something screamed in my ear, with brain-shredding force. And then everyone joined in.

'*Eeeeeee—ai—yack yack yack yack yack te yooo!*' answered every other giant male cicada, maniacally vibrating the timbals, drumskin membranes, in their cavity amplifiers, the megaphones built into their bodies.

'Shut up!' I shouted.

'*Wah Wah Wah Wah Wah!*' said four thousand frogs.

'Stop it at once!' yelled James.

'*Clatter clitter clatter*' went our mess tins over the shingle, being nosed clean by tree shrews.

The Iban laughed. The river grew louder in the darkness. Something hooted. Something screamed in earnest further off. Something shuffled and snuffled around the discarded rice and fish bits flung in a bush from our plates. A porcupine? A civet? A ground squirrel? The long-tailed giant rat? Why not a Clouded Leopard? Or, the only really dangerous mammal in Borneo, the long-clawed, short-tempered Sun Bear?

I switched off the torch and tried to sleep. But it was no good. The decibel-level was way over the limit allowed in discotheques. And, besides, the fire-flies kept flicking their own torches on and off; and some kind of phosphorescent fungus glowed in the dark like a 40-watt bulb.

I switched on again, clipped the right-angled torch on to my shirt, and settled down for a peaceful bed-time read with Hose and McDougall. Discussing the wars of the Kayan, Hose tells us that

If the defending party should come upon the enemy

struggling against a rapid—and especially if the enemy is in difficulties through the upsetting of some of their boats— they may fall upon them in the open bed of the river. Then ensues the comparatively rare event, a stand-up fight in the open. This resolves itself in the main into hand-to-hand duels between pairs of combatants, as in the heroic age. The short javelins and spears are first hurled, and skilfully parried with spear and shield. When a man has expended his stock of javelins and has hurled his spear, he closes in with his *parang*. His enemy seeks to receive the blow of the *parang* on his shield in such a way that the point, entering the wood, may be held fast by it. If one succeeds in catching his enemy's *parang* in his shield, he throws down the shield and dashes upon his now weaponless foe, who takes to his heels, throwing away his shield and relying merely on his swiftness of foot. When one of a pair of combatants is struck down, the other springs upon him and, seizing the long hair of the scalp and yelling in triumph, severs the neck with one or two blows of the *parang*.

It was definitely time to sleep.

At dawn the jungle was half-obscured in a heavy morning mist; and through the cloudy layers of rising moisture came the whooping call, the owl-like, clear, ringing hoot of the female Borneo Gibbon.

Replacing the dry socks, pants, trousers and shirt inside two plastic bags inside the damp Bergen pack, tying them tightly to keep out the ants, I shook the wet clothes. A double-barrelled charge of insects propelled itself from inside my trouser-legs. I groomed my pants free of visible bugs, covered myself in SAS anti-fungus powder until my erogenous zone looked like meat chunks rolled in flour, ready for the heat, and forced my way into clammy battle-dress for the day. It was a nasty five o'clock start; but in half-an-hour the mist would be gone, the sun merciless, and the river-water soaking one anyway.

After a breakfast of fish and rice, we re-packed the dugout and set off up-river. The gibbons, having proclaimed the boundaries of their territories, ceased calling. The world changed colour from a dark watery blue to mauve to sepia to pink and then the sun rose, extraordinarily fast.

Inghai put on his peaked cap to shield his eyes from the sun as he sat on the bow and scanned the turbulent water ahead for rocks and logs; Dana, in chiefly style, wore his round hat, as large and intricately patterned as a gaming-table; and Leon, proudly switching his outboard to full power, wore a mutant hybrid of pork-pie and Homburg. James adjusted his boater, stretched out his legs on his half of the duck-boards, and addressed himself to Swift.

Something large and flappy was crossing the river in front of us. Was it a bird disguised as a leaf-skeleton? Was it a day-flying bat disguised as a hair-net? Or was a lattice of tropical worms in transit across my retina? Very slowly, unconcerned, the something made its floating and dipping, floating and dipping, indecisive flight right over the boat: it was an odd idea indeed, *Hestia idea,* a butterfly with grey and white wings like transparent gauze, highly poisonous, and safe. In one of the richest of tropical rain forests, in a natural zone which actually contains more kinds of butterflies and moths than all other habitats of the world put together, it was ridiculously pleasing to have identified just one more species, even if, as I eventually had to admit to James, it was the most immediately obvious of them all.

James, momentarily, re-directed his critical gaze from Swift's sometimes defective scansion, and fixed it upon the surrounding jungle. With A–1 vision in both eyes which are set so far apart that he does, in this one respect, resemble a hammer-head shark, he announced, in a statement which later became formulaic and—for the Iban (and, well, just a little, for me)—the incantation of a shaman of immeasurable age and wisdom summoning the spirits of the forest to dance before him for a span: 'Redmond, I am about to see something *marvellous.*'

The canoe swung into the next bend and there, majestically perched upon a dead branch across an inlet, was a Crested Serpent Eagle.

'How's that?' said James.

The eagle was thick-set, black and brown and grey, his stomach lightly freckled, his head plumed flat. James was sitting up, boatered, bearded-black, his shirt dazzling white. James looked at the eagle. The eagle looked at James. The eagle, deciding that it was too early in the morning to hallucinate, flapped off into the jungle, puzzled.

Gradually, the rapids became more frequent, more difficult to scale. Leon would align the boat carefully in the deep pools beneath each one, open up to full throttle on a straight run, shut off the engine, cock the propeller well up out of the water as we hit the first curve of white foam, grab his pole as Inghai and Dana snatched up theirs, and then all three would punt the canoe up, in wild rhythm with each other.

They were lean, fit, strong with a lifetime of unremitting exercise, their muscles flexing and bunching, etched out as clearly as Jan van Calcar's illustrations to *De humani corporis fabrica*.

The solid tree-trunk keel of the hollowed-out canoe began to thud against the boulders beneath the cascades of water. It thudded lightly at first, and then with alarming violence as the day wore on. We had to jump out beneath each rapid, take the long bow-rope, walk up the stones strewn down beside the fall, wade into the deep current above and pull—guiding the bow up. The water pushed irregularly at our waist and knees, sometimes embracing us like a succubus might (after a year in prison), sometimes trying a flowing rugby-tackle, sometimes holding our ankles in a hydro-elastic gin-trap, but never in a way that could be described as friendly. With nothing but locked spines and clamped cartilages we leaned back against the great flow of water on its way to the South China Sea.

Just in time, by a deep pool, in a harbour formed by two massive fallen hardwoods, Dana ruled that it was noon and we were hungry. The boat was tied up, we collapsed, and Leon went fishing.

Spreading our wet clothes out on the burningly-hot boulders, James and I took a swim and a wash.

Dana, intrigued by Medicated Vosene, shampooed his glossy black hair and then rinsed it by swimming very fast across the pool underwater, a moving *V* of ripples on the surface marking his passage through the spins and eddies. He waded ashore, and even his dark-blue tattoos glistened in the sun. Dana was covered in circles and rosettes, whorls and lines (soot from a cooking pot, mixed with sweetened water, and punched into the skin with a bamboo stick and small hammer). On his throat (the most painful of all to suffer, and the most likely to produce septicaemia) a large tattoo testified to his immediate courage; on his thighs an intricate pattern of stylized Rhinoceros; and on the top joints of his fingers a series of dots and cross-hatchings suggested that he had taken heads in battle—probably from the bodies of invading Indonesian soldiers killed by the SAS, with whom he had sometimes served as a tracker, in the 1962–66 confrontation. Dignified, intelligent, full of natural authority, at forty an old man in the eyes of his tribe, Dana was the law-giver and judge of conduct, the arbiter of when to plant and when to harvest the *padi,* and, perhaps most important of all, the Chief Augurer to his people, the interpreter of the messengers of the gods: the birds.

He regarded us with protective amusement. We were like the white men he had met in the war, Leon had informed us in hushed tones; when we first met Dana, we had stayed in his long-house and behaved like guests he could trust, not offending against custom, well-mannered. James and I, in turn, decided that *Tuai Rumah* Dana, Lord of the House, a Beowulf, or, more accurately, a warrior-king out of Homer, was a great improvement on all our previous Headmasters, Deans and Wardens.

Leon surfaced by the far bank of the river, half-obscured by the roots of a giant tree which twisted into the water, but obviously excited, ferociously excited. He was yelling wildly to Dana and Inghai, '*Labi-labi*!', holding his harpoon cord with both hands, shouting in Iban; and, to us, 'Fish! Round fish! Big round fish!'

Dana and Inghai leaped into the dugout and swam fast across the current. It seemed a lot of fuss about a fish, however big and round.

Dana cut two lengths of our parachute cord, one for himself and one for Inghai and, tying the boat to a branch, plunged in. Something thrashed and splashed, churning up the water between the three of them. Lowering the cord, knotted into a noose, Dana pulled it tight, secured it to the stern of the dugout; and then all three paddled back, towing something. The boat beached; they hauled on the parachute cord. Gradually, a shiny olive dome broke surface, almost round, and about three feet across. Two pairs of webbed, thick claws were thrusting against the water, front and back. Pulling it ashore in reverse, the Iban cut two holes at the rear of its carapace and threaded a lead of rattan through each slit. It was a large Mud Turtle, *Trionyx cartilagineus,* one of whose specific characteristics, described by a so-called closet-naturalist in the nineteenth-century British Museum from trophies in the collection, had been, as Wallace liked to point out, these very same restraining holes at the back of the shell.

Left alone for a moment, the turtle's head began to emerge from a close-fitting sleeve, from folds of telescopic muscle. It had a flexible snout for a nose, a leathery green trunk; and a sad, watery eye. Dana's *parang* came down with great violence, missing the head, glancing off the cartilaginous armour, bucking the turtle, throwing up water and pebbles. The head retracted. Dana crouched, waiting. Some ten minutes later, the turtle once more began to look cautiously for its escape. Out came the head, inch by inch. With one blow, Dana severed the neck. The head rolled, quizzically, a little way across the sand.

After a lunch of rice and Sebarau, Dana and Leon heaved the turtle on to its back, slit open its white belly, and threw its guts to the fish. The meat was cut into strips, salted, and stowed away in a basket on the boat. The empty shell, the blood drying, we left on the shingle.

The river twisted and turned and grew narrower, and the great creepers, tumbling down in profusion from two hundred feet above our heads, edged closer. The rapids and cascades became more frequent. We had to jump out into the river more often, sometimes to our waists, sometimes to our armpits, pushing the dugout up the shallows, guiding it into a side-channel away from the main crash of the water.

'*Saytu, dua, tiga—bata!*' sang Dana, which even we could reconstruct as one, two, three, and push.

The Iban gripped the round, algae-covered stones on the river-bottom easily with their muscled, calloused, spatulate toes. Our boots slipped into crevices, slithered away in the current, threatened to break off a leg at the ankle or at the knee. It was only really possible to push hard when the boat was still, stuck fast, and then Headmaster Dana would shout '*Badas!*' 'Well done!' But the most welcome cry became '*Npan! Npan!*': an invitation to get back in, quick.

Crossing one such deep pool, collapsed in the boat, the engine restarted, we found ourselves staring at a gigantic Bearded Pig sitting quietly on his haunches on the bank. Completely white, an old and lonely male, he looked at us with his piggy eyes. Dana, throwing his pole into the boat, snatched up his shotgun; Leon, abandoning the rudder, followed suit. Inghai shouted a warning, the canoe veered sideways into the current, the shotguns were discarded, the boat re-aligned, and the pig, no longer curious, ambled off into the jungle, his enormous testicles swaying along behind him.

We entered a wide reach of foaming water. The choppy river-waves, snatching this way and that, had ripped caves of soil out of the banks, leaving hundreds of yards of overhang on either side. There was an ominous noise of arguing currents ahead. The rapids-preamble—the white water, the moving whirlpools, the noise ahead—was longer and louder than it ought to have been.

With the canoe pitching feverishly, we rounded a sweeping bend; and the reason for the agitated river became obvious. The Green Heave ahead was much higher than any we had met. There was a waterfall to the left of the river-course, a huge surging over a ledge. The way to the right was blocked by thrown-up trees and piles of roots that had been dislodged upstream, torn out in floods, and tossed aside here against a line of rocks. There was, however, one small channel through; a shallow rapid, dangerously close to the main rush of water, but negotiable. It was separated from the torrent by three huge boulders.

Keeping well clear of the great whirlpool beneath the waterfall, Leon brought the boat to the base of this normal-size rapid. Dana, James and I made our way carefully up with the bow-rope.

Dana held the lead position on the rope; I stood behind him and James behind me. We pulled, Leon and Inghai pushed. The boat moved up and forward some fifteen feet and then stuck. Leon and Inghai walked up the rapid, and, hunching and shoving, rolled small rocks aside to clear a channel. We waited on the lip of the rock above, pulling on the rope to keep the long boat straight. At last Leon and Inghai were ready. But the channel they had had to make was a little closer to the waterfall. To pull straight we must move to our right. Dana pointed to our new positions.

It was only a stride or two. But the level of the river-bed suddenly dipped, long since scooped away by the pull of the main current. James lost his footing, and, trying to save himself, let go of the rope. I stepped across to catch him, the rope bound round my left wrist, snatching his left hand in my right. His legs thudded into mine, tangled, and then swung free, into the current, weightless, as if a part of him had been knocked into outer space. His hat came off, hurtled past his shoes, spun in an eddy, and disappeared over the lip of the fall.

His fingers were very white; and slippery. He bites his fingernails; and they could not dig into my palm. He simply looked surprised; his head seemed a long way from me. He was feeling underwater with his free arm, impossibly trying to grip a boulder with his other hand, to get a purchase on a smooth and slimy rock, a rock polished smooth, for centuries, by perpetual tons of rolling water.

His fingers bent straighter, slowly, edging out of mine, for hour upon hour—or so it felt, but it must have been seconds. His arm rigid, his fingertips squeezed out of my fist. He turned in the current, spread-eagled. Still turning, but much faster, he was sucked under; his right ankle and shoe were bizarrely visible above the surface; he was lifted slightly, a bundle of clothes, of no discernible shape, and then he was gone.

'Boat! Boat!' shouted Dana, dropping the rope, bounding down the rocks of the rapid at the side, crouched, using his arms like a baboon.

'Hold the boat! Hold the boat!' yelled Leon.

James's bald head, white and fragile as an owl's egg, was sweeping round in the whirlpool below, spinning, bobbing up and down in the foaming water, each orbit of the current carrying him within inches of the black rocks at its edge.

Leon jumped into the boat, clambered on to the raised outboard-motor frame, squatted, and then, with a long, yodelling cry, launched himself in a great curving leap into the centre of the maelstrom. He disappeared, surfaced, shook his head, spotted James, dived again, and caught him. Inghai, too, was in the water, but he faltered, was overwhelmed, and swept downstream. Leon, holding on to James, made a circuit of the whirlpool until, reaching the exit current, he thrust out like a turtle and they followed Inghai down-river, edging, yard by yard, towards the bank.

Obeying Dana's every sign, I helped him coax the boat on to a strip of shingle beneath the dam of logs. James, when we walked down to him, was sitting on a boulder. Leon sat beside him, an arm round his shoulders.

'You be all right soon, my friend,' said Leon, 'you be all right soon-lah, my very best friend. Soon you be so happy.'

James, bedraggled, looking very sick, his white lips an open *O* in his black beard, was hyper-ventilating dangerously, taking great rhythmic draughts of oxygen, his body shaking.

'You be OK,' said Leon. 'I not let you die, my old friend.'

Just then little Inghai appeared, beaming with pride, holding aloft one very wet straw boater.

'I save hat!' said Inghai, 'Jams! Jams! I save hat!'

James looked up, smiled, and so stopped his terrible spasms of breathing.

He really was going to be all right.

Suddenly, it all seemed funny, hilariously funny. 'Inghai saved his hat!' We laughed and laughed, rolling about on the shingle. We giggled together until it hurt. 'Inghai saved his hat! Ingy-pingy saved his hat!' It was, I am ashamed to say, the first (and I hope it will be the last) fit of genuine medically-certifiable hysterics which I have ever had.

Dana, looking at James, decided that we would camp where we were. Finding a level plateau way above flood level on the bank behind us, the pole hut and the pole beds were soon built. I had a soap and a swim, re-covered myself in SAS super-strength insect repellent and silky crutch powder, re-filled our water bottles from the river and dosed everyone with water-purifying pills, took a handful of vitamin pills myself, forced James and the Iban to take their daily measure too, and then settled down against a boulder with my pipe (to discourage further mosquitoes), a mess-mug full of arak, and the third edition of Smythies' *The Birds of Borneo*.

James, covered in butterflies, was reading *Les misérables* and looking a little miserable himself.

'How are you feeling?'

'Not too good, Redmond. I get these palpitations at the best of times. I've had attacks ever since Oxford. I take some special pills for it but they're really not much help. In fact the only cure is to rest a bit and then be violently sick as soon as possible.'

'Can I do anything?'

'No,' said James, pulling on his umpteenth cigarette and concentrating on Victor Hugo.

He was, I decided, an even braver old wreck than I had imagined. Looking fondly at his great bald head I was really fairly pleased with

Leon for helping the future of English literature; for preventing the disarrangement of all those brain cells; for denying all those thousands of brightly-coloured little fish in the shallows the chance to nibble at torn fragments of cerebellum tissue, to ingest synapses across which had once run electrical impulses carrying stored memories of a detailed knowledge of literatures in Greek and Latin, in German and French, in Spanish and Italian. But all the same, I wondered, what would we do if an accident befell us in the far interior, weeks away from any hospital, beyond the source of the Baleh, marching through the jungle towards the Tiban range and well away, even, from the stores in the boat?

Dana took his single-barrelled shotgun, held together with wire and strips of rattan, and set off to find a wild pig. Leon and Inghai went fishing with their harpoons. My Balkan Sobranie tobacco, as ninety-per-cent humid as everything else, tasted as rich and wet as a good gravy.

The sky grew black suddenly. There was an odd breeze. Everyone—insects, monkeys, birds, frogs—stopped making a noise. Dana, Leon and Inghai ran to the dugout and re-tied it, bow and stern, with long ropes leading to trees on the high bank. Huge globules of water began to fall, splashing star-burst patterns on the dry hot rocks along the shore. We made for our bashas, changed fast, and slipped inside. Rain splattered on the tree canopy two hundred feet above, a whispery noise growing duller and increasing in volume to a low drumming. Drops hit our canvas awnings and bounced off; a fine spray came sideways through the mosquito net. A wind arrived; and we heard the first tree start its long crashing fall far off in the forest. Thunder rumbled nearer, and, every few seconds, the trunks of the trees immediately in view through the triangular gap at the foot of the basha were bright with lightning flashes. The reflected power from sheets and zig-zags of light picked out the clumps of lichen on the bark and tendrils of fungus with startling clarity: the stalks of spore-bodies looked like heads of unkempt hair.

I fell asleep and I dreamed of James's sister Chotty. She was coming at me with a particular knife she uses to make her beef stews, her pheasant pies. 'It's quite all right,' she said, 'it doesn't matter now that he's drowned. There's no need to apologize. I don't want to hear your explanations.'

This is the first of a two-part article.

COLIN THUBRON
NIGHT IN VIETNAM

In those late days anyone could go to Saigon who was rash enough to try. A few months before the Tet offensive, there were already hundreds of Vietcong hiding in the suburbs, and foreign travellers were reduced to a trickle of irresponsible intruders like myself.

I arrived with an unfocused idea of discovering something about war. I sweated along the streets in a threadbare tweed jacket which wouldn't fit into my rucksack (every photograph of myself at this time, whether in Burma, Japan or Cambodia, includes this ludicrous piece of clothing). The leather from my boots was shedding itself in dust-clogged slivers, but I barely noticed. I had grown into my clothes the way travellers do who haven't looked in a mirror for weeks.

I had little more than twenty-four hours in Vietnam. But I was refused transport to the surrounding country and I walked out into flatlands of such desolate similitude that I turned back after a few hours and explored Saigon instead.

I don't think it is hindsight that tinges the city with the colours of dying. The tree-lined boulevards of this 'Paris of the East' were no more than the fixed grin on a corpse. Behind the veil of chestnut trees, the concrete façades were cracked and discoloured, and the shops burrowed into their own darkness like rabbit-holes, or threw out cheap awnings and a sprinkle of neon signs. Here and there, between faceless apartment blocks, the architecture of nineteenth-century France intruded with a sad grace, or some government ministry piled upon itself in an impenetrable heap of wedding-cake Ionic.

As I tramped the streets, I rarely knew precisely where I was. My map pinpointed six official buildings and a few streets ending in *-ngi* or *-uyen*. The rest was an empty grid. I couldn't speak a word of Vietnamese. The posters pinned to walls or telegraph poles were printed in a Roman alphabet so flecked by cabalistic accent-marks that the language looked literally unutterable. I knew nobody. I was dreaming the traveller's arrogant dream of understanding things by an ignorant observing and listening. So Saigon interpreted itself to me only in clichés—US servicemen lumbering like intrusive giants among a fragile, hard-faced people, enigmatically beautiful.

The whole city was glazed in rain. Its peculiar noise was the *shush* of bicycle tyres over wet tarmac—bicycles and trishaws everywhere, a treadmill of lean yellow legs. On the outskirts, the streets faltered into tracks where ox-carts creaked and wobbled into the rice-fields and barracks of Vietnamese soldiers hid behind whitewashed walls crested in barbed wire.

I became mesmerized by the women. They wore split skirts over pantaloons, and high collars, aggressively chaste. They emerged from their sordid apartment blocks with the cold immaculacy of mannequins and tripped along rubble-strewn pavements in a titter of high heels. Their faces were urban and often exquisite, nested in Western hairstyles. But their incongruous illusion of wealth and separateness had not been bought with American money. An old and rigid culture incarcerated them in this defensive glamour. If they had been used, they yet seemed untouched.

I had no money for a decent hotel, let alone for a woman. The night-clubs in the million-strong Chinese quarter of Cholon were asleep in the mid-afternoon, and I wandered instead among fruit-markets filled with brown-skinned men come in from the country, and old women draped in Annamese black robes. Compared to the shifting townspeople, they were earthy, dark, rather solemn.

I was the only foreigner in the National Archaeological Museum. It had almost closed down. Nothing was lit. Fragments from extinguished dynasties were scattered indecipherably in its gloom. I searched the stone gods' faces for some secret that the people outside had withheld. The statues gazed back at me from the pilfered plinths of temples. Their faces were broad and thick-lipped: another race. Their stone haloes rose in flame-like mandorlas that had been worked into runnels like the excreta of worms. There were photographs of jungle-darkened temples in parts of Vietnam where I couldn't go. Their towers were tasselled in shrubs, and their stonework showed the same mysterious delicacy as the gods' haloes.

I felt excluded and restless. I was walking through Vietnam's past with the same ignorance as I had walked through its present. Why hadn't I read anything before coming? I had entertained ideas about encountering Vietnam free from prejudice; I would be a clean slate for the country to write upon. But the country had written nothing, and I was a blank.

I stopped beside another man, staring into a cabinet of worn sandstone faces.

'Are these portraits?' I asked the question to make contact.

Yes, he said, in a dry, guttural English. They were Champa sculptures from Huong Qua (or somewhere).

I nudged him into conversation. He had the face of a middle-aged boy. His hair was close-cropped, his eyes lidless and undreaming behind their spectacles. He taught physics at Saigon's university, he said. 'And you are with the army here...?' But his gaze on me was uncertain, as if something about me didn't fit.

'No, I'm English.' I added foolishly: 'I'm just looking around.'

He showed no surprise. He began asking me about conditions in Britain and how easy was it to get a work permit? He wanted to leave. 'Our top people have all got money or property in the States, ready for when the time comes.'

I wanted to ask him naive questions. What was really happening in this city that the powerful were deserting? What lay behind the hard, immaculate faces of those women? Or behind the peasant watchfulness in the markets? Were they filled with fear or just a habit of enduring? Did they expect anything any more?

But instead I found myself answering his questions about Britain and visas. The man seemed as far from his stricken country as I was. Whatever it had once meant to him had disintegrated. He was going to abandon it.

My plane was leaving at dawn for Singapore, and I planned to sleep in the civil airport. In the dusk, I flagged down a taxi and we bumped out of the last suburbs across a rain-sodden wasteland. I was set down in front of a military enclave that I did not recognize. Behind the barbed wire, helmeted heads muttered and coalesced.

Suddenly, as I hesitated there, I was bathed in floodlights. It was like being caught naked. I imagined myself in American military eyes—a figure in idiotic jacket and disintegrating boots (a civilian in war-time feels unmanned). But under the helmets the faces were all Vietnamese. When I shouted for the civil airport they merely raised the barrier-pole. They couldn't speak English. They waved me on.

I blundered down a malebolge of barbed-wire compounds and exercise grounds, through deepening rings of windowless barracks and ranked jeeps. Occasionally a lorry or an armoured personnel-carrier went grinding past me, and on either side dim constellations of lights were moving back and forth to muffled engines. Whenever I reached a check-point, the Vietnamese guards would peer into my face, salute, and lift the barrier. I was assumed to be an American. Nobody halted or questioned me. By now I was deep in the heart of the largest military air-base in Saigon.

I was appalled at this ease of penetration. My intrusion grew more incriminating at every step.

At the next military police barrier, I shouted: 'Are there any Americans here? I want an American!'

A sentry called into the dark, while I waited. A three-quarter moon was tangled in the barbed wire above me. I felt suddenly tired. My rucksack was buckling my shoulders forwards instead of bracing them back. I wanted to sleep somewhere: anywhere.

'Where the hell's the civil airport?'

Then a military police sergeant appeared. He was formidably big for a Vietnamese, and swung a baton. But as he advanced on me he grew more and more deferential. Even in clothes like mine, six foot of lanky Westerner was a *bone fide* American.

'Sir yes, sir yes,' he mumbled—it was the only English he knew. He gave an order. The pole-bar lifted. The sentry saluted. I marched through in secret despair.

Ten minutes later the concrete barracks and blockhouses fell away, and I found myself on the edge of the military airstrip—an asphalt plain gleaming with rain and faintly reflected lights. It was utterly still. The noise of lorry engines had thinned behind me to a susurration, indistinguishable from the sifting of wind through the stubbled grass. And there in front of me, in moonlit ranks of silver, spread scores of American jet bombers. They gleamed like ghosts on the asphalt sea. It was hard to believe in them. The breeze had died, and there was a sultry, almost liquid weight in the air.

Quarter of a mile across the runway, I saw the beacon of the civil airport. It beckoned with a fitful promise of sleep. It was eleven o'clock. My feet felt numb. Partly because the bombers looked so intangible, so unreal, I started to march across the runway towards the beacon. My boots scraped and rang with a desolate loneliness. I remembered war stories of soldiers too tired to care if they were shot.

I understood. Weariness can pass for heroism.

Even the next moments held a dream-like stupor. I saw a jeep slide over the tarmac and caught the wink of bayonets as its soldiers jumped out. They clattered towards me. I should have raised my hands, but the gesture was too melodramatic, too un-British. Instead I stood stock-still, like a witness at my own execution. They panted up to me.

My voice sounded oddly angry and unpleading: 'I'm looking for the civil airport.'

I'd walked clean across the military one and into its forbidden heart. Who would believe me? But the faces surrounding me were Vietnamese, bewildered. Their rifle-points dropped from my chest to my unshining boots and were then eased behind their shoulders. They muttered together a moment, then saluted ashamedly. The jeep glided away and disappeared.

I made for the airport beacon, racked by sudden, nervous laughter. I indulged a fantasy of myself as a Soviet saboteur with a rucksack full of limpet mines. I could have stuck one to each bomber as I went by. I imagined their detonation in the moonlight, like fat cigars exploding from their silver paper. Then I squirmed through a gap in the perimeter wire and trudged into the terminal.

It was almost empty. I peeled off my rucksack and stretched out across three seats in the shadow of a pillar. I closed my eyes. But something refused me sleep. My body was dog-tired and heavy as rock, but my head seemed detached from it and felt light with sensation. The whole day had been so steeped in unreality that I thought I might levitate.

But the day wasn't over. Voices rasped above me. I opened my eyes to see helmeted heads staring down: military police, Americans.

'You can't stay here,' they said.

'But I'm leaving early in the morning.'

'You can't stay here. Security risk.' But even they concluded I was a soldier. 'Are you British in this war now?'

I felt a quiver of submerged patriotism. Were the British so insignificant that American military police didn't know if we were fighting alongside them? 'Not yet,' I said.

'We'll drive you back into Saigon. Curfew starts at midnight, so get off the streets. They shoot on sight.'

Twenty minutes later from the centre of a half-sleeping city, I watched the lights of the jeep fading into the dark like a pair of cynical eyes. My watch said quarter to twelve. I made for the main boulevards, but an impenetrable perimeter of barbed wire cauterized the buildings that lined them. All about me, the windows were shuttered or darkened and the doors of the few hotels bolted and unlit. Every road was deserted. The street-lamps shed down long avenues of dimness, as if I were walking across a dilapidated stage, watched by an invisible audience. Once or twice, a door half-opened or a curtain shifted momentarily from a lamplit profile. But that was all. I was reduced by utter weariness. I was no longer quite myself. Myself was plodding Saigon ten minutes before curfew like a drunken GI, while I watched him with only a distant fear.

He hunted for a vestige of cover. But every thicket and roadside shrub—anything that could have lent refuge to a sniper—had been hacked from the paths. It was only on the stroke of midnight that he crawled through a wire fence into a small graveyard, whose sanctity had prevented the cutting of its trees. He heard the long ripping of his foolish jacket on the barbed wire. The tombstones glimmered in the grass. But he felt only relief. The dead, tonight, were more companionable than the living.

I curled up in the largest bush, which was barely thick enough to conceal me. I was trembling, pouring sweat. The glare of the nearest street-lamp struck me through a faint, leaf-sheltered patina. I eased my rucksack under my head and stared up into a sky littered with stars and a moon like a rotten cheese. Between these stars and me a whining canopy of mosquitoes hung. I could scarcely breathe, but I covered my head with my spare shirt and prayed for the dawn.

Soon afterwards, something sniffed and scuffed at my boots. I drew up my knees. Then, with a long, betraying growl, it threw back its head and sent its bark moaning and echoing over the city—the kind of measured cry that was set to last for as long as its victim remained. In my ears this sad, fluctuating call, prolonged minute after minute, seemed to waver almost into words, announcing my strange presence to every patrol. I bunched in a suffocated cocoon, my head still buried in my shirt, hearing my own breathing, fierce and frightened. But little by little the dog's barking was taken up and re-echoed by another dog, then another and another, until at last the whole air seemed to be howling and baying at the waxing moon, and nobody could have told where the alarm had originated or if it were not some huge, spontaneous requiem for the desecrated city.

However tired, I never slept. Six hours later the dogs in the most distant suburbs were still passing their lament into the scarred countryside, until the stars faded into dawn. As I scrambled back on to the road, my whole body streaked in dirt, the peasants' ox-carts were already lurching to market, and a few of those stone-faced and unfathomable women were treading the streets.

Even now, years later, when people ask me if I ever went to Vietnam, I find myself saying that I never did.

MARTHA GELLHORN
WHITE INTO BLACK

This is a cautionary tale, showing how travel narrows the mind.

I left my happy home in Mexico in February 1952 to spend five or six weeks in Haiti. I knew nothing about Haiti except the splendid name of Toussaint l'Ouverture, but Haiti as such was not the point. The point was scenery, weather, sea to swim in as background for sitting still and solitary and starting a novel. Resident travel. When you can't write at home, go someplace else. I had seen Haiti in passing, years earlier, and remembered high green mountains, cobalt sea and Port-au-Prince, a climbing white city festooned in flowering vines and bougainvillaea. Any Caribbean island would have suited; Haiti was a careless choice.

The years had done Port-au-Prince no good. A taxi-driver recommended the grandest hotel by the sea. The walls were peeling, a juke box deafened, drunks abounded, and the rooms were sticky with old dust. Bar talk whined in discouragement. Tourism was on the skids, people were selling up and leaving, president followed president, all crooks, and in the general chaos no one knew what would happen next. The streets of the city now looked like dust tracks, the black citizens wretchedly poor and glum. I should have left then, after a day. The vibes, which existed before being named, were very bad. Instead, at ten o'clock on the second night, I moved from the loud hotel to a pension higher up the hillside where I was the only guest. Here, too, everything was seedy but at least quiet.

It rained; unheard of. I took against Port-au-Prince and bought a map. South over the mountains, on a bay, was a tiny dot marked Jacmel. The manageress at the pension had never heard of the place. This sort of information cheers me instead of sensibly putting me off. I imagined Jacmel as unspoiled, unexcited, a sleepy fishing village where I would find a simple room with sea view and breezes. Work hard, swim in the bay, amble about, eat, sleep and repeat same. It took two days to make travel arrangements, now forgotten; no one seemed to have any reason to go to Jacmel. The delay allowed time for voodoo and a sprained ankle.

The waiter invited me to the voodoo ceremony. I was flattered and interested: exotic mysteries in the Haitian jungle. In those days voodoo was a secret religion; now it

95

figures in a popular TV serial. Slaves, in the seventeenth century in Haiti, invented voodoo from confused West African tribal memories. Voodoo remains the true religion of the peasants, the majority of Haitians. That night, in a crumbling shack lit by kerosene lamps, I wondered whether these barefoot ragged people looked much different from their slave ancestors. The priest, a bony fiery-eyed man in a cloak and trousers, crouched and cavorted, tracing magical signs on the dirt floor, but kept a calculating eye on the believers. He seemed a dubious manipulator. A woman, another woman, a man, became possessed by a voodoo god and thrashed about violently, ran, staggered, shouting in unintelligible unnatural voices. If enough people ended up foaming and fainting, presumably the priest was a success. The result of all the chanting and drumming and hysteria was fear. I could see it on the faces around me. When the priest grabbed a squawking chicken, preparatory to biting off its head in sacrifice, I moved silently out the door.

The bad vibes came back as I groped my way along the path. Uneasy, unlivable, country. But the night air was soft on my skin and sweet to breathe and the sky was true Caribbean, soft blackness, fur soft, with more diamond starlight than anywhere I know in the world and I told myself to buck up, nothing could be too wrong in such a beautiful place. Next morning the sun shone on sea and mountains and I leapt like a kudu downhill to finish departure chores. Skidding on a stone, I wrenched my ankle and hopped and limped into town, thinking this was a bruise that would soon cure itself. And so arrived in Jacmel with optimism and a badly swollen ankle.

At first sight, Jacmel charmed. What I saw was an unpaved street running back from the cliff that edged the bay. The far view was glinting blue water; the near view was wooden houses, two storeys high, with balconies and long windows (tropical French) and pillars and fretwork. They were painted strawberry pink, lemon yellow, white with green trimmings, pretty as a picture. Opposite the row of houses, a sort of village green was shaded by big feathery trees, flamboyante and jacaranda, and huge mangoes and others, perhaps Indian laurel. Lovely, I thought, what luck. I presented myself with winning smiles at the Pension Croft, middle house in the row, white with green trim, the only hotel.

Madame Croft received me icily in the ground floor dining-room. She was an ornate coal-black lady with a mountainous involved hair-do over mean eyes. She did not bother to answer and I stood there, weight on my operational foot, wondering if this was a bad morning or if she was always rude to guests. How was I to know that my skin colour revolted Madame Croft? Her skin didn't matter a hoot to me, though her manner did.

I had not thought of Haiti in terms of colour. Probably I knew it was a black republic. Good. No concern of mine. Most of the people in this part of the world were black or coppery brown or a mixture; non-white, anyway. Mexican Indians, whom I knew best, were one of the main reasons I loved living in Mexico. I had travelled a lot in the Caribbean and found the islanders specially kind and agreeable. Why should Haiti be different?

A maid, giggling from nerves, showed me my room. A corridor ran the length of the floor, doors opened on both sides to cubicles whose thin wood walls did not meet the ceiling. Primitive air conditioning. A window at either end of the corridor let in scant air and light. My cubicle had no window, a weak bulb on a cord from the ceiling, a bowl and pitcher, an iron cot, wobbly table and chair and a rope nailed to the wall for hanging clothes. I wanted to lie down but the sheets gave off a daunting sour smell, so I sat on the chair, my foot on the cot, listening to a man who yawned and spat, yawned and spat. And listened to the school next door where lessons had resumed. For four hours in the morning and two in the afternoon, little Haitians kneeled on their school benches and shouted in unison whatever they were learning. 'Deux fois deux font quatre, trois fois deux font six.' In due course I heard geography—les grands fleuves du monde sont—French kings and spelling. If it stunned my mind, what did it do to theirs?

Come lunch-time, I limped downstairs to the soiled table-cloths and the flies. The dining-room was a bare white room with seven or eight tables, opening to the street and village green. I was given a table stuck off in a corner. Nearby tables had been pulled away so that I sat in a cordon sanitaire of space. No one looked at me directly; sly glances took me in; no one answered my *bon jour* then, or ever after spoke to me. With prickly intuition, I knew that the whispering and bursts of laughter had to do with me. The food was inedible, tasting of garlic and sugar.

At stressful moments in travel, I try to console myself with worse moments elsewhere. Is this as ghastly as The Light of Shaokwan? Not quite, cheer up, it isn't raining, the weather is perfect, you can lie under a tree; for clearly, walking was a thing of the past.

My search for a tree out of sight of the Pension Croft led me close to a small shoebox-shaped building of cream-coloured stucco with a sign: Bibliothèque. A public library in Jacmel seemed a miracle, as did Monsieur Réné the librarian and his assistant Mademoiselle Annette, a girl so silent that she became invisible. Monsieur Réné was small, thin, brown not coal black, with receding greying hair, glasses and a proper dark suit. He smiled at me so that I wanted to kiss him and blubber thanks but instead told him that I was a writer with no place to write and could I work in the library. Monsieur Réné fluttered with enthusiasm; he had never met a writer; he would gladly give me an empty room in the back.

By way of confirming what I guessed, I asked Monsieur Réné if there was any other foreigner here. Such as a foreigner washed ashore from a wreck with permament brain damage, or a criminal foreigner hiding from the cops of three countries. Monsieur Réné was puzzled by my question. No, he said, we are all Haitians. Foreigners never come here; our village offers no distractions. I saw it, then. I was the only Negro in Jacmel. And, furthermore, a Negro who had gate-crashed an exclusive white club, the Pension Croft. The Pension Croft, I lied, was very nice but a bit noisy; could I rent a quieter room in someone's house? Monsieur Réné was amazed. The houses were filled with large families, nobody would wish to take in a guest. Not surprising. Few white families would welcome an unknown black visitor. I dared not ask, so soon, about transport back to Port-au-Prince, but when I did Monsieur Réné had no ideas; he never went himself; his car was not strong enough and Port-au-Prince seemed too far, too strange; no one from Jacmel went there.

Beyond the main library with its two rows of bookshelves, Monsieur Réné ushered me into an oversized empty closet. They found a table and chair, the window was luxury, the silence blessed. Since I hadn't brought anything with me, might I just sit here? Monsieur Réné hurried to find a writing-pad and two pencils and left on tiptoe so that creation could begin. I wrote on the pad 'Self pity, that way madness lies,' then stretched out on the clean floor, to rest my ankle. Monsieur Réné knocked and entered before I could scramble up. In this position, he saw what ailed me, was full of sympathy and insisted on driving me to the clinic.

The clinic has vanished from memory but I remember the smiling doctor, a slightly larger edition of Monsieur Réné, in a white coat. He produced an enormous syringe, suitable for a horse, and a gigantic thick needle, about six inches long. I was paralyzed by my new role, lonely Negro scared to offend white authority. With terror, I let that kind dangerous doctor plunge the needle into my hot puffed ankle and force in what seemed a pint of liquid. Novocaine, said the doctor, all goes well now. Monsieur Réné drove me back to the Pension Croft.

By four that afternoon, my left foot and ankle resembled elephantiasis and the pain was torture. I clamped the pillow over my face and groaned aloud; through the pillow I heard myself making animal noises. I wept torrents. I couldn't stop and was frightened to be so helpless among enemies: shivering, sweating, snivelling, half crazy. Madame Croft told a maid to inquire why the white-Negro was being a nuisance. Madame Croft appeared in the doorway to check for herself. She stared at me with glacial contempt, but did send up pitcher after pitcher of boiling water. For the next three hours I soaked my elephantine extremity in the washbowl and was finally beyond the howling stage. Madame Croft sent up greasy soup. I slept despite the cot smell and gruelling sounds from other rooms.

Suffering is supposed to ennoble; not me, it stupefies me. I could have saved myself by ordering a bottle of rum and getting sodden drunk, and then another bottle, though first finding a telephone to call the US Consulate in Port-au-Prince and demand evacuation on medical grounds. I thought drink was for pleasure among friends and never turned to consulates in an hour of need. In growing misery, I clung to one plan: survive until I could walk, then dump my suitcase and proceed on foot, hippety-hop over the mountains, to an airplane and flight from this doom island.

When I could return to the library, I did not report that the nice doctor had just about finished me but Monsieur Réné saw that I was barely mobile and brought me a cane. My creeping along with a cane, sneaker on right foot, cut-open bedroom slipper on left foot, added to my repellent skin colour, made me an irresistible target. When classes ended at noon the homing schoolchildren picked up stones and cheerfully stoned me. They were behind me and I didn't know what the yelling and laughing was about until a stone hit me. I thought this an accident and turned to smile forgiveness, only to see a bunch of pretty little kids, dressed in those French-style black school smocks, jumping up and down and aiming more stones. Which hit me. 'Blanc! Blanc!' they shouted, meaning 'Nigger! Nigger!' The stones weren't large, nor were the kids; I wasn't hurt. I was an old lame Negro, chivvied and harassed by white kids, and I burned with outrage. And with hatred for those adults on the street who watched, smiling approval.

There was nothing to do except retreat to the library, where again I suppressed the news of the day. The silent retreat shamed me. Shame was hardest to bear. I could see it would take a while to get used to humiliation. If anyone ever got used to it?

My unborn novel was by now a sad joke. All day, I sat on the hard library chair, resting my foot on an orange crate, and read and brooded. From whenever ideas first reach a child's mind, I had been indoctrinated by my parents' words and deeds never to condemn by race, creed, colour or even nationality. The history of our time gave that early teaching the force of moral law; I refer, above all, to the Nazis. But there was still plenty of repression in the world, by race, creed and colour, and I was wholeheartedly against it. Yet here I sat, in racist Jacmel, grinding my teeth in a fury of counter-racism. I wondered whether I was ruined for life and would become a disgrace to my parents, loathing blacks.

It is hard to believe that, in 1952, there were only two places on earth where blacks could not be insulted or mistreated simply because of their colour: Haiti and Liberia. The Caribbean colonies were intact though certainly benign by 1952, but the African colonies were far from guaranteed humane and insult was automatic: no dogs or natives allowed. The American South practised apartheid, discrimination and segregation, and deprived Negroes of the basic right to vote. Ugly and violent white racism: and the Civil Rights Act, which finally outlawed all this, was twelve years away. South Africa made customary apartheid into the law of the land, in 1948. But Haiti had been a sovereign state for just short of one hundred and fifty years. No living Haitian ever suffered here from white racism.

Hold on. Error. For twenty years, from 1915 until 1934, when Franklin Roosevelt recalled them, the US Marines were overlords of Haiti. They had been sent for allegedly humanitarian reasons, to quell disorder in Haiti; this action was justified by the Monroe Doctrine (the time-honoured precursor of the Brezhnev Doctrine). Ordinary Haitians resented the Marines who treated them like American Negroes. No Negroes were then accepted in the Marine Corps. But surely the Marines hadn't troubled remote little Jacmel? There is a sort of folk knowledge that drifts and stays in the air. Could I have been reaping what the Marines sowed: anger, revenge, insult for injury? Americans tend to forget, or never knew, how often our government through our soldiery has interfered in the domestic affairs of others in the Caribbean area; and certainly we ignore the after-effects, lingering on in collective memory.

Haiti baffled me then and baffles me now, decades later. It is, I think, the most beautiful country in the Caribbean. It has a marvellous healthy climate, fertile soil, plenty of water, some mineral resources, possible hydro-electric power, a surrounding sea full of fish. With responsible government, education, public health care, Haiti could long since have become happy and prosperous. It has never been happy, though, as a slave-owning French colony called Saint Domingue, for well over a hundred years it made French investors and local landowners rich. Saint Domingue was notorious for brutality to slaves, which means something in view of contemporary standards. Slaves were worked to death, with all the attendant punishments and degradations. Ten labouring years was average life expectancy. Saint Domingue was really an eighteenth-century forerunner of Nazi concentration camps. Half a million slaves finally rebelled in the bloodiest uprising of the slave world, fought French soldiers with raging bravery for three years, and won their freedom. It is a colossal story of will and courage. After the United States, Haiti was the second independent nation in the New World. Since 1804, Haiti has been misruled by Haitians.

Misrule is nothing new anywhere at any time. Perhaps Haiti never had a hope, poisoned from the beginning by its terrible past. There is something in this, looking around the world today. The worse the early oppression, the worse oppression continues, like battered babies maturing into baby batterers. It is rubbish to pretend, as the Reagan administration does, that communism alone assures misrule. Consider capitalist states in Central and South America, Turkey, Pakistan, the Philippines, most of Africa from north to south. Zaire is a model of rapacious corruption; as the Congo, it had a famously nasty rapacious past. Can the relentless siege mentality of the Afrikaners in South Africa be traced back to the Boer War? The rulers in the Kremlin are more understandable as lineal descendants of the Tsars; too bad they weren't all brought up in Sweden. How long does it take a people to outgrow and reject inherited misrule? However long, they have to do it themselves if they can.

Toussaint l'Ouverture, the hero slave leader, might have been the founding father Haiti needed, but he died in a French prison. Two self-styled Emperors, engrossed in their imperial life style, were followed by a turnover of greedy presidents, grabbing power by palace *putsch*, rigged elections, assassinations. The procession of presidents ended fatally in 1957 with Papa Doc Duvalier who locked his people in a sinister police state, ruling by terror through thugs in sunglasses, the Tonton Macoutes, by torture, murder and the ominous use of voodoo. Now Papa Doc's heir, Baby Doc, upholds the family tradition. Maybe the Duvaliers, Presidents-for-Life, have founded a dynasty and can give Haiti another hundred years of slavery.

After one hundred and seventy-nine years of home-grown misrule to date, Haiti is among the world's least developed countries, economically and socially. Haiti ranks 122. Only thirteen countries, mostly new African states, are more deprived. (The US ranks 7, Britain ranks 16.) These statistics are not a comment on style of government but on the material conditions, within each state, of the mass of the governed. In the western hemisphere, Haiti has the lowest per capita income; the fewest schools, teachers and literates; the fewest hospitals and doctors; the highest infant mortality; the lowest life expectancy. Misrule is an ongoing (as they say) fact from Haiti south, and can be measured in the same terms. (El Salvador 84, Guatemala 85, etc; but Cuba 36, far ahead of all countries in the Caribbean, in Central and South America with only Argentina, 37, a close rival. What do we make of that?) Haiti's sorry distinction is to be bottom of the bottom class in an area where public welfare is not the most urgent priority of government and poverty ranges from heavy to crushing.

People often say, with pride, 'I'm not interested in politics.' They might as well say, 'I'm not interested in my standard of living, my health, my job, my rights, my freedoms, my future or any future.' Politics is the business of governing and nobody can escape being governed, for better or worse. In the few fortunate societies where voting is free and honest, most people take the weird view that politics is a horse race—you bet on a winner or loser every so often, if you can bestir yourself; but politics is not a personal concern. Politics is *everything*—from clean drinking water through the preservation of forests, whales, British Leyland to nuclear weapons and the disposal thereof. If we mean to keep any control over our world and lives, we must be interested in politics.

The unlucky ignorant people of Haiti never understood that they had to take an interest in politics while they still had the chance. I think their brains were fuddled by three hundred years of voodoo. They were too busy propitiating a gang of demented malevolent gods to notice that men, not gods, were running their country and themselves into the ground. If they know now, it is late. Once you get a tyranny, you don't easily get rid of it. Much better to remember about eternal vigilance.

While I was brooding on my chair one morning, Monsieur Réné appeared with a book. He said it was the only book in English in the library, where I was always the only customer. No one could read English but perhaps it would interest me. The book was E.M. Forster's *Two Cheers for Democracy*. A miracle of the highest order. Oh, that beautiful book! It shines with reason, mercy, honour, good will and wit; and is written in those water-smooth sentences that one wants to stroke for the pleasure of feeling them. No longer isolated, I had Mr Forster's mind for company. When I finished the book, I wrote pages to Mr Forster, like a letter in a bottle, telling him that he was a light in the darkness and a moral example to mankind. I resolved to reform. I would not disgrace my parents or Mr Forster; no goddamned black racists were going to make a racist of me.

During these month-long days, I observed the weather but took no joy from it, though it was joyful. The sky went up in pale to darker translucent layers of blue, the air smelled of flowers and sea and sun, so delicious you could taste it. The Caribbean, my favourite sea, stretched out like a great smooth sapphire carpet with wind moving gently under it. I hungered for the sea and one afternoon nerved myself to chance the path down the cliff. With a dress over my bathing-suit, a towel around my neck, the usual footwear and cane, I made my way slowly to the beach. The sand was golden, empty and lovely; no boats, no people and no sign of there having been either.

I chucked my stuff and got into the sea like a crab, using my arms. Freedom returned; I could move. I swam far out in the silky water and floated, rejoicing. Jacmel washed off me, body and soul. Unable to sing, a felt lack, I made shouting noises of delight. Every day, until I had two sound legs, I would bring bread and papaya, the only edible pension food, to this glorious beach and swim and sunbathe. Happiness was possible, even in Jacmel.

When I started to drag myself up the sand to my clothes, I saw the boys. They were playing ball with my dress, footwear, cane, towel. There were eight of them, teenagers, fleet of foot and laughing their heads off. I stood up, with dignity, and informed them that they were too big for this game and please give me my effects. They instantly invented a new game. They ran in close and flicked me with dress and towel, twirled my sneaker against my face, feinted and jabbed with the cane. After lurching once for my dress, I realized that pleased them; also that it was useless. I imagined, with dread, hobbling up the street in my white bathing-suit while all Jacmel came out to jeer. But I could not make it, not without foot covering and cane.

I limped on the comfortable sand towards the path, maintaining cold silence and, I hoped, a calm face. They followed, same game, same taunting laughter. My good resolves left me. I wanted to cause them grievous bodily harm. Failing that, I wanted to curse them at the top of my lungs. But I was afraid to anger these white bully boys. They could do much worse to a defenceless Negro. And who would punish them, who would care? Monsieur Réné, the tolerant educated white, could hardly stand up to the whole nigger-baiting town. I had to conceal rage and alarm, as other Negroes have surely done, and stand and take it. Suddenly, they had had all the fun they needed, threw my things around the beach, and ran up the path. I collected them piece by piece, got organized, and climbed to the street, knowing I would not risk the sea again. Jacmel had defeated me.

Now it was Mardi Gras and Jacmel seethed with excitement because the Carnival Queen of Haiti was arriving by air to preside over the festivities. Everyone was costumed and painted and bouncing around the streets. Alone on the pension balcony, I watched this throng of merry Haitians and thought them grotesque and hideous, just as they thought me. My only interest in the event was the Queen; I had to get a ride back to Port-au-Prince. Neither the Queen nor her plane were available to a white-Negro but an ancient limousine had brought the Queen's mother, as chaperone and the Magistrate, whatever that meant. I elbowed through the crowd to this gentleman and made him a threatening speech. If I were left here, probably to die of gangrene, the entire world would know and blame Haiti; I was a famous journalist with powerful connections and etcetera. I don't think I have ever behaved worse and I didn't care.

They allowed me to pay for a place in the limousine. I was ordered to the front seat where the chauffeur, a servant, had to put up with me. The grand passengers in the rear did not deign to speak to me. If they thought I wanted to sit near them or talk with them, they were crazy. We were all racists together. And I had the best view of the country, lush and flowered like Douanier Rousseau jungle, and beautiful every mile of the way.

Air service between the islands was sketchy. I got to St Thomas where I met a man who frolicked about in a Piper Cub, an air bum. He gave me a lift to Philipsburg on the Dutch side of St Martin, an enchanting island that was, and still is by choice, half Dutch, half French. I had been blissfully becalmed on the French side, ten years earlier; why didn't I come here at once and spare myself Haiti? Because Haiti was the unknown, that's all, and that's enough. I haven't yet learned to be careful in travel.

Philipsburg had a dear dinky Dutch charm; freshly-painted shutters on little square houses, starched white curtains, neat gardens, swept streets. The houses belonged to friendly composed black people, speaking Caribbean English. Accommodation was in the Government Rest House, four barely furnished but spotless rooms. Here, at last, I would get to work. But I felt tender to myself, I deserved a long convalescence to recover from Jacmel. Beyond the village, I found a cove where I spent my days, swimming naked in aquamarine water, lying on white sand, dreaming a novel instead of writing it.

A handful of white people lived on the Dutch side of the island. We had no reason to foregather and didn't. The two races lived in amity under the guardian eye of a lone black policeman. Since no one despised and maltreated me because of my skin, I stopped being a racist. Much later I began to think, imagine, hope, that maybe, somehow, possibly I understood just the tiniest bit of what it really means to be black in a bad place.

BRUCE CHATWIN
A COUP

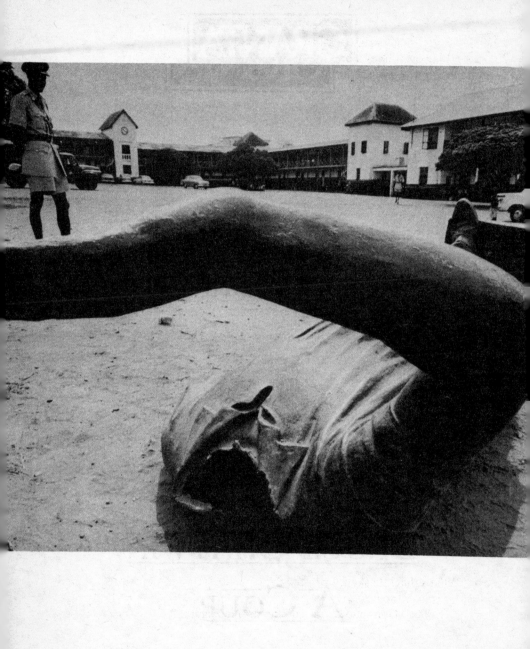

The coup began at seven on Sunday morning. It was a grey and windless dawn and the grey Atlantic rollers broke in long even lines along the beach. The palms above the tide-mark shivered in a current of cooler air that blew in off the breakers. Out at sea—beyond the surf—there were several black fishing canoes. Buzzards were spiralling above the market, swooping now and then to snatch up scraps of offal. The butchers were slaughtering, even on a Sunday.

We were in a taxi when the coup began, on our way to another country. We had passed the Hôtel de la Plage, passed the Sûreté Nationale, and then we drove under a limply-flapping banner which said, in red letters, that Marxist-Leninism was the one and only guide. In front of the Presidential Palace was a road-block. A soldier waved us to a halt, and then waved us on.

'Pourriture!' said my friend, Domingo, and grinned.

Domingo was a young, honey-coloured mulatto with a flat and friendly face, a curly moustache and a set of dazzling teeth. He was the direct descendant of Francisco-Félix de Souza, the Chacha of Ouidah, a Brazilian slaver who lived and died in Dahomey, and about whom I was writing a book.

Domingo had two wives. The first wife was old and the skin hung in loose folds off her back. The second wife was hardly more than a child. We were on our way to Togo, to watch a football game, and visit his great-uncle who knew a lot of old stories about the Chacha.

The taxi was jammed with football-fans. On my right sat a very black old man wrapped in green and orange cotton. His teeth were also orange from chewing cola nuts, and from time to time he spat.

Outside the Presidential Palace hung an overblown poster of the Head of State, and two much smaller posters of Lenin and Kim Il-Sung. Beyond the road-block, we took a right fork, on through the old European section where there were bungalows and balks of bougainvillaea by the gates. Along the sides of the tarmac, market-women walked in single file with basins and baskets balanced on their head.

'What's that?' I asked. I could see some kind of commotion, up ahead, towards the airport.

'Accident!' Domingo shrugged, and grinned again.

Then all the women were screaming, and scattering their yams and pineapples, and rushing for the shelter of the gardens. A white Peugeot shot down the middle of the road, swerving right and left to miss the women. The driver waved for us to turn back, and just then, we heard the crack of gunfire.

'C'est la guerre!' our driver shouted, and spun the taxi round.

'I knew it.' Domingo grabbed my arm. 'I knew it.'

The sun was up by the time we got to downtown Cotonou. In the taxi-park the crowd had panicked and overturned a brazier, and a stack of crates had caught fire. A policeman blew his whistle and bawled for water. Above the rooftops, there was a column of black smoke, rising.

'They're burning the Palace,' said Domingo. 'Quick! Run!'

We ran, bumped into other running figures, and ran on. A man shouted 'Mercenary!' and lunged for my shoulder. I ducked and we dodged down a sidestreet. A boy in a red shirt beckoned me into a bar. It was dark inside. People were clustered round a radio. Then the bartender screamed, wildly, in African, at me, and at the boy. And then I was out again on the dusty red street, shielding my head with my arms, pushed and pummelled against the corrugated building by four hard, acridly-sweating men until the gendarmes came to fetch me in a jeep.

'For your own proper protection,' their officer said, as the handcuffs snapped around my wrists.

The last I ever saw of Domingo he was standing in the street, crying, as the jeep drove off, and he vanished in a clash of coloured cottons.

In the barracks guardroom a skinny boy, stripped to a pair of purple underpants, sat hunched against the wall. His hands and feet were bound with rope, and he had the greyish look Africans get when they are truly frightened. A gecko hung motionless on the dirty whitewash. Outside the door there was a papaya with a tall scaly trunk and yellowish fruit. A mud-wall ran along the far side of the compound. Beyond the wall the noise of gunfire continued, and the high-pitched wailing of women.

A corporal came in and searched me. He was small, wiry, angular, and his cheekbones shone. He took my watch, wallet, passport and notebook.

'Mercenary!' he said, pointing to the patch-pocket on the leg of my khaki trousers. His gums were spongy and his breath was foul.

'No,' I said, submissively. 'I'm a tourist.'

'Mercenary!' he shrieked, and slapped my face—not hard, but hard enough to hurt.

He held up my fountain-pen. 'What?'

'A pen,' I said. It was a black Mont-Blanc.

'What for?'

'To write with.'

'A gun?'

'Not a gun.'

'Yes, a gun!'

I sat on a bench, staring at the skinny boy who continued to stare at his toes. The corporal sat cross-legged in the doorway with his sub-machine-gun trained on me. Outside in the yard, two sergeants were distributing rifles, and a truck was loading with troops. The troops sat down with the barrels sticking up from their crotches. The colonel came out of his office and took the salute. The truck lurched off, and he came over, lumpily, towards the guardroom.

The corporal snapped to attention and said, 'Mercenary, Comrade Colonel!'

'From today,' said the colonel, 'there are no more comrades in our country.'

'Yes, Comrade Colonel,' the man nodded; but checked himself and added, 'Yes, my Colonel.'

The colonel waved him aside and surveyed me gloomily. He wore an exquisitely-pressed pair of paratrooper fatigues, a red star on his cap, and another red star in his lapel. A roll of fat stood out around the back of his neck; his thick lips drooped at the corners; his eyes were hooded. He looked, I thought, so like a sad hippopotamus. I told myself I mustn't think he looks like a sad hippopotamus. Whatever happens, he mustn't think I think he looks like a sad hippopotamus.

'Ah, monsieur!' he said, in a quiet dispirited voice. 'What are you doing in this poor country of ours?'

'I came here as a tourist.'

'You are English?'

'Yes.'

'But you speak an excellent French.'

'Passable,' I said.

'With a Parisian accent I should have said.'

'I have lived in Paris.'

'I, also, have visited Paris. A wonderful city!'

'The most wonderful city.'

'But you have mistimed your visit to Benin.'

'Yes,' I faltered. 'I seem to have run into trouble.'

'You have been here before?'

'Once,' I said. 'Five years ago.'

'When Benin was Dahomey.'

'Yes,' I said. 'I used to think Benin was in Nigeria.'

'Benin is in Nigeria and now we have it here.'

'I think I understand.'

'Calm yourself, monsieur.' His fingers reached to unlock my handcuffs. 'We are having another little change of politics. Nothing more! In these situations one must keep calm. You understand? Calm!'

Some boys had come through the barracks' gate and were creeping forward to peer at the prisoner. The colonel appeared in the doorway, and they scampered off.

'Come,' he said. 'You will be safer if you stay with me. Come, let us listen to the Head of State.'

We walked across the parade-ground to his office where he sat me in a chair and reached for a portable radio. Above his desk hung a photo of the Head of State, in a Fidel Castro cap. His cheeks were a basketwork of scarifications.

'The Head of State,' said the colonel, 'is always speaking over the radio. We call it the journal parlé. It is a crime in this country *not* to listen to the journal parlé.'

He turned the knob. The military music came in cracking bursts.

Citizens of Benin . . . the hour is grave. At seven hours this morning, an unidentified DC-8 jet aircraft landed at our International Airport of Cotonou, carrying a crapulous crowd of mercenaries. . . black and white. . .

financed by the lackeys of international imperialism. . . .
A vile plot to destroy our democratic and operational regime.

The colonel laid his jowls on his hands and sighed, 'The Sombas! The Sombas!'

The Sombas came from the far north-west of the country. They filed their teeth to points and once, not so long ago, were cannibals.

'. . . launched a vicious attack on our Presidential Palace. . .'

I glanced up again at the wall. The Head of State was a Somba — and the colonel was a Fon.

'. . . the population is requested to arm itself with stones and knives to kill this crapulous. . .'

'A recorded message,' said the colonel, and turned the volume down. 'It was recorded yesterday.'

'You mean. . .'

'Calm yourself, monsieur. You do not understand. In this country one understands nothing.'

Certainly, as this morning wore on, the colonel understood less and less. He did not, for example, understand why, on the nine o'clock communiqué, the mercenaries had landed in a DC-8 jet, while at ten the plane had changed to a DC-7 turbo-prop. Around eleven the music cut off again and the Head of State announced a victory for the Government Forces. The enemy, he said, were retreating en catastrophe for the marshes of Ouidah.

'There has been a mistake,' said the colonel, looking very shaken. 'Excuse me, monsieur. I must leave you.'

He hesitated on the threshold and then stepped out into the sunlight. The hawks made swift spiralling shadows on the ground. I helped myself to a drink from his water-flask. The shooting sounded further off now, and the town was quieter. Ten minutes later, the corporal marched into the office. I put my hands above my head, and he escorted me back to the guardroom.

It was very hot. The skinny boy had been taken away and, on the bench at the back, sat a Frenchman.

Outside, tied to the papaya, a springer spaniel was panting and straining at its leash. A pair of soldiers squatted on their hams and were trying to dismantle the Frenchman's shotgun. A third soldier, rummaging in his game-bag, was laying out a few brace of partridge and a guinea-fowl.

'Will you please give that dog some water?' the Frenchman asked.

'Eh?' The corporal bared his gums.

'The dog,' he pointed. 'Water!'

'No.'

'What's going on?' I asked.

'The monkeys are wrecking my gun and killing my dog.'

'Out there, I mean.'

'Coup monté.'

'Which means?'

'You hire a plane-load of mercenaries to shoot up the town. See who your friends are and who are your enemies. Shoot the enemies. Simple!'

'Clever.'

'Very.'

'And us?'

'They might need a corpse or two. As proof!'

'Thank you,' I said.

'I was joking.'

'Thanks all the same.'

The Frenchman was a water-engineer. He worked up-country, on artesian wells, and was down in the capital on leave. He was a short, muscular man, tending to paunch, with cropped grey hair and a web of white laugh-lines over his leathery cheeks. He had dressed himself en mercenaire, in fake python-skin camouflage, to shoot a few game-birds in the forest on the outskirts of town.

'What do you think of my costume?' he asked.

'Suitable,' I said.

'Thank you.'

The sun was vertical. The colour of the parade-ground had bleached to a pinkish orange, and the soldiers strutted back and forth in their own pools of shade. Along the wall the vultures flexed their wings.

'Waiting,' joked the Frenchman.

'Thank you.'

'Don't mention it.'

Our view of the morning's entertainment was restricted by the width of the doorframe. We were, however, able to witness a group of soldiers treating their ex-colonel in a most shabby fashion. We wondered how he could still be alive as they dragged him out and bundled him into the back of a jeep. The corporal had taken the colonel's radio, and was cradling it on his knee. The Head of State was baying for blood—'Mort aux mercenaires soit qu'ils sont noirs ou blancs. . . .' The urchins, too, were back in force, jumping up and down, drawing their fingers across their throats, and chanting in unison, 'Mort-aux-mercenaires! . . . Mort-aux-mercenaires! . . .'

Around noon, the jeep came back. A lithe young woman jumped out and started screeching orders at an infantry platoon. She was wearing a mud-stained battledress. A nest of plaits curled, like snakes, from under her beret.

'So,' said my companion. 'The new colonel.'

'An Amazon colonel,' I said.

'I always said it,' he said. 'Never trust a teenage Amazon colonel.'

He passed me a cigarette. There were two in the packet and I took one of them.

'Thanks,' I said. 'I don't smoke.'

He lit mine, and then his, and blew a smoke-ring at the rafters. The gecko on the wall hadn't budged.

'My name's Jacques,' he said.

I told him my own name and he said, 'I don't like the look of this.'

'Nor I,' I said.

'No,' he said. 'There are no rules in this country.'

Nor were there any rules, none that one could think of, when the corporal came back from conferring with the Amazon and ordered us, also, to strip to our underpants. I hesitated. I was unsure whether I was wearing underpants. But a barrel in the small of my back convinced me, underpants or no, that my trousers would have to come down—only to find that I did, after all, have on a pair of pink-and-white boxer shorts from Brooks Brothers.

Jacques was wearing green string pants. We must have looked a pretty couple—my back welted all over with mosquito bites, he with his paunch flopping over the elastic, as the corporal marched us out, barefoot over the burning ground, and stood us, hands up, against the wall which the vultures had fouled with their ash-white, ammonia-smelling droppings.

'Merde!' said Jacques. 'Now what?'

What indeed? I was not frightened. I was tired and hot. My arms ached, my knees sagged, my tongue felt like leather, and my temples throbbed. But this was not frightening. It was too like a B-grade movie to be frightening. I began to count the flecks of millet-chaff embedded in the mud-plaster wall. . . .

I remembered the morning, five years earlier, my first morning in Dahomey, under the tall trees in Parakou. I'd had a rough night, coming down from the desert in the back of a crowded truck, and at breakfast-time, at the café-routier, I'd asked the waiter what there was to see in town.

'Patrice.'

'Patrice?'

'That's me,' he grinned. 'And, monsieur, there are hundreds of other beautiful young girls and boys who walk, all the time, up and down the streets of Parakou.'

I remembered, too, the girl who sold pineapples at Dassa-Zoumbé station. It had been a stifling day, the train slow and the country burnt. I had been reading Gide's *Nourritures terrestres* and, as we drew into Dassa, had come to the line, 'Ô cafés—où notre démence s'est continuée très avant dans la nuit. . . .' No, I thought, this will never do, and looked out of the carriage window. A basket of pineapples had halted outside. The girl underneath the basket smiled and, when I gave her the Gide, gasped, lobbed all six pineapples into the carriage, and ran off to show her friends—who in turn came skipping down the tracks, clamouring, 'A book, please? A book? A book!' So *out* went a dog-eared thriller and Saint-Exupéry's *Vol de nuit,* and *in* came the 'Fruits of the Earth'—the real ones—pawpaws, guavas, more pineapples, a raunch of grilled swamp-rat, and a palm-leaf hat.

'Those girls,' I remember scribbling in my notebook, 'are the ultimate products of the lycée system.'

And now what?

The Amazon was squawking at the platoon and we strained our ears for the click of safety catches.

'I think they're playing games,' Jacques said, squinting sideways.

'I should hope so,' I muttered. I liked Jacques. It was good, if one had to be here, to be here with him. He was an old Africa hand and had been through coups before.

'That is,' he added glumly, 'if they don't get drunk.'

'Thank you,' I said, and looked over my shoulder at the drill-squad.

'No look!' the corporal barked. He was standing beside us, his shirt-front open to the navel. Obviously, he was anxious to cut a fine figure.

'Stick your belly-button in,' I muttered in English.

'No speak!' he threatened.

'I won't speak.' I held the words within my teeth. 'But stay there. Don't leave me. I need you.'

Maddened by the heat and excitement, the crowds who had come to gawp were clamouring, 'Mort-aux-mercenaires! . . . Mort-aux-mercenaires!' and my mind went racing back over the horrors of Old Dahomey, before the French came. I thought, the slave-wars, the human sacrifices, the piles of broken skulls. I thought of Domingo's other uncle, 'The Brazilian', who received us on his rocking-chair dressed in white ducks and a topee. 'Yes,' he sighed, 'the Dahomeans are a charming and intelligent people. Their only weakness is a certain nostalgia for taking heads.'

No. This was not my Africa. Not this rainy, rotten-fruit Africa. Not this Africa of blood and laughter. The Africa I loved was the long undulating savannah country to the north, the 'leopard-spotted land', where flat-topped acacias stretched as far as the eye could see, and there were black-and-white hornbills and tall red termitaries. For whenever I went back to that Africa, and saw a camel caravan, a view of white tents, or a single blue turban far off in the heat haze, I knew that, no matter what the Persians said, Paradise never was a garden but a waste of white thorns.

'I am dreaming,' said Jacques, suddenly, 'of perdrix aux choux.'

'I'd take a dozen Belons and a bottle of Krug.'

'No speak!' The corporal waved his gun, and I braced myself, half-expecting the butt to crash down on my skull.

And so what? What would it matter when already I felt as if my skull were split clean open? Was this, I wondered, sunstroke? How strange, too, as I tried to focus on the wall, that each bit of chaff should bring back some clear specific memory of food or drink?

There was a lake in Central Sweden and, in the lake, there was an island where the ospreys nested. On the first day of the crayfish season we rowed to the fisherman's hut and rowed back towing twelve dozen crayfish in a live-net. That evening, they came in from the kitchen, a scarlet mountain smothered in dill. The northern sunlight bounced off the lake into the bright white room. We drank akvavit from thimble-sized glasses and we ended the meal with a tart made of cloudberries. I could taste again the grilled sardines we ate on the quay at Douarnenez and see my father demonstrating how his father ate sardines à la mordecai: you took a live sardine by the tail and swallowed it. Or the elvers we had in Madrid, fried in oil with garlic and half a red pepper. It had been a cold spring morning, and we'd spent two hours in the Prado, gazing at the Velasquezes, hugging one another it was so good to be alive: we had cancelled our bookings on a plane that had crashed. Or the lobsters we bought at Cape Split Harbour, Maine. There was a notice-board in the shack on the jetty and, pinned to it, a card on which a widow thanked her husband's friends for their contributions, and prayed, prayed to the Lord, that they lashed themselves to the boat when hauling in the pots.

How long, O Lord, how long? How long, when all the world was wheeling, could I stay on my feet. . . ?

How long I shall never know, because the next thing I remember I was staggering groggily across the parade-ground, with one arm over the corporal's shoulder and the other over Jacques's. Jacques then gave me a glass of water and, after that, he helped me into my clothes.

'You passed out,' he said.

'Thank you,' I said.

'Don't worry,' he said. 'They *are* only playing games.'

It was late afternoon now. The corporal was in a better mood and allowed us to sit outside the guardroom. The sun was still hot. My head was still aching, but the crowd had simmered down and fortunately, for us, this particular section of the Benin Proletarian Army had found a new source of amusement—in the form of three Belgian ornithologists, whom they had taken prisoner in a swamp, along with a Leica lens the shape and size of a mortar.

The leader of the expedition was a beefy, red-bearded fellow. He believed, apparently, that the only way to deal with Africans was to shout. Jacques advised him to shut his mouth; but when one of the subalterns started tinkering with the Leica, the Belgian went off his head. How dare they? How dare they touch his camera? How dare they think they were mercenaries? Did they look like mercenaries?

'And I suppose they're mercenaries, too?' He waved his arms at us.

'I told you to shut your mouth,' Jacques repeated.

The Belgian took no notice and went on bellowing to be set free. *At once! Now! Or else! Did he hear that?*

Yes. The subaltern had heard, and smashed his fist into the Belgian's face. I never saw anyone crumple so quickly. The blood gushed down his beard, and he fell. The subaltern kicked him when he was down. He lay on the dirt floor, whimpering.

'Idiot!' Jacques growled.

'Poor Belgium,' I said.

The next few hours I would prefer to forget. I do, however, remember that when the corporal brought back my things I cursed, 'Christ, they've nicked my traveller's cheques,'— and Jacques, squeezing my arm very tightly, whispered, 'Now *you* keep your mouth shut!' I remember 'John Brown's Body' playing loudly over the radio, and the Head of State inviting the population, this time, to gather up the corpses. Ramasser les cadavres is what he said, in a voice so hoarse and sinister you knew a great many people had died, or would do. And I remember, at sunset, being driven by minibus to the Gezo Barracks where hundreds of soldiers, all elated by victory, were embracing one another, and kissing.

Our new guards made us undress again, and we were shut up, with other suspected mercenaries, in a disused ammunition shed. 'Well,' I thought, at the sight of so many naked bodies, 'there must be some safety in numbers.'

It was stifling in the shed. The other whites seemed cheerful, but the blacks hung their heads between their knees, and shook. After dark, a missionary doctor, who was an old man, collapsed and died of a heart-attack. The guards took him out on a stretcher, and we were taken to the Sûreté for questioning.

Our interrogator was a gaunt man with hollow temples, a cap of woolly white hair and bloodshot slits for eyes. He sat sprawled behind his desk, caressing with his fingertips the blade of his bowie-knife. Jacques made me stand a pace behind him. When his turn came, he said loudly that he was employed by such and such a French engineering company and that I, he added, was an old friend.

'Pass!' snapped the officer. 'Next!'

The officer snatched my passport, thumbed through the pages and began blaming me, personally, for certain events in Southern Africa.

'What are you doing in our country?'

'I'm a tourist.'

'Your case is more complicated. Stand over there.'

I stood like a schoolboy, in the corner, until a female sergeant took me away for fingerprinting. She was a very large sergeant. My head was throbbing; and when I tried to manoeuvre my little finger onto the inkpad, she bent it back double; I yelled 'Ayee!', and her boot slammed down on my sandalled foot.

That night there were nine of us, all white, cooped up in a ramshackle office. The President's picture hung aslant on a bright blue wall and, beside it, were a broken guitar and a stuffed civet cat, nailed in mockery of the Crucifixion, with its tail and hindlegs together, and its forelegs splayed apart.

In addition to the mosquito-bites, my back had come up in watery blisters. My toe was very sore. The guard kicked me awake whenever I nodded off. His cheeks were cicatrized, and I remember thinking how remote his voice sounded when he said, 'On va vous fusiler.' At two or three in the morning, there was a burst of machine-gun fire close by, and we all thought, This is it. It was only a soldier, drunk or trigger-happy, discharging his magazine at the stars.

None of us was sad to see the first light of day.

It was another greasy dawn and the wind was blowing hard onshore, buffeting the buzzards and bending the coco palms. Across the compound a big crowd was jamming the gate. Jacques then caught sight of his houseboy and when he waved, the boy waved back. At nine, the French Vice-Consul put in an appearance, under guard. He was a fat, suet-faced man, who kept wiping the sweat from his forehead and glancing over his shoulder at the bayonet points behind.

'Messieurs,' he stammered, 'this situation is perhaps a little less disagreeable for me than for you. Unfortunately, although we do have stratagems for your release, I am not permitted to discuss your liberty, only the question of food.'

'Eh bien!' Jacques grinned. 'You see my boy over there? Send him to the Boulangerie Gerbe d'Or and bring us sandwiches of jambon, paté and saussisson sec, enough croissants for everyone, and three petits pains au chocolat for me.'

'Oui,' said the Vice-Consul weakly.

I then scribbled my name and passport number on a scrap of paper, and asked him to telex the British Embassy in Lagos.

'I cannot,' he said. 'I cannot be mixed up in this affair.'

He turned his back, and waddled off the way he'd come, with the pair of bayonets following.

'Charming,' I said to Jacques.

'Remember Waterloo,' Jacques said. 'And, besides, you may be a mercenary!'

Half an hour later, Jacques' bright-eyed boy came back with a basket of provisions. Jacques gave the guard a sandwich, spread the rest on the office table, sank his teeth into a petit pain au chocolat, and murmured, 'Byzance!'

The sight of food had a wonderfully revivifying effect on the Belgian ornithologist. All through the night the three had been weepy and hysterical, and now they were wolfing the sandwiches. They were not my idea of company. I was left alone with them, when, around noon, the citizens of France were set at liberty.

'Don't worry,' Jacques squeezed my hand. 'I'll do what I can.'

He had hardly been gone ten minutes before a big German, with a red face and sweeps of fair hair, came striding across the compound, shouting at the soldiers and brushing the bayonets aside.

He introduced himself as the Counsellor of the German Embassy.

'I'm so sorry you've landed in this mess,' he said in faultless English. 'Our ambassador has made a formal protest. From what I understand, you'll have to pass before some kind of military tribunal. Nothing to worry about! The commander is a nice chap. He's embarrassed about the whole business. But we'll watch you going into the building, and watch you coming out.'

'Thanks,' I said.

'Anyway,' he added, 'the Embassy car is outside, and we're not leaving until everyone's out.'

'Can you tell me what *is* going on?'

The German lowered his voice: 'Better leave it alone.'

The tribunal began its work at one. I was among the first prisoners to be called. A young zealot started mouthing anti-capitalist formulae until he was silenced by the colonel in charge. The colonel then asked a few perfunctory questions, wearily apologized for the inconvenience, signed my pass, and hoped I would continue to enjoy my holiday in the People's Republic.

'I hope so,' I said.

Outside the gate, I thanked the German who sat in the back of his air-conditioned Mercedes. He smiled, and went on reading the *Frankfurter Zeitung*.

It was grey and muggy and there were not many people on the street. I bought the government newspaper and read its account of the glorious victory. There were pictures of three dead mercenaries—a white man who appeared to be sleeping, and two very mangled blacks. Then I went to the hotel where my bag was in storage.

The manager's wife looked worn and jittery. I checked my bag and found the two traveller's cheques I'd hidden in a sock. I cashed a hundred dollars, took a room, and lay down.

I kept off the streets to avoid the vigilante groups that roamed the town making citizens' arrests. My toenail was turning black and my head still ached. I ate in the room, and read, and tried to sleep. All the other guests were either Guinean or Algerian.

Around eleven next morning, I was reading the sad story of Mrs Marmeladov in *Crime and Punishment*, and heard the thud of gunfire coming from the Gezo Barracks. I looked from the window at the palms, the hawks, a woman selling mangoes, and a nun coming out of the convent.

Seconds later, the fruit-stall had overturned, the nun bolted, and two armoured cars went roaring up the street.

There was a knock on the door. It was the manager.

'Please, monsieur. You must not look.'

'What's happening?'

'Please,' he pleaded, 'you must shut the window.'

I closed the shutter. The electricity had cut off. A few bars of sunlight squeezed through the slats, but it was too dark to read, so I lay back and listened to the salvoes. There must have been a lot of people dying.

There was another knock.

'Come in.'

A soldier came into the room. He was very young and smartly turned out. His fatigues were criss-crossed with ammunition belts and his teeth shone. He seemed extremely nervous. His finger quivered round the trigger-guard. I raised my hands and got up off the bed.

'In there!' He pointed the barrel at the bathroom door.

The walls of the bathroom were covered with blue tiles and, on the blue plastic shower-curtain, was a design of tropical fish.

'Money,' said the soldier.

'Sure!' I said. 'How much?'

He said nothing. I glanced at the mirror and saw the gaping whites of his eyes. He was breathing heavily.

I eased my fingers down my trouser pocket: my impulse was to give him all I had. Then I separated one banknote from the rest, and put it in his outstretched palm.

'Merci, monsieur!' His lips expanded in an astonished smile. 'Merci,' he repeated, and unlocked the bathroom door. 'Merci,' he kept repeating, as he bowed and pointed his own way out into the passage.

That young man, it struck me, really had very nice manners.

The Algerians and Guineans were men in brown suits who sat all day in the bar, sucking soft drinks through straws and giving me dirty looks whenever I went in. I decided to move to the Hôtel de la Plage where there were other Europeans, and a swimming-pool. I took a towel to go swimming and went into the garden. The pool had been drained: on the morning of the coup, a sniper had taken a pot-shot at a Canadian boy who happened to be swimming his lengths.

The frontiers of the country were closed, and the airport.

That evening I ate with a Norwegian oil-man, who insisted that the coup had been a fake. He had seen the mercenaries shelling the palace. He had watched them drinking opposite in the bar of the Hotel de Cocotiers.

'All of it I saw,' he said, his neck reddening with indignation. The palace had been deserted. The army had been in the barracks. The mercenaries had shot innocent people. Then they all went back to the airport and flew away.

'All of it,' he said, 'was fake.'

'Well,' I said, 'if it was a fake, it certainly took me in.'

It took another day for the airport to open, and another two before I got a seat on the Abidjan plane. I had a mild attack of bronchitis and was aching to leave the country.

On my last morning I looked in at the 'Paris-Snack', which, in the old days when Dahomey was Dahomey, was owned by a Corsican called Guerini. He had gone back to Corsica while the going was good. The bar-stools were covered in red leather, and the barman wore a solid gold bracelet round his wrist.

Two Nigerian businessmen were seated at lunch with a pair of whores. At a table in the corner I saw Jacques.

'Tiens?' he said, grinning. 'Still alive?'

'Thanks to you,' I said, 'and the Germans.'

'*Braves* Bosches!' He beckoned me to the banquette. 'Very intelligent people.'

'*Braves* Bosches!' I agreed.

'Let's have a bottle of champagne.'

'I haven't got much money.'

'Lunch is on me,' he insisted. 'Pierrot!'

The barman tilted his head, coquettishly, and tittered.

'Yes, Monsieur Jacques.'

'This is an English gentleman and we must find him a very special bottle of champagne. You have Krug?'

'No, Monsieur Jacques. We have Roerderer. We have Bollinger, and we have Mumm.'

'Bollinger,' I said.

Jacques pulled a face: 'And in Guerini's time you could have had your oysters. Flown in twice a week from Paris. . . Belons. . . Claires. . . Portugaises. . . .'

'I remember him.'

'He was a character.'

'Tell me,' I leaned over. 'What *was* going on?'

'Sssh!' his lips tightened. 'There are two theories and, if I think anyone's listening, I shall change the subject.'

I nodded and looked at the menu.

'In the official version,' Jacques said, 'the mercenaries were recruited by Dahomean emigrés in Paris. The plane took off from a military airfield in Morocco, refuelled in Abidjan. . .'

One of the whores got up from her table and lurched down the restaurant towards the Ladies.

' '66 was a wonderful year,' said Jacques, decisively.

'I like it even older,' I said, as the whore brushed past, 'dark and almost flat. . . .'

'The plane flew to Gabon to pick up the commander. . . who is supposed to be an adviser to President Bongo. . . .' He then explained how, at Libreville, the pilot of the chartered DC-8 refused to go on, and the mercenaries had to switch to a DC-7.

'So their arrival was expected at the airport?'

'Precisely,' Jacques agreed. 'Now the second scenario . . .'

The door of the Ladies swung open. The whore winked at us. Jacques puushed his face up to the menu.

'What'll you have?' he asked.

'Stuffed crab,' I said.

125

'The second scenario,' he continued quietly, 'calls for Czech and East German mercenaries. The plane, a DC-7, takes off from a military airfield in Algeria, refuels at Conakry. . . you understand?'

'Yes,' I said, when he'd finished. 'I think I get it. And which one do you believe?'

'Both,' he said.

'That,' I said, 'is a very sophisticated analysis.'

'This,' he said, 'is a very sophisticated country.'

'I know it.'

'You heard the shooting at Camp Gezo?'

'What was that?'

'Settling old scores,' he shrugged. 'And now the Guineans have taken over the Secret Police.'

'Clever.'

'This is Africa.'

'I know and I'm leaving.'

'For England?'

'No,' I said. 'For Brazil. I've a book to write.'

'Beautiful country, Brazil.'

'I hope so.'

'Beautiful women.'

'So I'm told.'

'So what is this book?'

'It's about the slave-trade.'

'In Benin?'

'Also in Brazil.'

'Eh bien!' The champagne had come and he filled my glass. 'You have material!'

'Yes,' I agreed. 'I do have material.'

ON THE BLACK HILL

BRUCE CHATWIN

Now in paperback, the brilliant, haunting novel from the author of *In Patagonia*

'It is the first novel I have seen in two years which begins to merit the accolade of "masterpiece"'
Auberon Waugh, Daily Mail

'The most refreshing novel I have read this year. He knows intimately the comedies, the tragedies and above all the passions and deceits of toil on the land . . . This is a very moving yet also often funny book'
V. S. Pritchett, Sunday Times

'Thomas Hardy, as a poet and as novelist would have liked this book. So would Ronald Blythe who wrote *Akenfield*. Close at home, Mr Chatwin earns his transcendence. The ordinary is made magical'
John Leonard, New York Times

'Nothing in Mr Chatwin's previous work quite prepares us for the dramatic intensity with which scene after scene of the novel is brought to light'
New York Times Book Review

'*On the Black Hill* signals the arrival of a major novelist who has come home to find his roots here, his truth in this soil'
Andrew Sinclair, The Times

PICADOR

OUTSTANDING INTERNATIONAL WRITING

RICHARD HOLMES
IN STEVENSON'S
FOOTSTEPS

The beginning of the journey was hard and rather unpleasant for us both.

For the whole of the first day, from Le Monastier to Le Bouchet, a distance of twenty-five kilometres over steep country roads, baked in hot golden dust, Robert Louis Stevenson had endless and humiliating trouble with his donkey, Modestine. She refused to climb hills, she shed her saddle-bag at the least provocation, and in villages she swerved into the cool of the beaded shop-doors. He was forced to beat her relentlessly, first with his own walking-cane, and then with a thorn-switch cut from a hedge by a peasant on the long hill up to Goudet.

At Costaros, the villagers even tried to intervene, taking the side of French donkey against foreign tyrant: 'Ah,' they cried, 'how tired she is, the poor beast!'

Stevenson lost his temper: 'Mind your own affairs—unless you would like to help me carry my basket?' He departed amid laughter from the Sunday loiterers, who had just come out of church and were feeling charitable.

Yet as he flogged her over the rocky, gorse-covered hillsides under a blazing afternoon sun, Stevenson's own heart revolted against the apparent brutality of donkey-driving. He later wrote in his route Journal: 'The sound of my own blows sickened me. Once when I looked at Modestine, she had a faint resemblance to a lady of my acquaintance who once loaded me with kindness; and this increased my horror of my own cruelty.'

As I laboured up the same noviciate slopes, sweating under my own pack, I found myself puzzling over these words. Were they just the famous Stevensonian whimsy? Or was he really thinking of some particular woman? It was intriguing; I would have liked to have asked him about it. But it was true. When travelling alone, your mind fills up strangely with the people you are fond of, the people you have left behind. It produces odd effects.

Stevenson described one of these odd little incidents:

We encountered another donkey, ranging at will upon the roadside; and this other donkey chanced to be a gentleman.

A hot summer in the Massif Central of southern France, some twenty years ago. The narrator is eighteen.

131

He and Modestine met nickering for joy, and I had to separate the pair and stamp out the nascent romance with a renewed and feverish bastinado. If the other donkey had had the heart of a male under his hide, he would have fallen upon me tooth and nail; and this is a kind of consolation: he was plainly unworthy of Modestine's affections. But the incident saddened me, as did everything that reminded me of my donkey's sex.

Stevenson eventually discovered that Modestine was on heat for almost the entire length of his journey. This disturbed him; for as I gradually came to suspect, problems of friendship, romance and sexuality were much on his mind throughout this lonely summer tour.

S itting up to my chin in the cool brown waters of the Loire tributary, on a sandy bank below the little bridge at Goudet, I mumbled over these questions and whistled to myself. I was wearing my hat, but nothing else to speak of, and was dissolving in the glittering flowing water which seemed, for a moment, like time itself, a fluid gentle medium through which you might move at will, upstream and down, wherever you chose, with a lazy kick of your feet.

There was a sharp giggle overhead; two children hung over the parapet, pointing: 'Mais qu'est-ce que c'est que ça! c'est un nomad—non, c'est un fou!'

I retreated to my clothes under the shadow of a tree, embarrassed. It was not so easy slipping out of time, or clothes, or conventions, even here. I turned again to the dusty road.

D espite his donkey troubles, Stevenson got into the inn at Le Bouchet shortly after nightfall, well ahead of me on this first day's run.

I began to appreciate how physically tough he must have been. Coming down to Costaros, in a hot low red sun, I started to shiver with exhaustion and at one point tumbled headlong into a ditch. My shoulders were bruised from the pack, and my right foot spectacularly blistered; my morale was low. I fell asleep on the bench of a little dark-panelled café, knocked over my green glass of *syrop*, and was turned out into the twilit street by an angry *madame la*

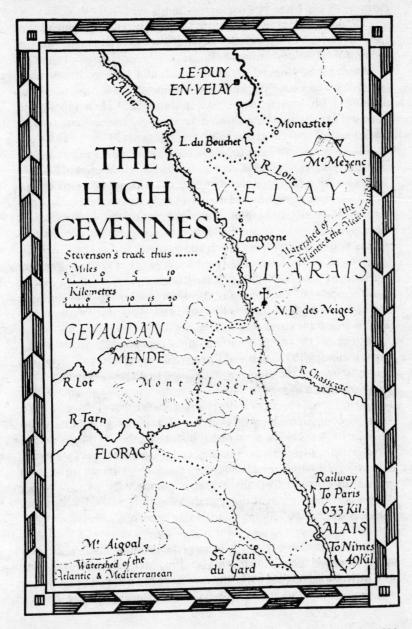

patronne. I felt I was not managing things very well.

'Désolé, madame,' I murmured. I was soon to recognize this feeling: it is how every traveller feels at the approach of night, and the lighting up of windows where he does not belong, and cannot enter in.

An old man stopped me, and talked, and took me by the arm. 'Mais oui, la route de Monsieur Steamson—' it was the local pronunciation—'c'est par ici, prenez courage....' He led me to the outskirts of the town, and showed me the *vieux chemin*, a mere cart-track heading into the darkening, pine-fringed hills for Le Bouchet.

Then, inexplicably, he took me back again, and I was suddenly sitting in a little shoemaker's cottage, under a yellow print of Millet's *Angelus*, eating omelette and drinking red wine from a pitcher and laughing. I remember the old man's dungaree blues, his black beret, his arthritic hands, still nimble and expressive on the red check table-cloth. He was one of those who knew the story, as if it were part of village history. He spoke of Stevenson as if he had done his *Travels* in living memory, in some undefined time 'avant la guerre', when he himself was young and full of adventure.

'You see,' said the old man, 'there is a time to kick up your heels and see the world a bit. I was like that, too. And now I make shoes. That's how things are, you will see.'

I slept out that night under an outcrop of pines, facing east on a slight incline, with the lights of Costaros far away to my left. The turf was springy, and the pine needles seemed to discourage insects. As I lay in my bag, a number of late rooks came out of the gloaming, and settled in the pine branches, chuckling to each other. They gave me a sense of companionship and even security: nothing could move up through the trees below me without disturbing them. Once or twice I croaked up at them (it was the wine), and they croaked back: 'tais-toi, tais-toi'. I fell asleep quickly. Only once, waking, I drank two ice-cold mouthfuls of water from my can and, leaning back, saw the Milky Way astonishingly bright through the pine tops, and felt something indescribable—like falling upwards into someone's arms.

At Le Bouchet, Stevenson slept in the same inn room as a married couple from Alais. They were travelling to seek work at St Etienne. Sharing rooms was normal practice in country *auberges* till the very end of the nineteenth century, but the woman was young and Stevenson was shy for all his bohemian manners.

> Honi soit qui mal y pense; but I was sufficiently sophisticated to feel abashed. I kept my eyes to myself as much as I could, and I know nothing of the woman except that she had beautiful arms, full, white and shapely; whether she slept naked or in her slip, I declare I know not; only her arms were bare.

In the morning the innkeeper made a goad for Modestine, while the innkeeper's wife briskly advised Stevenson about what should go into his travel book. 'Whether people harvest or not in such and such a place; if there were forests; studies of manners, what, for example, I, or the master of the house, say to you; the beauties of nature; and all that.' Stevenson wrote it all down in his most winning manner, adding that the wife—unlike the husband—could read, had a share of brains, but was not half so pleasant. '"My man knows nothing," he recorded her as saying, with an angry toss of her chin, "he is like the beasts." And the old gentleman signified acquiescence with his head as if it were rather like a compliment.'

Their youngest daughter, who looked after the cattle, was rude and mischievous, until her father—without a flicker of expression—abruptly announced that he had sold her to the foreign *monsieur* to be his little servant girl. The father appealed to Stevenson for confirmation.

Stevenson solemnly took up the game. '"Yes," said I, "I paid ten half-pence; it was a little dear, but...."'

'"But," the father cut in, "Monsieur was willing to make a sacrifice."'

A little while after, the girl ran out of the stone-flagged kitchen, and the sound of sobs came through from the stable next door. Stevenson hurried after her, and put everything right, closing the game in wild laughter. He had a quick rapport with children, and played instinctively on their sense of mystery and adventure, half-entrancing and half-terrifying them. To be sold to a long-haired foreign traveller with a huge blue woollen sack, was not much better than to be pursued by Blind Pew, tap-tapping with his stick, at the door of the Admiral Benbow inn.

Stevenson's route now swung almost due south, up over the last high farmlands of the Velay to Pradelles, and then down to the little market town of Langogne on the River Allier. Here, he came to a new wild country and a new phase in his pilgrimage of the heart.

He described the bleak prospect with the relish of an Edinburgh lowlander set free.

On the opposite bank of the Allier, the land kept mounting for miles to the horizon; a tanned or sallow autumn landscape, with black dots of firwood, and white roads wandering far into the Gévaudan. Over all this, the clouds shed a uniform and purplish shadow, sad and somewhat menacing, exaggerating height and distance, and throwing into still higher relief the twisted ribands of highroad. It was a cheerless prospect, but one stimulating for a traveller. For I was now upon the limit of the Velay, and all that I beheld lay in another country—wild Gévaudan, mountainous, uncultivated, and but recently disforested from *the terror of wolves.*

All that morning, as I tried to catch Stevenson up, I thought of wolves. Clambering over the flint farm-tracks, I watched the dark hills of Gévaudan before me, and saw no one but the figures of distant labourers working in the fields around me.

A curious gnawing pain began at my heel. Before Pradelles, the ball of my right foot split open, leaving something like a slice of best back bacon, which I held under the village pump. The doctor at Landos, with half-moon gold spectacles, hung out of his window and announced that he was having lunch. Then seeing me so crestfallen, added, 'Mais montez, montez quand-même.'

Scissors snapped, patent ointments oozed, bandages twirled, money was waved aside. I limped out of Landos in a cloud of Pernod fumes, menthol, and cocaine-gel.

Beyond Pradelles I bathed in another stream, this time discreetly shrouded by bullrushes. The heat was still stunning and I lay back in the cool water, my bandaged foot raised solemnly in the air. I dozed, and the grumbling of distant thunder mixed in my dreams with the growling of those wolves of long ago.

But Stevenson was still three or four hours ahead of me. He crossed the stone bridge into Langogne in·the early afternoon of Monday 23 September 1878, 'just as the promised rain was beginning to fall.' Here, however, he decided to settle for the rest of the day at the inn, and this I knew would give me my chance to catch up with him. Modestine was fed and stabled, and Stevenson sent his rucksack out for repair, and sank into a corner seat to read up about the legendary 'Beast of Gévaudan'.

The Beast had terrorized the region in the mid-eighteenth century. Its exploits held a peculiar fascination for Stevenson. Roving in the remote hills between Langogne and Luc, it had viciously attacked small children guarding sheep, or lone women returning from market at dusk. These attacks lasted throughout the 1760s. When the victims were found, their bodies were always drained of blood, though not wholly devoured, and there were wild rumours of vampirism or worse. The Bishop of Mende ordered public prayers to be said in the country churches on Sundays, and the Intendant of Languedoc organized armed wolf-hunts with parties of dragoons. The king himself eventually offered a reward of six thousand *livres* to whoever should slay the Beast.

It proved strangely elusive for several seasons, and myths about the Beast grew: its appearance on nights of the full moon, its liking for thunderstorms (endemic to the region), its power to leap from one hilltop to the next or to appear in two places at once. Finally, in September 1765, a local shepherd called Antoine shot a huge wolf weighing nearly ten stone. Its body was stuffed and sent to the court at Versailles amid great rejoicing. The local people felt a curse had been lifted from them.

How great was their horror when, less than two years later, in the spring of 1767, the attacks began again with even more frenzied violence. On the hills of the Lozère, two teenage boys were virtually torn to pieces. The entire population of the Gévaudan lapsed into a state of superstitious panic; farming was neglected and almost no one crossed their doorstep after dark.

The end when it came was curiously muted. One late June evening in 1767, Jean Chastel, a local woodsman, out hunting for the Beast, was attacked in a forest-clearing by a large wolf which he shot at point-blank range with a single musket ball. The killing brought the reign of terror to an end, and Chastel himself became a kind of folk hero. Yet this second wolf was a common animal, with a tatty pelt, and weighing two stone less than its predecessor. In a way, it served to protect the mystery. The Beast of Gévaudan always remained, and continued to haunt the region even in Stevenson's time. He read a novel on the subject by Elie Berthet at Langogne.

'If all wolves had been as this wolf,' Stevenson remarked, 'they would have changed the history of man.'

I found several modern studies of the subject, rich in explanations, each one more fantastic than the last. One school followed the vampire theory; another proposed a sadistic Gévaudan land-owner who terrorized his tenants with a trained pack of hunting wolves; and a third, deeply psychological, produced Jean Chastel himself as a pathological killer dressed up in wolf-hides. My favourite had a sinister simplicity. It proposed, as a strict zoological possibility, a rogue family of *three* wolves (like The Three Bears) who, ostracized from the main pack, had tasted the delights of human flesh, and thereafter attacked in combination. Hence the inexplicably ferocious power of the Beast; and also its ability to be in two places at once. This theory also had the great attraction of leaving *one wolf still unaccounted for.* I liked this very much.

It was sheer coincidence that on the final leg of my walk over the hills to Langogne, I had my first brush with a Cevennes storm. The storms are peculiar to this highland region; they are localized and extremely intense, move quickly from one hilltop to the next, and produce a forked lightning that frightened me. It overtook me rapidly from the west, and seemed to chase me over the bare pastures until, to my relief, I came upon a hamlet in the fold of the hill, with a tiny *café-épicerie* in which I took shelter for an hour. The storm passed, banging and snarling and flashing overhead.

The café-owner, a small man in an extravagantly dirty apron, polished glasses philosphically in the doorway, as the rain beat on the green awning. We talked disjointedly of Stevenson and storms.

'It is not always wise to go over the hills,' he observed, while cigarette ash from his yellow *papier-maïs* fell on his apron in the hot damp wind. There was something lugubrious about his down-turned mouth. He craned his head outside, looked sharply up at the louring clouds and shrugged. 'There,' he added, 'it is clearing away now.'

He returned to the little zinc-topped bar, flapped at the thunder flies, coughed, shook his head (more ash) and wished me well in his own fashion. 'So, you are going into Gévaudan. You will see him again, *alors.*'

At least, I think that's what he said. I departed, draped in my waterproof sheet, my hat at a combative angle. The sun came out, and I made the last descent to Langogne, through drenched fields full of gleaming buttercups. I felt oddly elated.

At a little after eight in the evening, I at last crossed the bridge over the Allier into Langogne, the shadows lengthening along the streets. The shopkeepers were closing up their stalls, and the air was full of the smell of crushed fruit and frying garlic. The town had a fine eleventh-century church and a medieval covered market. It was the biggest place I'd been in for days. It was cheerful and bustling, with family groups sitting out on the pavements, and couples strolling arm in arm along the riverbank. There were children fishing with pink and yellow nets for minnows.

But here something strange happened. The feeling that Stevenson was actually waiting for me, in person, started to grow. It was overwhelmingly strong. It was almost like a hallucination. I began looking for him in the crowds, in the faces at the café doors, at the hotel windows.

I went back to the bridge, took off my hat—rather formally as if to meet a friend—and paced up and down, waiting for some sort of sign. People glanced at me. I felt an oddity, not knowing quite what I was doing, or what I was looking for. The twilight thickened, and bats appeared over the river. I watched their flight, flickering over the glistening surface, from one bank to the other.

And then I saw it, quite clearly against the western sky. I saw the old bridge of Langogne. It was about fifty yards downstream, and it was broken, crumbling, and covered with ivy. So Stevenson had crossed *there*, not on this modern bridge. There was no way of following him, no way of meeting him. His bridge was down. It was beyond my reach over time, and this was the true sad sign.

This discovery put me in a black gloom. It was stupid, but I was almost tearful. I could not bear to stay in Langogne and, after a distracted supper, I climbed the steep hill of rustling plane trees towards St Flour and Fouzilhac. It was pitch black, but I was anxious to plunge myself into the Gévaudan. Below, to my left, I could hear a small river running through what I took to be a gentle sloping water-meadow, and I fancied I would camp there. Turning off through the plane trees, I jumped over a low wall and seemed to drop into a bottomless pit.

In fact, it was a fifteen-foot, stone-banked wall, and ending in a mass of thorn briars; below them, the ground shelved away directly into the river and, skidding and cursing through the blackness, I slid down to it. It took an hour to return to Langogne, where I signed myself into the only hotel that would take a doubtful traveller after midnight. I was wet to the waist. I had lost maps and various bits of equipment from my rucksack. In my pocket I found my pipe broken off at the stem.

As I dropped off to sleep in my luxurious broom-cupboard, I thought I would give the whole damn thing up.

I had mad dreams about children dancing round me in a mocking circle. They were waving nets and singing: 'Sur le pont d'Avignon/On y dance, on y dance....' I thought a good deal about this dream. It seemed, in part, to be a projection of Stevenson's own experiences, when on the following night, he was lost on the paths between Fouzilhac and Fouzilhic. He could find nowhere to stay as darkness came on, and no one to give him directions. Instead, he too met strange and dreamlike children.

As I came out on the skirts of the woods, I saw near upon a dozen cows and perhaps as many more black figures, which I conjectured to be children, although the mist had already unrecognizably exaggerated their forms. These were all silently following each other round in a circle, now taking hands, now breaking up with chains and reverences. A dance of children appeals to very innocent and lively thoughts; but, at nightfall on the marshes, the thing was eerie and fantastic to behold. Even I, who am well enough read in Herbert Spencer, felt a sort of silence fall for an instant on my mind.

But there was, also in part, something else to my dream. I came to think that it was a warning: a warning not to be so childish and literal-minded in my pursuit of Stevenson. The children were dancing and singing of the old bridge of Avignon: the bridge that is broken, just like the old bridge of Langogne. You could not cross such bridges any more, just as you could not cross literally into the past.

Even in imagination the gap was there. It had to be recognized. You could not play-act into the past; you could not turn it into a game of make-believe. There had to be other methods of reaching it. Somehow you had to produce the living effect, while remaining true to the dead fact. The adult distance—the critical distance, the historical distance—had to be maintained. You stood at the end of the broken bridge, and looked across carefully, objectively, into the unattainable past on the other side. You brought it alive, you brought it back, by other sorts of skills and crafts and sensible magic.

Have I explained myself at all? It is the simplicity of the idea, the realization, that I am after. It was important for me, because it was probably the first time that I caught an inkling of what the process (indeed the entire vocation) called 'Biography' is really about. I had never thought about it before. 'Biography' meant a book about someone's life. But, for me, it was to become a kind of pursuit, a tracking of the physical trail of someone's path through the past, a following of footsteps. You would never catch them; you would never quite catch them. But maybe, if lucky, you might write about the pursuit of that fleeting figure in such a way as to bring it alive in the present.

I awoke next morning in a different mood, and climbed, in bright sunlight, the same hill which I had failed to cross the night before in the company of a shepherd with his small black-and-white collie dog. The shepherd had been on the road eight days, he said, going to his cousins' farm across the Tarn. He mended my pipe with a piece of waxed twine, cunningly tied.

Stevenson had a rough day on those hills. The weather was bad. He fell into bogs, lost his way in woods, and finally found himself benighted in a storm at the inhospitable village of Fouzilhac. No one would cross their doorstep to put him on the path for Cheylard. 'C'est que, voyez-vous, il fait noir,' they told

him. Stevenson implies that it was memories of the Beast of
Gévaudan that made the men so reluctant. But he himself could not
have looked a very inviting figure by then: gaunt, long bedraggled
hair, trousers caked in mud, and a strong whiff of the brandy flask.
No wonder everyone refused his requests to be shown the way with a
lantern. The hour grew later, the rain heavier. He blundered on,
alone.

Stevenson, for all his reputation as a dilettante, was determined
and resourceful. He camped alone that night in the howling wind,
under the lee of a dry-stone wall, tethering Modestine to a nearby
pine-branch and carefully feeding her hunches of black bread. He
spread his sleeping-sack by the light of his spirit-lamp tucked into a
crack of the wall. After removing his soaking boots and gaiters, he
drew on 'a pair of long, dry woollen stockings', stuck his knapsack
under the canvas top flap of the bag for a pillow, slid into the warm
woolly interior of the bag (still containing his books, pistol and spare
clothes) and strapped himself in with his belt 'like a bambino'. Here
he dined on a tin of Bologna sausage and a cake of chocolate, washed
down with plenty of brandy from his flask, rolled and smoked 'one of
the best cigarettes in the world', and dropped off to sleep like a child,
contentedly lulled by the stormy sounds of wild Gévaudan. It struck
me as an admirable feat in all the circumstances.

The next morning, Wednesday 25 September, he woke warm and
refreshed, beneath a clear grey light of dawn and a brisk dry wind.
Closing his eyes, he reflected for a moment how well he had survived,
without once losing his temper or feeling tempted to despair. Opening
them again, he saw Modestine gazing across at him with an
expression of studied patience. Hastily pulling on his boots, he fed her
the remaining black bread, and wandered about the little beech wood
where he now found himself, cheerfully consuming more chocolate
and brandy. He was filled by one of those sensations of early-morning
rapture, which only seem to affect people who have slept rough in the
open. He later wrote:

> Ulysses, left on Ithaca, and with a mind unsettled by the
> goddess, was not more pleasantly astray. I have been after
> an adventure all my life, a pure dispassionate adventure,
> such as befell early and heroic voyagers; and thus to be
> found by morning in a random woodside nook in

Gévaudan—not knowing north from south, as strange to my surroundings as the first man upon the earth, an inland castaway—was to find a fraction of my daydream realized.

I loved this idea of the 'inland castaway'. It seemed to me such a subtle, almost poetic idea, as if real travel were concerned with disorientation rather than merely distance. It was losing yourself, and then finding yourself again: casting yourself, at least for one moment, into the lap of the gods, if only to see what happened. Of course I could understand that the literary talk of Homer, and later Bunyan, was partly whimsical. But then it seemed to me it was partly serious as well, and that the 'daydream' was a real thing for Stevenson, and that his travels were also a pilgrimage.

But what puzzled me was that 'goddess'. Did Stevenson have some particular Circe in mind? Some woman who had cast a spell over him, perhaps? Were his own thoughts secretly 'unsettled' by her, and was this pilgrimage perhaps an attempt to escape her—or appease her? Padding along the silent woodland trails, deeper and deeper into Gévaudan, it slowly dawned on me that I might be pursuing a woman as well. Beyond Fouzilhac, which I was never to find, even in daylight, I stopped for an adder slowly uncurling off a large flat rock in my path. It was small and handsomely zigged: glossy black on soft beige. It moved aside with perfect dignity. At Cheylard, which is little more than a clearing with a few farms and a shrine, I stood for a long time beneath the wooden statue of Our Lady of All Graces.

We were now heading for the Trappist monastery of Notre Dame des Neiges. Stevenson, I supposed, had a conscience to examine. Our path went eastwards, over high moorland beyond the shelter of the Forêt de Mercroire, to Luc; and then turned south again down a remote valley of the Allier towards La Bastide, where the Trappists lived on a thickly-wooded hillside, in their ancient vows of poverty, chastity, obedience—and silence. Lay people from the outside would occasionally be granted permission to stay there 'on retreat', sharing the monks' harsh routine, meditating and praying, and taking stock of their lives. For a lapsed Calvinist like Stevenson, it was a not entirely foreign idea; for a lapsed Catholic like me, it was only too familiar. A brief visit seemed unavoidable.

This leg of the journey took two days, broken by a night at Luc. Stevenson slept at the comfortable *auberge*, after his Fouzilhac adventure; while I crossed the river and camped in a fragrant barn full of new-mown hay. I had again been caught by a storm crossing the moors between Cheylard and Luc, and I was glad of a roofbeam and the friendly, reasuring sound of munching cattle.

I had another dream. My track was an endless one of grey-stone chippings that passed through mauve heather against a bare sky. It seemed deserted, but it was full of unknown presences and pine-stumps—ghastly stumps all, lightning-struck and dead-white. The storm-rain approached me from behind, and thunder booms set me running, gasping, with my pack growing heavier and heavier. Someone was coming, chasing, and prongs of lightning snapped down on the hill—to my right, to my left, then directly overhead. My heart was beating with fear. I ran and ran over the lonely moor, and my hair turned snow white.

I sat up and it was the whiteness of dawn. The cattle were chomping and the hay smelled sweet.

In the morning a farmer gave me a big bowl of coffee and *tartines*, and I was sick. I went down to the Allier, and bathed from a rock, and scrubbed some clothes. A fisherman, carrying a long cane rod, walked by with a sideways glance, curious. I could see the gleaming tip of the rod moving on down the valley in the direction of La Bastide, long after he was gone, like the antenna of a predatory insect. I felt like another species myself, a sort of animal cut off from the human world. I lay on the rock all morning in the hot sun, listening to the call of peewits, and the sounds of the river.

I found that Stevenson wrote that day:
Why anyone should desire to go to Cheylard or to Luc is more than my much inventing spirit can embrace. For my part, I travel not to go anywhere, but to go; I travel for travel's sake. And to write about it afterwards—if only the public will be so condescending as to read. But the great affair is to move; to feel the needs and hitches of life a little more nearly; to get down off this feather bed of civilization, and to find the globe granite underfoot and strewn with cutting flints.

It is one of his most memorable formulations, and I learned it by heart. At night I would mumble it to myself, in the solitariness of my sleeping-bag. Again, I took it quite literally, on trust. Or rather, I took it by compulsion—this, I felt, is what I had to do; though if anyone had asked me why, I could not have explained. The fact that Stevenson was also making something of a profession of his bohemian wanderings, and deliberately searching for picturesque copy, did not occur to me at first. (He did not use that sentence about his reading public in the published version of his *Travels*; it revealed his hand too far.) But I now think that my critical innocence allowed me to learn other things, far more important, about the personal life that is hidden in, and below, the printed page. To learn by heart has more than one meaning.

On Thursday 26 September, Stevenson turned east again away from the Allier, climbed along the high forested ridge above La Bastide, and with much misgiving came down with Modestine to the gateway of Our Lady of the Snows. He stayed there for one night and most of two days. I came to think of this as one of his most complicated human encounters. It threw into relief for me much of his Scottish inheritance and upbringing, and eventually revealed some of the deepest preoccupations of his journey.

The faintly jocular tone in his Journal was, I was sure from the start, something of a disguise. I felt the same real twinges myself.

> Here I struck left, and pursued my way, driving my secular donkey before me and creaking in my secular boots and gaiters, towards the asylum of silence. I had not gone very far 'ere the wind brought to me the clanging of a bell; and somehow, I can scarce tell why, my heart sank within me at the sound. I have rarely approached anything with more hearty terror than the convent of Our Lady of the Snows; this is what it is to have had a Protestant education.

His first sight of the monk Father Apollinaris planting out a long avenue of birch trees, in his flapping robed habit, immediately startled childhood memories. It reminded him of the old prints of the medieval friars in the Edinburgh antique shops. The white gown, the black and pointed hood, the half-revealed yellow pate, all stirred forgotten terrors. Moreover, what was the etiquette for dealing with the Trappist vow of silence? 'I doffed my fur cap to him, with a faraway, superstitious reverence.'

He was surprised to find, however, that a foreign traveller was most kindly and indeed volubly greeted. Once it was established that he was not a pedlar, 'but a literary man', he was regaled with a liqueur, assigned a white-washed cell in the guest-wing, and bidden to attend the community services and meals at will. Father Apollinaris asked Stevenson if he were a Christian, 'and when he found that I was not, or not after his way, he glossed over it with great good will.' Later, an Irish brother, when he heard that the guest was a Protestant, 'only patted me on the shoulder and said, "you must be a Catholic and come to heaven".'

Stevenson read the notice pinned over the table in his cell, for those attending official retreats, with a mixture of amusement and gravity. 'What services they were to hear, when they were to tell their beads, or meditate, when they were to rise or go to rest. At the foot was a notable NB: "Le temps libre est employé à l'examen de conscience, à la confession, à faire de bonnes résolutions, etc."' But he was decidedly impressed by the severe regime of the Trappists themselves: rising at two in the morning to sing in the choir, then regulating the entire day between work duties and prayer accordingly as the bell rang, eating a sparse vegetarian diet, and never speaking—except by special dispensation to strangers like himself.

At the same time La Trappe had its measure of worldly good sense. Every monk was encouraged, indeed required, to work on a hobby of his own choice. Stevenson found monks binding books, baking bread, developing photographs, keeping rabbits, or peacefully cultivating potato patches. The monastery library was open to all, with a collection that not only included the sacred texts and holy fathers of the church, but Chateaubriand, Molière, and the *Odes et Ballades* of Victor Hugo. 'Let me whisper in addition what I only heard by way of report, a great collection in another room, under orthodox lock and key, where Voltaire and Walter Scott, in God knows how many volumes, led the dance.'

That night, in the conduct of the kind old Irish brother, he attended the service of Compline in the candle-lit choir, greatly moved by the stern simplicity of the plain, white-painted chapel, and the 'manly singing' of the cowled figures, alternately standing and bowed deep in prayer. 'These things have a flavour and significance

Le·Puy·en·Velay.

St Julien· Chapteuil

R. Loire

Le Monastier

R. Gazeille

L. Bouchet

Ussel

St Martin· de Frugeres

St Nicolas du Bouchet

Chateau Beaufort

Goudet

Stevenson's track ○○○○○○

Miles
1 0   5

R. Allier

Pradelles

Kilometres
1 0   5   10

THE VELAY
ON A LARGER SCALE

Langogne

that cannot be rendered in words. Only to the faithful can this be made clear; or to one like myself who is faithful all the world over and finds no form of worship silly or distasteful.'

As he retired to his cell for the night, Stevenson began to think about the force of prayer—a subject not especially familiar to his tolerant but sceptical mind. Partly he was thinking back to the old childish certainties of his Presbyterian boyhood, the attendance at the kirk, the teachings of his beloved nanny, Cummie, and the nostalgic confidences of the counterpane which he was to capture so brilliantly in the land of Leerie the Lamplighter, of *A Child's Garden of Verses*. But partly he was also realizing that, even as a man, he had continued to pray; only in a different sense. Not in the form of superstitious supplications or 'gasping complaints', which he could no longer regard as real prayers at all. But in the form of deliberate meditations, a particular turning and concentrating of the mind when alone. Sometimes, he recollected, he had even found himself taking pleasure in giving these prayers verbal form, 'as one would make a sonnet'.

He realized that his voyage through the Gévaudan had been peculiarly fruitful in this respect: that through the physical hardships and the plodding loneliness, a particular kind of consciousness had been released in him. And this consciousness made him more, not less, aware of his place in the scheme of things outside; of his friendships, his loves, his duties; of his common fate. He wrote:

> As I walked beside my donkey on this voyage, I made a prayer to myself, which I here offer to the reader, as I offer him any other thought that sprung up in me by the way. A voyage is a piece of autobiography at best.

He then entered not one, but three short prayers in his Journal, of which the last is a Prayer for Friends.

> God, who hast given us the love of women and the friendship of men, keep alive in our hearts the sense of old fellowship and tenderness; make offences to be forgotten and services to be remembered; protect those whom we love in all things and follow them with kindness, so that they may lead simple and unsuffering lives, and in the end die easily with quiet minds.

I sensed in all this that Stevenson was telling himself, quite simply, that he was not made to be alone, either in the human or the divine scheme of things. Paradoxically, the Trappists were teaching him that he belonged outside: he belonged to other people; he belonged especially to the people who loved him.

It is here that I later discovered one of the most suggestive differences between the original Journal and the published *Travels*. For, on reflection, Stevenson removed all these passages from the published version. They were, I think, just too personal and became part of an emotional 'autobiography' he was not prepared, at that date at least, to deliver up to his readers. Instead he struck a more romantic, raffish pose, remarking only of his feelings after the Compline service: 'I am not surprised that I made my escape into the court with somewhat whirling fancies, and stood like a man bewildered in the windy starry night.' Cutting out all mention of the prayers, he reverted to his bohemian persona, and added instead a snatch of bawdy French folk-song,

> Que t'as de belles filles
> Giroflé! Girofla!

It served to remind him, he said, that the Trappists were after all 'the dead in life—there was a chill reflection.' He could only bless God that he was 'free to wander, free to hope, and free to love.' An interesting contradiction.

But La Trappe is full of contradictions. They knew all about Stevenson when I passed through: a hundred years, they told me, is not so long in the eyes of eternity. Father Apollinaris's line of birch trees still stood. There were the white blocks of the monastic buildings perched bleakly on the forested hillside, rows of square unrelieved windows, part military and part industrial in appearance, and a bell chiming a flat commanding note—what memories it stirred!—from the rugged church tower. Yes, they said, it was all rather like a power station: so think of it as a spiritual generator, pumping out prayers.

Yet the original buildings which Stevenson saw had been burned down in 1912. His small guest-wing for travellers and retreat-makers had been replaced by a brightly-painted café-reception house astride the main drive, constructed like a Swiss chalet, with a self-service food bar and souvenir counter. Under the trees a score of cars were parked, transistors played, and families picnicked at fixed wooden tables. I walked through like a ghost, dazed with disappointment, and headed for the church, remembering now what my farmer at Luc had said: 'Ah, La Trappe, they make an *affaire* of the holy life up there'; though he added with a Gallic shrug, 'but good luck to them! We must all live in our own way, and le Bon Dieu has always liked a little money, as proof of good intentions.'

In the church a young monk, with a snappy Cicero haircut and amused grey eyes, suddenly rose out of the sacred book-stall and gently tugged at my rucksack. English? On the trail of Stevenson? Sleeping rough? Ah yes, he had wanted to be a writer himself. That too was a vocation! Well, it was a happy chance that had brought me to la Trappe. A happy Providence. So now I must lay down my burden (he said this with a smile, the grey eyes almost teasing) and he would take me to visit the monastery. But first things first! And here he peered at me with what I took to be a frown, and I thought I was to be put through my catechism. Protestant, lapsed-Catholic, atheist, poetic agnostic....

'You are hungry, my friend,' Father Ambrose cut into my thought, 'so come along with me.' And he gave me another of those Trappist smiles.

I was whisked away without ceremony to the kitchens, and made to sit down at a huge wooden table. Behind me, a large electric dishwasher turned like a Buddhist prayer-wheel. All round, tiles gleamed and scoured pots bubbled on brand new gas ranges. The kitchen monk in a pressed white apron considered me thoughtfully. 'One must feed the corpse as well as the spirit,' he observed, in a heavy Provençal accent, and grinned seraphically. He was as thin as a fence-pole, with the marks of asceticism like the marks of an axe over his long face and frame. He disappeared into an echoing pantry and came out with plate after plate balanced on his arm. I could not believe such a feast, and later listed it all in my diary: dish of olives, black and green; earthenware bowl of country paté with wooden scoop; whole pink ham on the bone, with carving knife; plate of melon slices; hot bowl of garlic sausage and mash; bowl of salad and radishes; board of goat cheeses; basket of different breads; canister of home-made butter; two jugs of wine, one white, one red. *Spécialité de la maison*, thin slices of fresh *baguette* spread very thickly with a heavy honey-coloured paste which turned out to be pounded chestnuts, *marrons*, and tasted out of this world. I was told simply: 'Mangez, mais mangez, tout-ce que vous voudrez!' And he was right, I had the hunger of the devil.

Much later I smoked my pipe and fell asleep in the monastery gardens, under a mulberry tree, wondering at the wisdom of monks. Father Ambrose woke me as his sandals came tapping along the terrace. 'Better now?' was his only comment. I was taken on a tour of the buildings: long bare corridors of polished pinewood, a chapter house full of afternoon sunlight and smelling of beeswax, a library like that of an academic college, with a special history section including the complete works of Winston Churchill. Then a large bleak dormitory, with iron bedsteads in rows of cubicles, which brought back bad memories; and a shadowy choir-stall with, for me, the eternally ambiguous smell of incense.

The monks' timetable had shifted little since Stevenson's day. Prime began a little later, at 3.30 in the morning; but the vegetarian fast was maintained from January till Eastertide. Prayer and hard physical work remained the staple of their lives. The cemetery stood behind a wall of the vegetable garden, a cluster of plain white crosses on a neat lawn, like a war grave in Passchendaele.

'And here at La Trappe,' said Father Ambrose as we stood again upon the terrace, 'the summer visitors soon depart. We are alone again with Our Lady. Her snows fall from November until April. Sometimes we are cut off for days. Cut off from everything…except from God. And sometimes it is so…. But you must pray for us. Pray for us on your road. You will do that, my friend, I think? And come back again, we will be here. Your rucksack is a light one.'

Father Ambrose smiled and turned rapidly away, slipping his hands into the long white sleeves of his habit, and stepping off into silence. Only the sound of his sandals retreated along the stone-flagged terrace. I was left strangely confounded, perplexed; this was not what I had expected. In a sense I felt they had found me out.

NORMAN LEWIS

VILLAGE OF CATS

When I went to live in Farol, the Grandmother who owned the house gave me a cat. 'Don't feed it,' she said. 'Don't take any notice of it. It can sleep in the shed and it'll keep the rats away.' Farol was full of cats, for which reason it was often called Pueblo de los Gatos—Cat Village. There were several hundred of them living in whatever accommodation they could find in the village, and in caves in the hill behind it. They were an ugly breed, skinny with long legs and small, pointed heads. You saw little of them in the daytime, but after dark they were everywhere. The story was that Don Alberto, the local landowner, who was also a bit of an historian, claimed that they had always been there, and produced a fanciful theory based on some reference made to them by an early traveller that they had some connection with the sacred cats of Ancient Egypt. Mentioning this, the fishermen of Farol would screw their fingers into their temples and roll their eyes in derision as if to say, what will he come up with next? Their version was that the cats had been imported in the old days to clean up the mess left when they degutted fish on the spot before packing them up to be sent away. No one in this part of the world would ever kill a domestic animal, so their numbers soon got out of control. In addition to scavenging round the boats, they hunted lizards, frogs, anything they found edible, including fat-bodied moths attracted to the oleanders on summer evenings, which they snatched out of the air with their paws. Whenever a cat became too old or sick to have about the place, it would be put in a bag and taken to the cork forest and there abandoned. The people who owned this part of the forest lived in the village of Sort, about five kilometres away. They had no cats but were overrun by dogs, and as they, too, were squeamish about taking life, they brought down unwanted animals, borrowed a boat, and left them to die of hunger and thirst on an island a hundred yards or so off-shore.

It soon became clear that the Grandmother was a person of exceptional power and influence in the village. All the domestic aspects of life—and largely the financial ones, too—came came under the control here of the women, 'dominated', to use the local word, by the Grandmother, just as the males were dominated by the five senior fishermen owning the major shares in the big boats. In each case the domination was subtle and indirect, a matter rather of leadership accorded to experience and vision.

The Grandmother had gathered a little respect in deference to her money, but most of it was based on sheer spiritual force. She was large, dignified and slow-moving, dressed perpetually in black, with the face of a Borgia pope, a majestic nose and a defiant chin, sprouting an occasional bristle. A muscular slackening of an eyelid had left one eye half-closed, so that she appeared at all times to be on the verge of a wink. Her voice was husky and confiding, although in a moment of impatience she was likely to burst into an authoritarian bellow. Everything she said carried instant conviction, and the villagers said that she was inclined to make God's mind up for him, because whenever people left a loophole of doubt about future intentions by adding the pious formula, 'if God is willing', she would decide the matter there and then with a shout of, '*Sí* que quiere'—of *course* he's willing.

As a matter of routine the Grandmother meddled in the family affairs of others. She provided instruction on the mechanics of family planning, investigated the household budgets of newly-married couples to decide when they could hope (if ever) to afford a child, and put forward a suitable name as soon as it was born. All the names suggested for male children were taken from a book she possessed on the generals of antiquity, and the village was full of inoffensive little boys called Julio César, Carlos Magna (Charlemagne), Mambró (Marlborough), and Napoleón.

Above all, she was an expert on herbal remedies and the villagers saved on the doctor's fees by prescriptions provided after a scrutiny of their faeces and urine. 'Mear claro y cagar duro' (clear piss and hard shit), she claimed—quoting a saying attributed to Lope de Vega—was at the base of health and prosperity. She also offered a sporadic supply of the urine of a woman who had recently given birth, locally regarded as effective in the treatment of conjunctivitis and certain skin ailments—although in a village where the birthrate must have been one of the lowest in the world, it was rare for a donor to be available.

My room in the Grandmother's house was odd-shaped and full of sharp edges, with a ceiling slanting up in four triangles to a centre point, and dormer windows throwing segments of light and shade across walls and floor. In Farol they were nervous about using colour, so it was all stark white, and living in this room was rather like living inside a crystal, in which the Grandmother, when she came on the scene, appeared as a black, geometrical shape.

A tiny cubicle contained a charcoal-burning stove, and another a floor of ceramic tiles. It was a feature of the house that illuminated a nook in the Grandmother's mind inhabited by poetic fancies, for the tiles' pattern—made to the Grandmother's own design—depicted flowers on intertwining stems, growing from a central hole beside which a powerful disinfectant in an amphora-shaped container had been placed.

I was taken into the garden to admire another feature of the accommodation: three strands of barbed-wire twisted together round the top of the wall, cut from a roll the Grandmother had bought as an extravagance. Beyond the wall a rampart of sunflowers besieged by goldfinches hung their heads, and through their stalks I could see the beach with the glossy, translucent pebbles glittering among the coarse limestone chips, and a rank of purple and yellow fishing boats leaning on it. I asked the price of the room, and the Grandmother's eyes became misted with introspection. She passed her tongue very slowly in a clockwise direction round her teeth inside the lips, and said, 'Five pesetas a day. Here,' she continued, 'you will enjoy great tranquillity.'

This proved true; to find the place had been an immense stroke of luck. I had been attracted to Farol by its reputation of being the least accessible coastal village in north-east Spain, and I had spent my first week being driven out of the *fonda* (inn), largely by the smell of cat. The inn was run by two shy, silent brothers I never saw except at mealtimes, when one or other of them would bring the food, drop the plate on the table, head averted, and scuttle away. The food was always tinned sardines—a luxury in this place where they caught fresh sardines sometimes by the ton—and hardboiled eggs. The brothers kept sixteen cats in their cellar, and had taken four more away and left them in the cork forest only the week before I arrived.

My room in the Grandmother's house had been occupied until a few days before my arrival by the Grandmother's eldest daughter, her son-in-law and their two small children, who—as I was later told—had been hugely relieved after some years of living in the shadow of the Grandmother's personality, to be able finally to make their escape.

There were fifty or more such houses in Farol built in an irregular and misaligned fashion into a narrow zig-zag of street, and a few more squeezed where space could be found among the semi-circle of massive rocks almost enclosing the village. Standing aloof were several mansions originally belonging to rich cork-merchants, who came here for their holidays at the end of the last century; all the mansions were in varying states of decrepitude, and decorated with stone coats of arms to which their owners had not been entitled.

Farol catered for basic needs with a small, decayed church, a ship's chandlers, a butcher's shop, and a general store selling a wide range of goods, from moustache wax to hard black chocolate that had to be broken up with a hammer and was kept in a sack, and a single book: Alonso Barros's *Eight Thousand Familiar Sayings and Moral Proverbs*, published in 1598, of which almost every house possessed a copy and by which people regulated their lives. The bar offered thin acidulous wine for half a peseta a glass, and was notable for its display of the mummified corpse of a dugong, known locally as 'the mermaid'. This grotesquely patched and repaired object, with its mournful glass eyes, sewn-on leather breasts and flap covering the sexual parts, was believed to vary its expression, whether pensive, sceptical or malicious, according to the weather, and it was noticeable that strangers who took refuge in the bar from the horrors of the *fonda*—generally agreed to be the worst in Spain—seated themselves so as not to be depressed by the sight of this macabre trophy.

In a village enjoying the brand of democracy, the absence of status-seeking, imposed by a manageable, shared-out poverty, a few influential people emerged in addition to the Grand-mother.

The formal head of the community, the Alcalde, an outsider who had been inflicted on the village, had almost been forgiven for serving in the Nationalist Forces in the Civil War by convincing the villagers that he had been a Nationalist not by choice, but by the geographical accident of having been born in territory taken over by the Nationalists. Shopkeepers in Farol acted as bankers, supplying goods on credit throughout the winter in anticipation of sardines and tunny to be caught in summer, and were therefore entitled to some grudging respect. Inevitably, the butcher wielded power through his control of the rare meat supplies—more importantly, of the blood hot from the veins of slaughtered animals, given to sickly children. My next-door neighbour attracted attention to himself in a community that hardly understood the usages of property, through his marriage to a rich peasant girl, who had brought him some fields and trees he had never seen. Five senior fishermen expected to be listened to when any matter relating to the village weal came under discussion. The survivor of the great storm of 7 January 1922, carried in his small boat almost to Italy before being picked up, was never allowed to sit in a bar alone, owing to the belief that his luck was communicable by physical contact. Don Ignacio, the priest, in so far as he could be considered a villager, was well thought of, because he had lived with a mistress quite openly, and had learned to mind his own business.

The other person of consequence would have been seen by most outsiders as a prostitute, although a villager might have pretended, or even felt, surprise at such a suggestion. Sa Cordovesa, possessor of a delicate beauty and charm, had arrived as a child refugee from Andalusia, and now conducted multiple affairs with discretion, even dignity, behind the cover of making cheap dresses. By common consent the community wore blinkers in this matter, a posture of self-defence adopted to cope as painlessly as possible with a situation in which most men could expect to reach the age of thirty before they could afford to marry. Taking refuge in self-deception, Farol invested Sa Cordovesa with a kind of subjective virtue. She had allies—such as the Grandmother—by the dozen, and was made welcome in any house. It was not long before I discovered that there had been a succession of Sa Cordovesas in the past. Farol had solved a social problem in its own unobtrusive way.

This, then, was Farol, cut off more by secret human design than by the accidents of nature, since the narrow, winding and precipitous road leading to it had been dynamited by a landlord within living memory, to keep outsiders away. By reason of its continuing isolation it remained a repository of past customs and attitudes of mind. Life had always been hard—an existence pared to the bone—and local opinion was that it was getting harder, purely because mysterious changes in the sea were directing the fish elsewhere. In most years catches were a little sparser than the year before, but there were optimists who believed that the decline was not necessarily irreversible, and they awaited in hope the end of the cycle of lean years.

The fishermen were totally absorbed by the sea, almost oblivious of the activities of those who lived by the land, wholly ignorant of the fact that only a few miles away a catastrophe was in the making. Three miles back from the shore the cork-oak forest began— hundreds of thousands of majestic trees, spreading their quilt of foliage into the foothills, and up and over the slopes into the low peaks of the sierra. The great wealth of cork belonged to the days before the invention of the metal bottle-top, but even now with slumped sales and low prices the oaks provided a livelihood for hundreds of tree-owning peasant cultivators of Sort, village of dogs, and many other forest hamlets.

In the year before my arrival in 1948, people in Sort began to notice that something was happening to the trees, that the early spring foliage had changed colour and was withering. Word of their neighbours' alarm reached Farol, but the fishermen shrugged their shoulders and went on preparing their lines or mending their nets. It was impossible for them to understand that their destiny could be in any way linked with that of peasants with whom they had little contact and from whom they were separated by huge differences of temperament and tradition. For the fishermen of Farol the peasants of Sort might have been the inhabitants of another planet, and they found it difficult to interest themselves in their fate, whatever misfortune might have befallen them.

My next-door neighbour, Juan, was the only man in Farol who should at least have had some slight interest in the fate of the oaks, for his wife, Francesca, had brought fifty oaks as her dowry to this dowry-less village, and another seventy had passed to her on her father's death. She was a lively, high-stepping, intelligent woman who wore a silk dress on all occasions, and had strutted about in high-heeled shoes until the Grandmother had warned her in a tactful fashion that all articles made from leather were taboo in the village. Her gaunt but imposing young husband with his seer's face, who always seemed on the verge of prophetic utterance, had expressed doubt about the morality of property acquired in the way his had been. Juan salved his conscience by neglecting to visit the trees and the few barren acres that had gone with them, although he agreed to accompany his wife on mushroom-hunting trips in the vicinity, from which they returned with basketfuls of the celebrated *amanita caesaria,* used by one or more Roman empresses to poison their husbands.

Francesca confirmed that the trees were ailing, about half those on her property being affected. She was worried about the possible loss of revenue from cork, but even more so by the fact that only about half the normal crop of mushrooms had come up the last autumn. Like the rabbits, the mushrooms needed cover and shade. Sort was full of men who had spent their life with trees, and knew all that was to be known about cork oaks, but nobody had ever seen anything like this before. Juan and the rest of the fishermen withheld their sympathy. It was firmly believed that every peasant had a boxful of thousand-peseta notes buried under his floor. 'They'll never go short of anything. Let them live on their fat,' was the general verdict.

The first signs of hard times in Sort was that their dogs were clearly getting even less food than usual and were therefore becoming more venturesome in their forays into Farol territory, where they managed to catch and devour not only an occasional cat, which no one grudged them, but a chicken here and there, which was a grave and unpardonable offence.

Whereas the cats of Farol needed no more than the presence and companionship of man, the dogs of Sort were not wholly independent in the matter of feeding themselves. Their function was to hunt game in the forest, and they were rewarded with the skins, the heads and the feet of the rabbits they caught. Apart from that, they had to make do with the sparse offal to be picked up around the village, and rare cannibal feasts when one of their own kind perished through accident or disease.

Unlike the people of Sort, who were individualists, those of Farol, accustomed to the communal enterprises of the sea, lost no opportunity to work as a team. In both villages women helped to make ends meet by keeping chickens. These, in Sort, would be shut up in cages at night, suspended from trees to keep them out of the reach of the dogs, or the rare fox that ventured into the village once in a while. In Farol, although this kind of protection was less essential, a communal coop had been built for the use of the aged and infirm, and a week after my arrival a pack of famished dogs from Sort managed to break into this and carry off many of the hens.

This was a calamity for which there was no redress. Sort denied responsibility. A peasant from the dog village who had driven a cart-load of vegetables over to Farol to barter them for fish, was tackled in the Alcalde's bar about what was to be done. His reply was, 'How do you know they were our dogs? You can't tell one dog from another.'

The fishermen, who were given to informal meetings, held one on the spot; after which they told the man he could take his vegetables back. At a second meeting reprisals were decided upon. The view was that if the Sort people were not prepared to cut down on their dog population, the fishermen would have to take their own measures to reduce their numbers. But how? It was impossible to conceive of anybody taking an axe or a club and killing a dog outright and the idea of using rat poison went against the grain. The final solution was to procure a number of dried sea-sponges, and fry these in olive oil to provide a flavour irresistible to dogs. When, a few days later, the animals had recovered from the surfeit of chickens, the sponges were put out for them on the periphery of the village. It was a time-honoured method, and as ever, successful. The dogs gorged themselves on the dried sponges, which swelled up as they absorbed the gastric juices, until in the end the dogs' stomachs ruptured. A dog that had come on the scene too late to partake of the fatal meal, was trapped and then, as a traditional gesture of defiance and contempt, castrated and sent home with a black ribbon tied round its neck. The black ribbon symbolized cowardice.

After that, the Sort people kept their dogs under control by fastening them to heavy logs which they had to drag about wherever they went. From this time on, the relationship between Sort and Farol—never more than a watchful neutrality—fell into decline, and the shadow of the vendetta fell across the villages. Despite the annual visit of a clairvoyant who cast horoscopes, consulted the Tarot cards, and thus directed their affairs, the people of Farol had no way of knowing that the great shoals of fish of the past would not return, and the predicament they faced was at least as great as that threatening the villagers of Sort. It was a time for enmities to be put aside, and alliances cemented wherever they could be found, but Farol and Sort turned their backs on one another, and went their separate ways towards an obscure fate.

SAUL BELLOW
OLD PARIS

Changes in Paris? Like all European capitals, the city has of course undergone certain changes, the most conspicuous being the appearance of herds of tall buildings beyond the ancient gates. Old districts like Passy, peculiarly gripping in their dinginess, are almost unrecognizable today with their new apartment houses and office buildings, most of which would suit a Mediterranean port better than Paris. It's no easy thing to impose colour on the dogged northern grey, the native Parisian *grisaille*—flinty, foggy, dripping and, for most of the year, devoid of any brightness. The gloom will have its way with these new *immeubles*, too; you may be sure of that. When Verlaine wrote that the rain fell into his heart as it did upon the city (referring to almost any city in the region), he wasn't exaggerating a bit. As a one-time resident of Paris (I arrived in 1948), I can testify to that. New urban architecture will find itself ultimately powerless against the *grisaille*. Parisian gloom is not simply climatic, it is a spiritual force that acts not only on building materials, on walls and roof-tops, but also on your character, your opinions and judgments. It is a powerful astringent.

But the changes—I wandered about Paris not very long ago to see how thirty-odd years had altered the place. The new skyscraper on the boulevard du Montparnasse is almost an accident, something that had strayed away from Chicago and come to rest on a Parisian street corner. In my old haunts between the boulevard du Montparnasse and the Seine, what is most immediately noticeable is the disappearance of certain cheap conveniences. High rents have done for the family bistros that once served delicious, inexpensive lunches. A certain decrepit loveliness is giving way to unattractive, over-priced, over-decorated newness. Dense traffic—the small streets make you think of Yeats's 'mackerel-crowded seas'—requires an alertness incompatible with absent-minded rambling. Dusty old shops in which you might lose yourself for a few hours are scrubbed up now and sell pocket computers and high-fidelity equipment. Stationers who once carried notebooks with excellent paper now offer a flimsy product that lets the ink through. Very disappointing. Cabinet-makers and other small artisans once common are hard to find.

My neighbour, the *emballeur* on the rue de Verneuil, disappeared long ago. This cheerful specialist wore a smock and beret and, as he worked in an unheated shop, his big face was stung raw. He kept a cold butt-end in the corner of his mouth—one seldom sees the *mégots* in this new era of prosperity. A pet three-legged hare, slender in profile, fat in the hindquarters, stirred lopsidedly among the crates. But there is no more demand for hand-hammered crates. Progress has eliminated all such simple trades. It has replaced them with boutiques that sell costume jewellery, embroidered linens or goosedown bedding. In each block there are three or four *antiquaires*. Who would have thought that Europe contained so much old junk? Or that, the servant class having disappeared, hearts nostalgic for the bourgeois epoch would hunt so eagerly for Empire breakfronts, Récamier sofas and curule chairs?

Inspecting the boulevards, I find curious survivors. On the boulevard St Germain, the dealer in books of military history and memorabilia who was there thirty-five years ago is still going strong. Evidently there is a permanent market for leather sets that chronicle the ancient wars. (If you haven't seen the crowds at the Invalides and the huge, gleaming tomb of Napoleon, if you underestimate the power of glory, you don't know what France is.) Near the rue des Saints Pères, the pastry shop of Camille Hallu, Aîné, is gone, together with numerous small bookshops, but the dealer in esoteric literature on the next block has kept up with the military history man down the street, as has the umbrella merchant nearby. Her stock is richer than ever, sheaves of umbrellas and canes with parakeet heads and barking dogs in silver. Thanks to tourists, the small hotels thrive—as do the electric Parisian cockroaches who live in them, a swifter and darker breed than their American cousins. There are more winos than in austere post-war days, when you seldom saw *clochards* drinking in doorways.

The ancient grey and yellow walls of Paris have the strength needed to ride out the shock-waves of the present century. Invisible electronic forces pierce them, but the substantial gloom of courtyards and kitchens is preserved. Boulevard shop windows, however, show that life is different and that Parisians feel needs they never felt before. In 1949 I struck a deal with my landlady on the rue Vaneau: I installed a gas hot-water heater in the kitchen in exchange for two months' rent. It gave her great joy to play with the faucet and set off bursts of gorgeous flame. Neighbours came in to congratulate her. Paris was then in what Mumford called the Paleotechnic age. It has caught up now with advancing technology, and French shops display the latest in beautiful ktichens—counters and tables of glowing synthetic alabaster, artistic in form, the last word in technics.

Once every week during the nasty winter of 1950 I used to meet my friend, the painter Jesse Reichek, in a café on the rue du Bac. As we drank cocoa and played casino, regressing shamelessly to childhood, he would lecture me on Giedion's 'Mechanization Takes Command' and on the Bauhaus. Shuffling the cards I felt that I was simultaneously going backwards and forwards. We little thought in 1950 that by 1983 so many modern kitchen shops would be open for business in Paris, that the curmudgeonly French would fall in love so passionately with sinks, refrigerators and microwave ovens. I suppose that the disappearance of the *bonne à tout faire* is behind this transformation. The post-bourgeois era began when the maid of all work found better work to do. Hence all these *son et lumière* kitchens and the velvety pulsations of invisible ventilators.

I suppose that this is what 'Modern' means in Paris now.

It meant something different at the beginning of the century. It was this other something that so many of us came looking for in 1947. Until 1939, Paris was the centre of a great international culture, open to Spaniards, Russians, Italians, Rumanians, Americans; to the Picassos, Diaghilevs, Modiglianis, Brancusis and Pounds at the glowing core of the modernist art movement. It remained to be seen whether the fall of Paris in 1940 had only interrupted this creativity. Would it resume when the defeated Nazis had gone back to Germany? There were those who suspected that the thriving international centre had been declining during the thirties, and some believed that it was gone for good.

I was among those who came to investigate, part of the first wave. The blasts of war had no sooner ended than thousands of Americans packed their bags to go abroad. Among these eager travellers, poets, painters and philosophers were vastly outnumbered by the restless young—students of art history, cathedral lovers, refugees from the South and the Mid-west, ex-soldiers on the GI Bill, sentimental pilgrims—as well as by people no less imaginative, with schemes for getting rich. A young man I had known in Minnesota came over to open a caramel-corn factory in Florence. Adventurers, black-marketeers, smugglers, would-be *bon vivants,* bargain-hunters, bubbleheads—tens of thousands crossed on old troop-ships seeking business opportunities, or sexual opportunities, or just for the hell of it. Damaged London was severely depressed, full of bomb holes and fire weed, whereas Paris was unhurt and about to resume its glorious artistic and intellectual life.

The Guggenheim Foundation had given me a fellowship and I was prepared to take part in the great revival when and if it began. Like the rest of the American contingent I had brought my illusions with me, but I like to think that I was also sceptical (perhaps the most tenacious of my illusions). I was not going to sit at the feet of Gertrude Stein. I had no notions about the Ritz Bar. I would not be boxing with Ezra Pound, as Hemingway had done, nor writing in bistros while waiters brought oysters and wine. Hemingway the writer I admired without limits; Hemingway the *figure* was to my mind the quintessential tourist, the one who believed that he alone was the American whom Europeans took to their hearts as one of their own. In simple truth, the Jazz Age Paris of American legend had no charms for me, and I had my reservations also about the Paris of Henry James—bear in mind the unnatural squawking of East Side Jews as James described it in *The American Scene.* You wouldn't expect a relative of those barbarous East Siders to be drawn to the world of Mme de Vionnet, which had, in any case, vanished long ago.

Life, said Samuel Butler, is like giving a concert on the violin while learning to play the instrument. That, friends, is real wisdom. I was concertizing and practising scales at the same time. I *thought* I understood why I had come to Paris. Writers like Sherwood Anderson and, oddly enough, John Cowper Powys had made clear to me what was lacking in American life. 'American men are tragic without knowing why they are tragic,' wrote Powys in his *Autobiography.* 'They are tragic by reason of the desolate thinness and forlorn narrowness of their sensual mystical contacts. Mysticism and Sensuality are the things that most of all redeem life.' Powys, mind you, was an admirer of American democracy. I would have had no use for him otherwise. I believed that only the English-speaking democracies had real politics. In politics continental Europe was infantile and horrifying. What America lacked, for all its political stability, was the capacity to enjoy intellectual pleasures as though they were sensual pleasures. This was what Europe offered, or was said to offer.

There was, however, another part of me that remained unconvinced by this formulation, denied that Europe—as advertised—still existed and was still capable of gratifying the American longing for the rich and the rare. True writers from St Paul, St Louis and Oak Park, Illinois, had gone to Europe to write their American books, the best work of the twenties. Corporate, industrial America could not give them what they needed. In Paris they were free to be fully American. It was from abroad that they sent imaginative rays homewards. But was it the European imaginative reason that had released and stirred them? Was it Modern Paris itself or a new universal Modernity working in all countries, an international culture, of which Paris was, or *had* been, the centre? I knew what Powys meant by his imaginative redemption from desolate thinness and forlorn narrowness experienced by Americans, whether or not they were conscious of it. At least I thought I did. But I was aware also of a seldom-mentioned force visible in Europe itself to anyone who had eyes—the force of a nihilism that had destroyed most of its cities and millions of lives in a war of six long years. I could not easily accept the plausible sets: America, thinning of the life-impulses; Europe, the cultivation of the subtler senses still valued, still going on. Indeed, a great European pre-war literature had told us what nihilism was, had warned us what to expect. Céline had spelled it out quite plainly in his *Voyage to the End of the Night.* His Paris was still there, more *there* than the Sainte Chapelle or the Louvre. Proletarian Paris, middle-class Paris, not to mention intellectual Paris which was trying to fill nihilistic emptiness with Marxist doctrine—all transmitted the same message.

Still, I had perfectly legitimate reasons for being here. Arthur Koestler ribbed me one day when he met me in the street with my five-year-old son. He said: 'Ah? You're married? You have a kid? And you've come to *Paris*?' To be Modern, you see, meant to be detached from tradition, traditional sentiments, from national politics and, of course, from the family. But it was not in order to be Modern that I was living on the rue de Verneuil. My aim was to be free from measures devised and applied by others. I could not agree, to begin with, on any definition. I would be ready for definiton when I was ready for an obituary. I had already decided not to let American business society make my life for me, and it was easy for me to shrug off Mr Koestler's joke. Besides, Paris was not my dwelling-place, it was only a stopover. There was no dwelling-place.

One of my American friends, a confirmed Francophile, made speeches to me about the City of Man, the City of Light. I took his rhetoric at a considerable discount. I was not, however, devoid of sentiment. To say it in French, I was *aux anges* in Paris, wandering about, sitting in cafés, walking beside the green, medicinal-smelling Seine. I can think of visitors who were not greatly impressed by the City of Man. Horace Walpole complained of the stink of its little streets in the eighteenth century. For Rousseau, it was the centre of *amour propre*, the most warping of civilized vices. Dostoyevsky loathed it because it was the capital of Western bourgeois vainglory. Americans, however, loved the place. I, too, with characteristic reservations, fell for it. True, I spent lots of time in Paris thinking about Chicago, but I discovered, and the discovery was a very odd one, that in Chicago I had for many years been absorbed in thoughts of Paris. I was a long-time reader of Balzac and of Zola, and knew the city of Père Goriot, the Paris at which Rastignac had shaken his fist, swearing to fight it to the finish, the Paris of Zola's drunkards and prostitutes, of Baudelaire's beggars and the children of the poor whose pets were sewer rats. The Parisian pages of Rilke's *Die Aufzeichnungen des Malte Laurids Brigge* had taken hold of my imagination in the thirties, as had the Paris of Proust, especially those dense, gorgeous and painful passages of *Time Regained* describing the city as it was in 1915—the German night bombardments, Mme Verdurin reading of battlefields in the morning paper as she sips her coffee. Curious how the place had moved in on me. I was not at all a Francophile, not at all the unfinished American prepared to submit myself to the great city in the hope that it would round me out or complete me.

In my generation the children of immigrants *became* Americans. An effort was required. One made oneself, free-style. To become a Frenchman on top of that would have required a second effort. Was I

being invited to turn myself into a Frenchman? Well, no, but it
seemed to me that I would not be fully accepted in France unless I had
done everything possible to become French. And that was not for me.
I was already an American, and I was also a Jew. I had an American
outlook, superadded to a Jewish consciousness. France would have
to take me as I was.

From Parisian Jews I learned what life had been like under the
Nazis, about the round-ups and deportations in which French
officials had co-operated. I read Céline's *Les Beaux Draps*, a
collection of crazy, murderous harangues, seething with Jew-hatred.

A sullen, grumbling, drizzling city still remembered the
humiliations of occupation. Dark bread, *pain de seigle*, was rationed.
Coal was scarce. None of this inspired American-in-Paris fantasies of
gaiety and good times in the Ritz Bar or the Closerie des Lilas. More
appropriate now was Baudelaire's Parisian sky weighing the city
down like a heavy pot lid, or the Paris of the Communard *pétroleurs*
who had set the Tuileries afire and blown out the fortress walls. I saw
a barricade going up across the Champs Elysées one morning, but
there was no fighting. The violence of the embittered French was for
the most part internal.

No, I wasn't devoid of sentiments but the sentiments were sober.
But why did Paris affect me so deeply? Why did this imperial,
ceremonious, ornamental mass of structures weaken my American
refusal to be impressed, my Jewish scepticism and reticence; why was
I such a sucker for its tones of grey, the patchy bark of its sycamores
and its bitter-medicine river under the ancient bridges? The place was,
naturally, indifferent to me, a peculiar alien from Chicago. Why did it
take hold of my emotions?

For the soul of a civilized, or even partly civilized, man, Paris was
one of the permanent settings, a theatre, if you like, where the greatest
problems of existence might be represented. What future, if any, was
there for this theatre? It could not tell you what to represent. Could
anyone in the twentieth century make use of these unusual
opportunities? Americans of my generation crossed the Atlantic to
size up the challenge, to look upon this human, warm, noble,
beautiful and also proud, morbid, cynical and treacherous setting.

Saul Bellow

Paris inspires young Americans with no such longings and challenges now. The present generation of students, if it reads Diderot, Stendhal, Balzac, Baudelaire, Rimbaud, Proust, does not bring to its reading the desires born of a conviction that American life-impulses are thin. We do not look beyond America. It absorbs us completely. No one is stirred to the bowels by Europe of the ancient parapets. A huge force has lost its power over the imagination. This force began to weaken in the fifties and by the sixties it was entirely gone.

Young MBAs, Management School graduates, gene-splicers and computerists, their careers well started, will fly to Paris with their wives to shop on the rue de Rivoli and dine at the Tour d'Argent. Not greatly different are the Behavioural Scientists and members of the learned professions who are well satisfied with what they learned of the Old World while they were getting their BAs. A bit of Marx, of Freud, of Max Weber, an incorrect recollection of André Gide and his Gratuitous Act, and they had had as much of Europe as any educated American needed.

And I suppose that we *can* do without the drama of Old Europe. Europeans themselves, in considerable numbers, got tired of it some decades ago and turned from art to politics or abstract intellectual games. Foreigners no longer came to Paris to recover their humanity in modern forms of the marvellous. There was nothing marvellous about the Marxism of Sartre and his followers. Post-war French philosophy, adapted from the German, was less than enchanting. Paris, which had been a centre, still *looked* like a centre and could not bring itself to concede that it was a centre no longer. Stubborn de Gaulle, assisted by Malraux, issued his fiats to a world that badly wanted to agree with him, but when the old man died there was nothing left—nothing but old monuments, old graces. Marxism, Eurocommunism, Existentialism, Structuralism, Deconstructionism could not restore the potency of French civilization. Sorry about that. A great change, a great loss of ground. The Giacomettis and the Stravinskys, the Brancusis no longer come. No international art centre draws the young to Paris. Arriving instead are terrorists. For them, French revolutionary traditions degenerated into confused leftism and a government that courts the Third World make Paris a first-class place to plant bombs and to hold press conferences.

The world's disorders are bound to leave their mark on Paris. Cynosures bruise easily. And why has Paris for centuries now attracted so much notice? Quite simply, because it is the heavenly city of secularists. 'Wie Gott in Frankreich' was the expression used by the Jews of Eastern Europe to describe perfect happiness. I puzzled over this simile for many years, and I think I can interpret it now. God would be perfectly happy in France because he would not be troubled by prayers, observances, blessings and demands for the interpretation of difficult dietary questions. Surrounded by unbelievers He, too, could relax towards evening, just as thousands of Parisians do at their favourite cafés. There are few things more pleasant, more civilized, than a tranquil *terrasse* at dusk.

TriQuarterly

Fiction • Poetry • Art • Criticism
Three times a year

The New York Times has called **TriQuarterly** "perhaps the pre-eminent journal for literary fiction" in the nation. **Chicago** magazine describes it as "one of the best, issue after issue." But see for yourself—subscribe now...

Recent and forthcoming contributors:

William Goyen
Pamela White Hadas
Amos Oz
Tobias Wolff
Michael Harper
Robert Coles
John Cage
Leslie Marmon Silko
Richard Ford
Maxine Kumin
Theodore Weiss
Jay Wright

Linda Pastan
Robert Stone
Alan Sillitoe
Carlos Fuentes
Eugenio Montale
Gerald Graff
Robert Pinsky
Stanley Elkin
Cyra McFadden
Joyce Carol Oates

...and many others

PATRICK MARNHAM
HOLY WEEK

In Mexico City, Trotsky was murdered. The details are notorious. The disciple who was really a Stalinist agent; the blast-proof steel doors, which opened to welcome the assassin; the ice pick, suddenly produced from a raincoat; *the weight, post mortem, of the great man's brain.* I heard the story first from a follower.

'Did you know that after his death they weighed his brain? It was *vast.* It weighed three pounds.'

I remember the awe in the voice of this normally cynical man. I had presumed that now, as research had revealed that brain size and weight are unrelated to intelligence, the myth of Trotsky's brain had begun to die. But it takes more than facts to destroy a myth. Something of my friend's awe remains with me still. It became my obsession to visit the house of Trotsky, where this vast brain had fed and grumbled and snored.

Mexico City is extremely large. Exhausted by the altitude and suffocated by the pollution, I found my resolve to work my way through it weakening day by day. Anyway it was Holy Week. The newspapers were full of the impending holiday carnage. '*Already—1,350 accidents, 152 dead!*' In a country where children are given little chocolate skeletons as a *memento mori*, the bank holidays have a special entertainment value. Roused eventually by the carnival atmosphere, I decided to pierce the descending cloud of smog and seek *la casa Trotsky*. I asked a travel agent how to get there but it was not on his itinerary. He thought that it was in the suburb of Coyoacán, 'Coyote'. He assured me that any taxi-driver would know it. This was not true of mine. For over an hour we asked our way around that suburb. It was frequently stated that the Trotskys still lived there and I began to believe this. Eventually we found it.

The house is just as it should be. It has a watch tower and steel doors, and there are gun slits in the watch tower and bullet scars on the doors. When He lived there, the house stood alone. Now it is surrounded by pleasant villas with gardens and garages and in the streets clean cars are being washed yet again. Coyoacán is a fashionable suburb. The district around the house has been gentrified, like the ideas of its former occupant.

I knocked on the gate. No answer. My taxi-driver, by now completely committed to my quest, knocked much louder. A steel peep-hole slid open in the steel door and an eye looked out. It filled the vacant space. It was a brown eye. I thought what a wonderful target it would make. It looked so vulnerable, one soft brown eye piercing this expanse of grey steel. A voice rendered sinister by the unblinking eye said '*Cerrado*'; closed, now *and for Holy Week*. The peep-hole snapped shut. We drove back to the city, through the stinging yellow murk. I paid the driver a very large sum. The quest for Trotsky was not cheap.

That evening I met Sonia de la Rozière. As a teenager she used to blow up trains for the French Resistance. Since the war she has lived in Mexico and has written a book called *Mexico and the Agony of Christ*. She advised me to avoid the more notorious Passion centres during Holy Week; instead I went to the little town of Amecameca where, she assured me, the most fervent religious devotion could be observed unaccompanied by tourists. I hired a car and drove there on Good Friday.

The road to Amecameca was extremely slow. It was formerly the main road to Veracruz and once the route chosen by Cortes for his invasion. But it has been superseded by a motorway and there should have been very little traffic on this road. When the turning to Amecameca appeared, the whole traffic jam took it—one slow-moving line of cars, all Mexican, all packed with families and all heading for this little town. I was impressed with Mexican devotion. For so many cars to leave the city and come here on pilgrimage on a day which the rest of the Christian world treated as a mere holiday seemed rather remarkable. At the entrance to the town the traffic jammed solid. There was a dirt track leading off to the right, and by following it I was able to work past the deserted shanties on the outskirts and so round to the central square. Here I discovered that the queue of family cars was passing out of town again on the other side. Mexico City was not going on pilgrimage to Amecameca after all; it was merely passing through Amecameca and on to a recreational area beyond it. The entire delay was caused by the distracted efforts of a single policeman to allow pedestrians to cross the road; something they were quite capable of doing without his assistance.

Good Friday was market day in Amecameca; the stalls, huddled together in the plaza in front of the church, were selling everything from cooked food to full suits of conquistadors' armour scaled down for children. In the church a service was in progress. So many people were trying to get into it that they were queueing right out into the market. The crowd, to the last worshipper, consisted not of car-drivers from the city but of Indians, the people of the countryside around who had come to town to trade and pray.

It was midday. To the side of the church, around the walls of a small cloister with romanesque arches and octagonal pillars, the Indians rested in the shade. They lay on the stone flags and slept, their heads pillowed on the sandals they had removed from their feet. Inside the church a terrible black figure had been raised on a high cross. He was supported by the two thieves. Unlike the Christ, the two thieves appeared to be gringos. I wondered if the Indian carver had derived some secular pleasure from crucifying these two white men. The Indians have a knack of turning a wonderful tale from a distant country to bear an unintended and very local meaning. On the high altar the voice of the priest giving out the stations of the cross boomed on. He was a gringo too.

The Indians of Amecameca bury their dead on a hill outside the town called Sacromonte. The dead Christ is called 'the Lord of Sacromonte'. On Good Friday, before the evening procession, the pilgrims carry their picnics up to the top of the hill and spread the food out on the gravestone of a relative and tuck in. Some of the graves are shaded by the branches of trees, or by large awnings that catch the wind blowing across the lip of the ridge. All the way up the hill the stations of the cross are picked out in coloured tiles. It is a very dusty track in the dry season and on Good Friday it was very hot.

The children wandering up with their parents were garlanded with white flowers; spiky white daisies. Bound loosely round the head they looked more like stars than thorns. Some of the men also wore these garlands; they resembled ancient pagans on their way to a Bacchic celebration. Good Friday is a black day in the Christian calendar. It is the one day of the year when Mass cannot be said; altars and images everywhere are decked in purple. But not so in Amecameca. The Indians of Mexico are well aware of the horror of death, but it is precisely that horror which they wish to celebrate: it seems to lift their spirits. On the track up the hill the children with their flowery 'crowns of thorns' were able to buy paper windmills or candy floss or holy pictures. These holy pictures were not the usual reproductions of the art of Raphael or Botticelli. Here the pictures were printed in such a way that the eyes moved. You could get the Pope or the Virgin with eyes that followed you as you passed, and there were close-ups of the Crucified Christ, eyes closed in death, then eyes and mouth open in agonized greeting. If the children got tired of that, they could try on pink plastic fangs which fitted over their own teeth to horrible effect.

On the hilltop I found an empty tomb and lunched on it. It contained Francisco Ortega who died in 1841. For some reason his descendants had not turned up that year.

The afternoon wore on and still the penitential procession did not form. The Mexican church authorities have had some success recently in controlling the enthusiasm associated with Holy Week. Live crucifixions have been restricted to once every seven years, but flagellants are still quite frequent. One Mexican newspaper carried a report from the Philippines stating that in a suburb of Manila nine devotees had been nailed to crosses by four-inch stainless steel nails soaked in alcohol. It was a detailed report. One of those nailed up was a woman. Another was the illegitimate son of a wartime GI who was trying to attract his father's attention. Needless to say, the GI's boy was a carpenter. Now aged thirty-six, he had hung there for less than a minute and had screamed when the nail was pulled out of his left palm. Blood had flowed from his left palm but not from his right. There seemed to be something wistful in the minute observation of the Mexican news-report: those were the days.

After a while I grew tired of the confusion and disturbance of the town. There were several bars open; one offered a *cocktail femenino* which I was curious to know more about. Instead, I decided to remain sober and drove out of town and up to the *Paso de Cortes,* the high pass by which the *conquistadores* had broken through the Aztec defences. These are the foothills of the Sierra Madre Oriental and on a clear day the view from Amecameca is dominated by the two volcanoes, Popocatepetl and Ixtaccihuatl. This was not a clear day. The heat haze pressed down beneath a layer of high cloud which hid the mountain peaks. The road started to climb through thick woodland. Indian women stood in some of the clearings, tending fires. They held out the tortillas they had been cooking, hoping for a sale. Their horses were tethered nearby; presumably they were on the last stage of their journey to the fair. They would be in town by nightfall, in time for the procession.

As I emerged from the woods, the clouds, which had hidden Popocatepetl for several weeks, suddenly lifted and the peak stood distinct in the cold blue air. The peak was covered in snow and from the tip of this arose a thin plume of smoke. Below the ring of snow the volcanic slopes were rumpled into pleats of soft brown and grey. Not a tree or a blade of grass could be seen on those slopes.

The Aztecs believed that Popocatepetl was a former king and that Ixtaccihuatl, 'the Sleeping Woman', was his faithful wife who accompanied him in death. I wondered what Cortes would have thought of all this beauty as he was guided between the volcanoes and knew that the guardian saints of the Aztecs were nothing more than volcanoes. It was as deserted now on the brown windy plateau as it was on the day he passed. Cortes is not honoured in Mexico—there are only two statues to him in the entire country—but on the Paso de Cortes a small bas-relief has been set into a stone. This shows him advancing, mounted on an armoured horse, a crowd of men around him and the Indian interpreter, Princess Marina, who bore his son, showing him the way. Without Marina, the Spanish could never have left the coast. They numbered only five hundred, but their arrival had been prophesied in the Aztec religion, of which, with Marina's help, they were able to take advantage and save themselves from Montezuma's sacrificial altars.

In truth Cortes needs no monuments in Mexico; the whole country is the result of his reckless adventure. Every church in Mexico is his monument, just as much as the mediaeval suits of armour which were being sold to the children in the town below the pass. A chill wind from the volcano started to blow and I returned to the warmth of the forest and the mist.

O utside the church as dusk fell, festivities took on a new life. The fair was now lit by neon signs and flares. Where there would once have been a band of trumpeters there was a loudspeaker blaring out pop music. A snake pit had been set up on the churchyard steps. The snakes were in an open-topped trough. One could not see into the trough until one had paid for a ticket and then climbed a wobbly ladder on to an equally wobbly platform. Most of the snakes were fast asleep, being deaf they would not have heard the pop music anyway. The Indian children, on seeing the snakes, jumped up and down in excitement. This was not a country with very high standards of public safety. It was easy to foresee the chaos in the crowd when the platform collapsed, the trough tipped over and the snakes made their bid for freedom.

The last light of Good Friday picked out the chequerboard façade of the church, white and ochre. One could still see the places where the ochre had run and stained strips of the white. On the churchyard wall a notice banned all commerce in the churchyard, by order of the Federal District. But by now of course the fair had spread inside the walls and right up to the church. So often in Mexico the simplest way to discover where a particular event will take place is to find the notice forbidding it.

In the darkness, people started to leave the fair and crowd back into the church. The cloister was now packed. For the poorest pilgrims it would provide a roof for the night. Some of them had spread matting on the flagstone floor; others, still poorer, had spread cardboard. On this they lay, wrapped in their blankets, whole families together, mothers feeding babies, slightly older children nursing younger ones. The evening service was amplified so that it could be heard in the cloister and many of the Indians were sitting up on their improvised beds saying the responses to the litany. They made a considerable noise but the sleepers, like the snakes in the trough, dozed on.

Inside the church the altar was hidden by a roll of Lenten purple suspended from the ceiling, giving the raised sanctuary the appearance of a stage. The performance now proceeded as, once more, the Black Christ was taken down from the cross and carried around like an outsize doll. The lights flickering in the cloister, the lulling responses of the rosary, the quiet laughter among the sleepers, the occasional shouts from children playing in the darkness outside, the women oblivious to all this, holding their babies and murmuring their prayers—somehow it all drew to mind the fantastic comparison with a house in Somerset thirty years earlier. The cloister, the rosary, the shouts of ten-year-old children, the devotion and inattention mixed, the carved stone pillars and the flagstone floor: I sat by the base of a pillar and tried to remember exactly what it was about Lent in an English boarding school that should have sprung to life again.

An Indian girl, aged about seven, in a red gingham dress and a red shawl with a pigtail hanging down her straight back sat down beside me, cradling a sleeping baby half her size. The baby was invisible within the shawl except for one white shoe and sock sticking out. The girl, her back still straight, still holding her burden, fell asleep, head slightly to one side to ease the weight she supported.

Opposite us a young couple spread out their mats. They had two children of their own and were accompanied by the mother of the sleeping girl and baby. On top of their mat they spread a quilt to add to their comfort. Sometimes the woman sat at her husband's side, leaning her back against his knees and holding his hand. Sometimes she lay down beside her children and tried to sleep. Sometimes, catching the words of a litany, she joined in. Noticing that her niece, the seven-year-old beside me, was asleep, she called her across and put the baby down on the already crowded quilt. There was no room for the girl who spread some sacking of her own. It was far too small for her to stretch out on, so she curled up to fit it and was immediately asleep again. Soon afterwards her mother returned from the church and woke her. The girl sat up and smiled again, but looked tired enough to cry.

'*Perdona tu pueblo, Señor,*' said the distant voice of the priest.

'Pardon us, Lord,' the Lord's people replied.

And in his sermon the priest introduced the familiar reflection about Mary's reaction to the death of her son. 'What can she have thought? How can we imagine her suffering?'

In the cloister another woman wrapped herself in a striped blanket. Her husband crossed himself, then lay down on his back in the space beside her. He closed his eyes. She, supported on one elbow, glanced down at him and stroked his face. They noticed no one around them. It was as though they were at home in bed. It was how they slept every night. In the centre of the cloister there was a flower garden; above it, the stars stood bright in a moonless sky.

It was by now quite dark and the high point of the day's devotion had been reached. Slowly a procession began to form up behind the

Cristo, once more recumbent in its crystal bier. The litany had stopped and the priest was nowhere to be seen.

They carried the life-size wooden figure lying in the glass case out of the main doors of the church and into the churchyard. Everyone in the congregation joined the procession. Sixteen men staggered beneath the weight of the bier. One of them was the young husband who had been sitting opposite me in the cloister. He had fought his way at the last moment to the altar rails to secure this honour. Immediately behind the Cristo other men, who had been pushed aside in the struggle, pressed forward, eager for signs of failing strength among those who had succeeded. Behind them, sixteen women staggered in the same way under another litter supporting the rocking but upright statue of Christ's mother. Behind them trailed the rest of the penitents. The procession was lit by a few candles. Beyond the churchyard wall there was all the noise and brilliance of the fair. Against this explosive background the dark figures of the worshippers seemed all the more intent on their unlit purpose. What they were doing had to be done in the dark space between funfair and church. There was a terrible determination in the scattered chorus of voices that sustained a mournful hymn against the thunder of commerce. Real grief was evident. It was as though a real mother was following the dead body of her real son. If the sixteen men had been carrying one of their own family, they could not have mourned him with more passion. This was what the Indians understood by belief. They did not in fact believe in Christ. They went further. They *invented* him. From the shadows at their feet occasional voices still called out; there were still a few traders rattling rattles, offering food, crying their wares to those who processed by. And yet there was no feeling of irreverence. The Indian imagination could as easily manage the discord of commerce and religion as it could bridge the space between grief for the dead of today and grief for the dead God.

An onlooker could be moved by the feelings of this wild congregation, but he could not share them. Mysteriously these Indians, while observing a Christian rite, managed to exclude the Christians who were foreign to their world. They had taken the characters of Christ and Mary out of the Gospel story and recast them in an entirely Indian tragedy. To an outsider the words of the drama seemed familiar, the figures in the cast were authentic.

Nothing had been omitted; but all kinds of meaning, inaccessible to the stranger, had been added. The grief of this *pueblo del Señor* was far too genuine and far too private. Cristo had been kidnapped, overwhelmed, diminished.

The procession ended, the penitents disappeared silently into the night. The bier was laid down again beside the high altar. Those still awake queued up to touch it. They held their children up, as they had done by the snake pit, to gaze down at the sight within. Then they crossed the children with their hands. Their lips, in supplication, moved constantly. Like a corpse at a funeral, the Lord of Sacromonte was surrounded by flowers; lilies, roses and thistles. What the children saw as they looked down was a twisted body; black, matted hair thinly spread; the face blackened and dead, blank, rejecting, caved in. It was more the corpse of a man dug up than one due to rise on the Third Day. There was nothing supernatural about the figure who had died again in this town on this day. He seemed as powerless as Popocatepetl and the Sleeping Woman who had been powerless to stop Cortes.

After Holy Week I returned to the house of Trotsky and knocked again. This time when the peep-hole opened it was for a blue eye. I asked if I could come in. The blue eye remained silent but the steel gate creaked open to reveal a slight figure wearing a powder blue jump suit. She had curly brown hair and rosy cheeks.

'Do you speak English?'

She replied in a clear Scottish accent that she ought to. She had only been living in Casa Trotsky for some months. Behind her I could see a lawn on which two small blonde children were busy at play. The house of Trotsky seemed to be occupied by an *au pair* girl from Ayrshire. On the wall of this once pleasant villa a great cluster of climbing roses hides a small steel door. You enter the house by this door, and by stepping over a steel plate which has been cemented into the wall. It is like entering a submarine. You can only move through the house by passing through a succession of steel doors, steel steps and steel shutters. Most of this was installed by the Mexican government in May 1940, after the failure of an attempt on Trotsky's life mounted by the Mexican surrealist painter, David Alfaro

Siqueiros. Siqueiros and his men had attacked with heavy machine guns but only managed to kill a gringo—'Trotskyist'—in fact a secret member of their plot. The bedroom wall is heavily scarred by their machine gun shells. In the whole house the only unprotected entry I could find was the bathroom window. I wondered if, as he lay there in his suds, Trotsky fantasized about the sudden arrival through the window of some Stalinist Charlotte Corday. All these precautions availed for only three months. Ramón Mercader, the trusted disciple, carried his ice pick through those steel gates in August of the same year.

The interior of the house is today covered in dust and plastic sheeting, preserved as exactly as possible in the state it was on that day. The deed was done not in Trotsky's bath but in his study as he bent over his desk. On that desk today are *The Statesman's Year Book for 1939* and several of Gollancz's Left Book Club series. One is called *If Germany Attacks* by Capt. Wynne. Beside it is *Trade Unionism Today*, by G.D.H. Cole. This is melancholy. Could it be that just before the Brain died it was pondering some footnote in G.D.H. Cole, the Englishman, the old Pauline, the detective-story writer, *the Fabian*?

It is appropriate that the interior of the house is so carefully preserved, for this too is a major shrine. Time has nothing to add to the truth as it was discerned within these walls. The steel doors, like the doors of a tabernacle, protect the mystical body of correct conclusions.

Throughout my tour I had the feeling of being watched very closely by my guide, the *au pair* girl. It was almost as though she were trying to read my thoughts. You could not help remembering that a man was once admitted to this room who had been trusted with a hideously misplaced trust; and under the eyes of this guide, you could not help feeling slightly in the same position yourself. The house was as much a period piece as any Spanish colonial church, and its guardians were as devout as any Indian congregation. The red and yellow roses pouring over the steel door symbolized what happens to an idea whose time has passed, though once it was bullet-proof, strong enough to move the world.

On my way out the Scottish girl showed me the stone column in the garden which stands beneath a tall tree and marks the place where

His ashes are interred—last resting place of the Brain. The column is engraved with the hammer and sickle, the emblem of the state whose agent murdered him.

Before I left Mexico City I returned to the house once again; I could hardly keep away from the place. This time the gates were opened by the presumed owner of the original brown eye, the curator in person. He was a youngish Frenchman wearing a white beret and a lugubrious expression that was somehow professional, as though he were employed as an ideological mute. He would explain some detail of the furnishings and then look at me in unspecified sorrow, some aspect of the familiar story having awakened his original grief. Once again I had a sense of a shrine in a parallel church. Unconsciously and in vain I searched for an alms box at the exit. Perhaps in the future an Indian Trotskyist will succeed the Frenchman, the missionary will be replaced by a native priest. You can see how the legend of the Great Brain might appeal to the Indian mind. So Trotsky may be absorbed into an Indian version of the past, and sit with Cristo, beside Popocatepetl, one day.

The monthly magazine for the Radio Three listener

'3' Magazine goes to studio and concert hall, theatre and opera-house to bring you the stories behind the music, plays and documentaries on Radio Three.

The highlights of all programmes for a month ahead are selected for preview and in-depth articles deal with major events: new works—new ideas—new performers—together with the latest records.

Place a regular order with your newsagent or register an annual, postal subscription by completing the form below and sending to Room 2816, King's Reach Tower, Stamford Street, London SE1 9LS.

JAN MORRIS
INTERSTATE 281

It was like entering another, and more nationalistic, country—like entering France, say, out of Switzerland. The moment I crossed the Red River out of Oklahoma, the nationality of Texas assaulted me almost xenophobically, and I seemed to be passing into another sensibility, another historical experience, another scale of values, perhaps. I was about to drive all the way down US 281, one of the several highways which run clean across Texas north to south: not because it is the fastest of them or the most important, or even I dare say the most scenic, but because it is one of the oldest of all the tracks by which the original Texans, long ago, drove their cattle northward to Kansas City and the rich markets of the north. Nobody seems quite sure which was actually the Chisholm Trail, the most famous of these routes: but we can be quite certain that along the line of 281 generations of herdsmen came and went, and that up and down it, too, so to speak, passed many of those impulses, influences and instincts which brought Texas to its own manifest destiny, and united it with the greater republic to the north.

It is rather more than six hundred miles down 281, from Red River in the north to Rio Grande in the south, across pleasant flatland counties with names like Jack or Archer, through the wooded hill country of the centre, across the wider rolling ranchlands south of San Antonio into the tropic territories of the Rio Grande valley, where the palm trees stand in lordly enfilade, where the fruit and vegetables grow like lush weeds, and there seems to hang upon the very air some potent radiation of the south.

Yet hardly was I over that bridge when all the conventional shapes and symptoms of Texas rose up around me: massed bluebonnets on the verges, smells of sage and barbecue, Stetson-hatted heads silhouetted through the rear windows of pick-ups, horses corralled in village yards, cattle roaming like wild beasts over evidently limitless ranges, the indefatigable shapes of Texan oil-pumps, the uncontrollable shapes of Texan countrymen, the shape of Texas itself, that assymetrical lump of tenderloin on maps and guides, on road signs and posters, on T-shirts and dishcloths and key-rings in souvenir shops and windows. The weather of Texas variously lifted my heart and squashed my spirits. From earth and air, creek and camper, I was hounded by the curse of Texas—country and western music.

So I began my journey, assaulted by Texanity, and the great sky of Texas seemed to close like a door behind me, as though I were in some separate cosmos now, spinning to another rhythm, tugged by different laws of gravity.

'Good grief!' cried the girl in the bank at Wichita Falls, 'Wales! Do you hear that, Mary-Lou?' But without a second thought she pressed a computer button for instant confirmation that my bank account in Llanystumdwy was in credit, and handed me my money.

The insularity of Texas has always entertained travellers, coupled as it is with extreme technical sophistication, and Texans of course love to make the most of it, flying their flag as if it were still their own republican emblem, using their dialect like another language. The scale of everything certainly contributes to the illusion: often Texas felt to me not even like a country, but like a continent of its own, and 281 suggested to me the sort of strategic thoroughfare that European wars were fought for, and frontiers adjusted to accommodate.

Yet Texas is not in the least separate really: even the Texanest of Texan families must have come here from somewhere else not so very long ago, and hardly a nation of Europe has not contributed to the style that advertises itself to the world nowadays as Texan to the core. As the writer Philip Bailey once said of America as a whole, in Texas there is 'something good and bad of every land', and all along Route 281, down the decades, immigrants from many parts have set up shop, dug down roots, turned themselves into something of Texas and Texas into a little of themselves.

Sometimes the foreign allusions are newer—there are no better pizzas in America, I swear it, than the pizzas of the minuscule Italian café recently established by an immigrant chef in Jacksboro—and sometimes they are more direct. The first I saw of Windthorst was the proud tower of its church on a hillock above the interminable plain—a mediaeval silhouette it seemed, bold against the blazing sun that day, dominating the prosperous farmland of Archer County all around. Windthorst is German through and through, settled by German Catholics in 1891, and is a place of intense corporate personality. The great Benedictine church, which was the focus of the original settlement, is the core of it still, with its school, its convent, and a great grotto of the Virgin Mary, 'Our Lady of Highway 281', which was built by the contributions of all those young men of Windthorst who fought in the Second World War.

Their names are recorded in the church, stout old German names almost without exception, and you can meet them, their sons and their grandsons, any day at Ed's Café along the road. Magnificent big men they are, with capable-looking wives and stalwart children—all related to each other, it seems, all more than ready for a plate of hash, all talking about swabbers and tornado warnings, all such devoted churchgoers to this day, they told me at Ed's, that every Sunday they have three Masses up at the church (where there is a sound-proof cry room, by the way, in which the mothers of the more difficult little Hoffs and Schreibers can listen to the sermon, over the audio system, without disturbing the more hard-of-hearing Ostermanns, Wolfs or Schroeders.

The town of George West is named for a Mr West. The present Mayor of Hamilton is a Mr Hamilton. Pleasanton is the Birthplace of the Cowboy, Lampasas the Heart of the Cow Country, Blanco the Gem of the Hills, and beside the court-house at Stephenville a large figure of a cow is labelled, MOO-LA! 42 MILLION GALLONS ANNUALLY!

Ah, the little towns of Texas, as one by one I passed through them on the long road south—the stately pride of their court-houses, classical or castellated, Georgian or Frenchified, stone, red brick or, in the case of Burnet, raw concrete decorated with bas-reliefs of pioneering scenes in the Assyrian mode! They greeted me in a regular, almost mathematical succession—some twenty miles between one and the next, as a rule, representing a day's journey in the old horse days. I thought them rather like a Texas index, for each had its own particular origins, or its own especial purpose: one an old military base, supervising the wild Indian country to the west, another a market town or a health resort—this one settled by Germans or Norwegians, the next full of Campbells or McTavities—a college here, to generate energy for the place, a refinery or a railroad somewhere else.

And in the course of Texas's headlong rush through history, they have also had their individual ups and downs. Some have been transfigured by strokes of good fortune, like the birth of Lyndon Johnson at Johnson City, or the presence of uranium at Alice (which is the home of the Yawn Motor Company, as it happens, but is very much awake). Some look wistfully back to lost glories: the ex-spa of Mineral Wells, for example, which is dominated still by the enormous but long-vacant Baker Hotel—'Oh', as a wistful resident sighed to me, 'the parties we used to have up there, the people who came, Tom Mix and Jean Harlow and I don't know who else!' Some have vanished, like Bridgetown, where nothing is left of a rumbustious past but a few faithful oil-pumps, still bowing incessantly down the generations, and some archaeological kinds of bumps in the ground. And some just seem to meander fatalistically on, like the one best left nameless, under whose chamber of commerce door, all locked up at 2.30 in the afternoon, I slipped a note to say that, alas, I had called for advice about how best to invest $10m in the town, but could not wait....

At Stephenville, I went to watch the kids playing baseball one evening, and found myself wallowing no less, in the fabled charm of Home Town. It was like a stage show for me, illuminated as it was by the lights of the diamonds, and orchestrated by you-know-what from the radios of cars parked all around. It was as though everyone were acting a part. Small boys burbled authentically here and there, slurping from cans and kicking footballs. Girls shrieked support to boyfriend pitchers, gossiped sibilantly in corners or carried errant baby-sitters back to mom. Young matrons sat in twos or threes talking about clothes and coffee mornings. And beyond the mesh, in that somewhat ghostly light, the young sportsmen played their allotted roles to perfection—the fat freckled one, the tall skinny one, the lovable one who tried so hard, the All-American who never failed—all like figures of a provincial allegory, performing to the smell of popcorn from the snack-bar cabin, and the scooting here and there, like insects in and out of the headlights, of exuberant youths on bicycles.

At Three Rivers, I think it was, stopping for a hamburger, I found that I had locked my car keys in the trunk. Small town Texas swung instantly to my rescue—well, eased itself slowly out of its chairs, tipped its Stetsons over its eyes, strolled into the car-park and stood meditatively eyeing the problem, saying things like 'Huh', or 'Kindofa problem there.' In easy stages they approached the task, sniffing it, feeling it, and when in the end they got the hang of it, enlarged the right aperture, unscrewed the right screws, and found that the keys were not in there at all, since I had left them on the Dairy Queen counter, they seemed not in the least disconcerted, but deftly re-assembling the mechanism, tilting their Stetsons back again, they drifted once more into the café murmuring, 'You bet, lady, any time.'

But the town I liked best of all was Hico. 'Why then, you should move right in yourself,' suggested the town barber, whom I chanced to meet walking home to his lunch between short-backs-and-sides, and I wouldn't mind. You could do a lot worse than Hico. It does not, perhaps, look anything very special—just the classic American huddle of houses around an intersection, where State Highways 6 and 220 join US 281: built of brick mainly, I think, with overlays of clapboard, and the usual suggestion of wasteland at one edge where the railroad used to run, and a hint of suburbia in the comfortable gardened houses away from the highway, towards one of which, as it happens, the barber was making his way that day. But there are green trees speckling the town all over, and cheerful weathered faces in the streets, and an air of family comradeship laced with a proper ration of gossip.

Yes, you could do a lot worse than Hico. In Hico (pronounced *Hy-co,* they told me, if you're sober; *Hicko* if you're drunk), you can have your car washed by Junior High School pupils next Saturday in the park. In Hico, you can get your hair done at Chat-'n-Curl prior to the Friday Nite Special Catfish Buffet. In Hico, the Hico Meat Company will Process your Deer for you, the motel is OWNED BY TEXANS, and at the drug store you are welcome to pick up a complimentary copy of the Ladies' Almanac. In Hico, Firemen Only Are Allowed On Fire Trucks.

I am half a Hican already. See that figure down there by the Bosque River, way down by the willows, this side the bridge, chewing hickory-smoked jerky and reading the social intelligence in the *Hico News Review*? Yeah, that's me.

'What do I do?' said a man in the Koffee Kup Kafe, 'I don't do
nothin'. What does he do? He don't do nothin' either. We're
all retarded here.'

I was going for a walk along the river at Lampasas one evening
when three motor-cyclists approached me very slowly in line
ahead. They were all tremendously old, and absolutely identical.
They wore jaunty baseball caps, but beneath the peaks their faces
were hide-like, like the faces of tortoises: and as they passed me, one
by one those visages momentarily split, with a 'Hi', or a 'Hi there',
before sealing themselves once more into leatheriness.

They were like visitors from another world, or from some
Unidentified Retirement Object, and there were times as I travelled
through Texas when I thought that the aged were about to take over
the state. It is true that in most parts of the western world the old are
coming into their inheritance, assisted by greater affluence, greater
leisure and the vagaries of the birth-rate, but I never observed the
phenomenon more vividly than I did along 281. Whole towns seemed
to be seized already. Whole counties were occupied by squadrons of
Kamping Koaches, encampments of Mobile Homes, and cult-like
images of geriatry haunted me everywhere. Through the big windows
of the CIA Retirement Club at Wichita Falls I saw them, I saw them,
conspiring there in their eye-shades over the card tables. At the Crazy
Woman Hotel at Mineral Falls I found them already in possession,
for it had been turned into a retirement home, and a notice above the
reception desk ominously warned me:

If you must spit be sure to spit
Some place else than where I sit.

Almost anywhere along Highway 281, if you go down to the town
camper park in the evening, you will find the old folk plotting their
next move, crouched beneath the awnings of their recreational
vehicles beneath dim lights over paper cups of stimulant, like tank
commanders in the field....

Actually in the rural reaches of north and central Texas the senior
citizens are mostly survivors. They are representatives of a less
aggressive army—the rural rearguard, still entrenched in the
countryside they were born to, as all around them youth, hope and

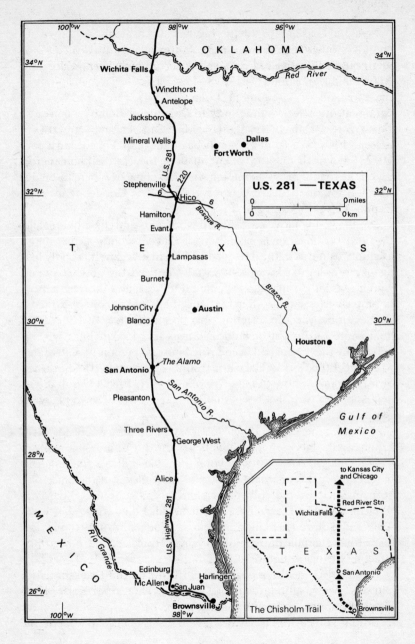

OKLAHOMA

34°N   34°N

Red River

Wichita Falls

Windthorst

Antelope

Jacksboro

Mineral Wells

Dallas

Fort Worth

U.S. 281

220

Stephenville

32°N   32°N

6   Hico   6

Bosque R.

U.S. 281 — TEXAS	
0 ⊢⊣ 0 miles	
0 ⊢⊣ 0 km	

Hamilton

Evant

T   E   X   A   S

Lampasas

Burnet

Brazos R.

Johnson City

Austin

Blanco

30°N   30°N

Houston

The Alamo

San Antonio

San Antonio R.

Pleasanton

Gulf of
Mexico

Three Rivers

George West

28°N

Alice

M   E   X   I   C   O

Rio Grande

U.S. Highway 281

Edinburg

Harlingen

McAllen   San Juan

26°N

100°W

Brownsville

98°W

to Kansas City
and Chicago

Red River Stn

Wichita Falls

T   E   X   A   S

San Antonio

The Chisholm Trail

Brownsville

199

opportunity hastens by to the big cities. All along 281, as along countless other highways in every continent, one feels the pull of metropolitan life, like some massive unseen magnet over the horizon. In England I sometimes feel the whole island is tilted imperceptibly in the direction of London; in India, a whole race, a whole sub-continent often seems on its way to Calcutta or Bombay; in Texas, Fort Worth, Dallas, Austin, Houston, San Antonio, are always present, however remote they may be on the map. For the most part US 281 avoids the big towns, but all along the way their names crop up on the road signs like come-on signals—come over here to Big D, next left for the lights of Cowtown, Taste The Good Life in Your Capital City!

So the young move on, where the action is and the jobs are, and the survivors linger on in a countryside that sometimes seems almost as empty as it was in the days when Texas first began. It is oddly like history running backwards. I actually noticed the absence of the young—visually, I mean, as one might notice a lack of street-lamps, or motor-cycles. All too often the dance-halls and saloons of 281 have long been boarded-up, offering only spectral shades of yesterday's honky-tonk. 'Run out of kiddos!' I was told in Antelope, when I asked why the school had been turned into a community centre, and when Mrs Effie Cork of Hamilton County demonstrated to me on her own front porch how to make a poke bonnet, I felt I was in direct living contact with the Texas that was there before the young were born.

On the other hand, down in the warm south, where the land softens and palms itself into the valley of the Rio Grande, age really is on the march. Down there young people still abound, in the prosperous market-garden country of the valley, but the place has been invaded by old folk from elsewhere. Go South, Old Man! 'Welcome Winter Texans', says a sign outside Edinburg, 'Valley Folk Are Glad You're Here', and it seems a prudent attitude to me: for there, mile after mile the Adult Retirement Homes extend, powerfully affecting the whole nature of the country, swarmed in and out of by vigorous elderly denizens on their daily forays to garage sales and flea markets. 'We're all retarded here,' said the man in the Koffee Kup Kafe, but he said it grimly, tongue-in-cheek.

And if you have a taste for the symbolisms of age, how about the retired couple I found mowing the grass at Lynn Creek cemetery near Jacksboro? This lonely little garden, having long outlived the communities it once served, is a *memento mori* in every way: elegiac winds blow through its cedars and live oaks, memorial irises blossom wild among its tombs, and Texan clans lie in their generations all around. My senior citizens were mowing it for the first time, having just undertaken the contract, and were finding it heavy going. As the husband said, 'It takes a million turns in and out of the gravestones—I only hope I don't fall right in one of the graves myself!' I laughed rather hollowly at the quip, as the breeze stirred the leaves above my head, but later took the opportunity, when they kindly allowed it, of mowing a few square feet of grass myself. It is not everyone who has mown a Texan graveyard: besides, if you can't beat them....

Half-way through my journey, rather more than three hundred miles south of Red River, I passed tangentially through the delectable hill and lake country west of Austin, where the rich scudded around in motor boats visiting each other in luxurious lake-side condominiums, and the village stores had turned themselves into delicatessens and were selling Earl Grey tea and Rumanian canned rhubarb. But hardly had I emerged from that happy Shangri-La when I entered another sort of hallucination, for I arrived at San Antonio in the middle of its annual fiesta. Generally speaking, I am told, San Antonio is a reasonably down-to-earth working town, the third largest in Texas and some say the nicest: but the night I arrived was the night of the great water-parade along the San Antonio river, meandering through its artificial canyon among the downtown buildings: and so, falling into the hands of hospitable San Antonians, I was ushered into a dream.

What phantasmagoric gulley was that stream beneath our windows, lined along its curling course with what inconceivable multitudes? What shapes were those on the water passing by, those drifting baubles of light and colour, those gesticulating figures weirdly dressed? Whose flags were these, thick across every street, and what manner of people, these sombre men with Mickey Mouse balloons? From what exotic divisions did these generals come, with their massed medals of unrecognizable campaigns, their drooping epaulettes and their theatrically-gilded caps?

The talk in that town seemed a kind of gibberish to me, of Ugly Kings and Fabergé Courts, of Cavaliers and Coronations, of curtseying instructions and sixty thousand dresses. The whole city seemed seized in an arcane ecstasy all its own, jumping up and down with the excitement of it, discussing nothing else. We dined at a club which, with its great white portico among the palm trees, seemed to have been transported there from Calcutta, and as we walked across the lawn at the end of the day we saw a great grey armadillo, itself like some beast of the imagination, scuttling through the half-light into the shrubbery.

> *'My statement,' an artist told me in Stephenville, 'is that we're all goin' to die out one day'—and he pointed to a forlorn sort of bird-object, made of feathers, wire and pampas grass, hanging from the ceiling and entitled, if I heard him right, 'The Last Mating.' 'That's my statement.'*

The last Texan mating seemed a long way off to me, but still it is true that Texas and war, if not Texas and Armageddon, rather go together. Everywhere down 281, itself designated the American Legion Memorial Highway, I heard the rumours of old conflicts, because for years this old cattle trail passed dangerously close to the Indian country of the west. It was, I suppose, a Hell Fire Alley of long ago, and from its forts and encampments the military made their reconnaissances and forays into the territories of the Apaches, the Comanches or the Wichitas. It looks like fighting country still, with its hidden gullies for ambushes, its crests for warriors to silhouette themselves upon: and even now, if you put your mind to it, and look away to the west over these silent prairies, you may imagine the smoke of the tribes rising on those horizons.

The mementoes of the Indian wars are vivid still in these parts. Here was a massacre, here an abduction, here for the first time an Indian was tried in a white man's court, and here at Burnet soldiers and Comanches fought a bloody battle in the eerie pitch-black of a cave. Once I noticed an old dirt track running east to west across my route, and thought it had a somehow epic look: I was right, for it turned out to be the Marcy Trail, by which the Texas Rangers travelled to their outposts on the remotest frontier of the day—a strategic highway straight as a die still, still heroically rutted, from limit to limit of my vision.

Nor were they only Indian enemies that the folk-memory of 281 recalled for me. Think of it—as recently as 1915 infantry was on guard to protect the King Ranch against Mexican raiders! And when at Windthorst I spoke thoughtlessly of 'the last war,' meaning as Europeans do the Second World War, they looked at me a little sadly: ninety-one of their young men, out of a total population of four hundred and nine, fought in Korea and Viet Nam. No wonder Texas has a military air. Half the towns down my road seem to have their military bases. Fighters zip now and then across your line of sight; soldiers in fatigues tumble out of trucks into Jack-in-a-Box cafés; Fort Hood, the city of Lampasas proudly tells you, is 'the biggest military base in the Free World'.

The central shrine of my journey, as of Texas itself, was the Alamo. I happened to get there on the day of its annual pilgrimage, and the military virtues were certainly paramount then. White-scarved soldiers of the Old Guard stood statuesque behind the dais, colonels in dark glasses were everywhere, American Legionaires were in attendance, bands played, ribbons blazed, a general assured us (ambiguously, I thought, since all its heroes died) that the story of the Alamo showed us what it meant to be an American, and most formidably of all, the Daughters of the Texas Republic themselves, shock troops with a vengeance, were in parade in full front-line regalia of pearls and Neiman-Marcus hats.

For me, it all came more disturbingly to a head, though, at Harling in the south: for there on a former air-base two of the most relentlessly military institutions in America live cheek-by-jowl in machismo, presided over gigantically by the original plaster-cast of the Iwo Jima Memorial. To one of pacifist leanings this is a daunting place. You come first to the Marine Military Academy, described variously as 'the toughest prep school in the world' and 'a vanguard against terrorism', whose boys are educated to the sternest precepts of the US Marine Corps and whose teachers are former Marines themselves. Slogans of Free Enterprise, Traditional Morality, Discipline and Respect resound through this forbidding campus; the pupils live in barrack blocks and are kept up to the mark by retired Marine Corps drill instructors. Ronald Reagan, after a visit once, told some satisfied parents (Mr and Mrs Gene Snuggs, actually, of Snuggs Diversified Investments) that it gave him 'a new sense of security about the future of our country'; but my own heart sank, as I tried to imagine leaving a child of mine, smiling goodbye through his tears no doubt, and possibly clutching his teddy bear, in the care of General Spanjer and his sergeant majors.

There is worse up the road, for there the self-styled colonels of the Confederate Air Force have turned the idea of war and all its squalors into a species of celebration. There, on the tarmac, stand the hideous bombers of the Second World War, preserved not in loathing, but in love; there in the museum are the guns, bombs, torpedoes and battle-plans that cost the world so many millions of lives, presided over by kindly local ladies, and offered as 'a warm and exciting step back into yesteryear.' It is also, they claim, 'an injection of uncut inspiration all of us could use from time to time:' but I distrusted its pretensions from the start, and detested its gung-ho enthusiasm. I think they love it all. Outside the Operations Room a place is permanently reserved for the aircraft of the Confederate Air Force's commanding officer, Colonel Jethro E. Culpeper, who is described as having fought in all branches of the US armed forces in every theatre of action throughout the Second World War: but I was glad to find that this gentleman was only mythical, or we might have got into an argument.

Now, I have some news for you ranchers of Texas. The Hereford bull, who comes originally from my own part of the world, does not pronounce himself Hearford, as you seem to suppose, but Herreford. 'Is that right? Well, he pronounces himself Hearford on my ranch.'

Hunched, purposeful, tingling with energy, a Santa Gertrudis bull glowered at me over the fence of the King Ranch, but only briefly, for he had better things to do. He was preparing himself for lust. By striking the ground savagely with his front hoof, he was throwing dirt all over himself, and with each shower of soil he made a kind of grunt, a muted bellow, louder with each successive lunge, until at last he felt himself ready: and shaking his great head without another glance at me, off he loped towards his apprehensive herd.

The fauna of Texas is a mighty pageant, from the twitchy long-tailed birds of the telegraph wires to such noble ruffians of the range. I watched coots swim through bayou weeds; I saw deer bounce across shrublands; I mourned the passing of a hundred squashed opossums; I marvelled at the grace of the quarter-horse; I heard tales of coyotes and wild cats; I lay in wait for jack-rabbits; I saw an armadillo at the Argylle Club. You cannot escape the Texan bestiary. When I stopped at McDonald's Food Store near Lampasas to buy a carton of milk, Mr McDonald asked me if I would care to buy a horse at the same time.

Earthiness is a Texan grace—some might say a saving grace. If it sometimes expresses itself in crudity, it also reveals a closeness to things original and organic that you would never feel in California, say, even among the healthiest of health-food farmers, or even I think in the great farmlands of the wheat belt. It is true that all too many beasts of Texas are destined for the slaughter-house—raised for profit, killed for cash—but still one feels in this state, more than in most places, some old working partnership with the rest of God's creatures: a rough-and-ready, take-it-or-leave-it, but essentially honest sort of relationship, as frank in the abattoir as it is in the stables.

So all down 281 I made the acquaintance of animals. And the animals I admired most I saw in the open range one stormy day, when the sun was black with thundercloud and hailstones were beginning to slap upon my windscreen. I looked to my left as I braced myself for the tempest, and there advancing across the scrub, illuminated marvellously now by flashes of lightning, and swirled about by the vapour rising from the warm ground, a team of Angora goats was on the move, heads down, muscles taut, and led by a fine old bearded patriarch, all raunch and guts, who seemed to me the very image of Old Texas, two- or four-legged as you please.

Me: 'Where are you from?'
Hotel maid: 'I'm not from nowhere, I'm from Mexico.'

The Hispanicity of Texas did not strike me much at first—a Tex Mex restaurant here and there, a few bilingual signs, snatches of mariachis. But as I went south, gradually I felt the complexion of the place changing: not just the skin complexion, but the complexion of life itself, the pace and temper of it. As in some flickering old movie, I seemed to see Texas changing its character before my eyes, as the ethnic balance shifted, until down in the southern counties, Wilson, Live Oak or Jim Wells, small dark ladies in enormous limousines seemed to be shooting into 281 at every intersection, hypnotically beautiful black-eyed babies gazed at me in grocery stores, and half the people I inquired the way of seemed to know the neighbourhood rather less intimately than I did myself. It is true that in the course of my journey I passed through nine degrees of latitude—from 34 to 26, like going from Berlin to the French Riviera: even so, this transformation of temperament and appearance took me rather by surprise.

At a small town called Evant, well to the north, I first heard the whisper of a Mexican Issue. There, spying an enclave that looked to me beguilingly like a gypsy encampment, all scampering animals, discarded bedsteads and tumble-down huts, I inquired of a neighbouring resident who it was that lived there. 'Mexicans, that's who,' she said. 'This town used to be all white, no coloured people, no nothing. Then those Mexicans moved in.' She did not say it unkindly exactly, only cautiously, and indeed they did not seem to have moved in very far—an ethnic nibble, no more, on the fringe of the little town. But by the time I reached San Antonio the matter lay more thickly on the air. This has always been a Spanish city, once the capital of Spanish Texas indeed, but it is getting more Spanish every day—so Spanish it often seemed to me more like a South American than a North American city. Old undercurrents of resentment sharpened the edge of that tumultuous fiesta, and conversations were full of ethnic allusion and innuendo. Everybody talked to me about illegal immigration, about indentured labour, about border-guard bribes and sweat-shop wages: and here, as so often in contemporary

America, all around me I felt the growing power of the Spanish-speaking people, the pulse of their music, the flow of their tongue, the revival perhaps of their pride.

Of course Texas itself is very Spanishy. Spaniards founded it, Spaniards named it, Spanish words, customs, foods and artefacts are part of its everyday fabric. The very style of the state speaks, if only obliquely, of conquistadores and grandees. But it is a new kind of Hispanicization that is changing it now—not the grand Castilian kind, or the dashing cowboy kind, but something different out of Mexico—the Spanishness above all of poor, troubled or angry people, who have nothing much to lose, and who have come to the United States, I sometimes speculate, as much in resentment as in hope.

They are making a new Texas, I think. Indeed, by the time I got to the Rio Grande Valley I felt I was hardly in Texas at all, or at least only in some heavily-mutated version of the Lone Star State we know and love. Gone, I felt, was its easy grandeur of heritage and purpose. Three parallel thoroughfares run through the valley from McAllen to Brownsville. In the north is Expressway 82, all speed and exit signs. In the middle is Business Route 82, all trailer havens, business malls and First National Banks—forty-two miles of Main Street, they like to call it down there. In the south is my own 281, running hangdog and outclassed now through the wide fields of fruit and vegetables, beneath the spindly palms, saluted only along the way by listless Hispanic villages and direction signs to Mexico. And to the south again is the Rio Grande itself, where the wetbacks wade, where the socialites of San Antonio get their housemaids, where the vegetable-packers get their cheap labour, and the border patrols keep their ceaseless but less than incorruptible watch.

It is like a topographical allegory—those four parallel lines upon the map, each expressing a different origin, a different intention, a different style. Fields of tension seemed to me to lie between them all, giving the whole valley, for all its warmth and colour, some indefinable air of bitterness or suspicion. It is no longer a very beautiful vale. The early travellers thought it a kind of paradise, with its richness of foliage, its benign climate and its miraculously fertile soil: but it has long since been tarnished by the developers, and looks today more a Limbo than an Elysium. Still, it does remain undeniably exotic, a kind of Texas Riviera beneath those avenues of palms, and this makes its nuances of conflict all the more disturbing. Sometimes it seemed to me that the houses of the richer residents, couched in sprinkled lawns and jacaranda, were like the homes of colonial settlers in some sub-tropical empire: and when a notice warned me that I was entering a Tick Eradication Zone, as I drove through the potato fields, I was reminded obscurely of no-man's-lands and neutral zones, where misunderstanding armies eye each other across the wire, wondering what will happen next.

Before I left the valley I paid a visit to the Shrine of the Virgin at San Juan, one of the holiest places of Mexican Catholicism in the United States. I thought it might soothe me, and indeed there was a profound sanctity to the great modern church, its massed displays of grateful votaries, the discarded crutches of its faithful cured and the beloved figure of the Madonna itself, high on the eastern wall. But the longer I watched those Mexican families at their devotions, the less serene I felt. Anxiety was writ upon those kind fathers' faces, sacrifice upon the features of their wives, and the little children kneeling at the rail, so reverent, so hushed, looked all too poignantly like lambs for the world's slaughter.

'If you don't like the weather, wait a minute:' Old Texan saying, repeated to me twice a day for three weeks.

Rain and sun, dry and wet, all the way through Texas the weather had been mocking me, shifting my mood from day to day and doubtless warping my perceptions. But though the sun shone brightly on me when I arrived in Brownsville, where 281 finally deposits its travellers upon the International Bridge to Mexico, and though it was proper to end such a journey upon a frontier line, still I found myself a little melancholy.

Brownsville is hardly the best of Texas, being at once tumultuous of motion and hangdog of manner. It reminds me of several other towns—Port Said, Panama, Trieste—where cultures are tossed against each other by history, now one pre-eminent, now another, but it somehow lacks the sting or fizz of confrontation. Its shapes and symptoms are threadbare, or exhausting: bazaar-like shops of china and cheap toys, humped scurrying figures loaded with tote-bags and brown-paper parcels, hooting horns, bumpy tarmac, lines of cars at border posts. Only a certain sad excitement attends the bridge itself, with all its mixed emotions—this is after all one of the supreme boundaries of the world, the boundary between the richest society ever established, and the world of poverty, frustration, ill-health and ignorance which, starting just over there in Mexico, extends in so ominous a swathe from here to Bangladesh.

These were not the sensations I wanted of the Lone Star State. In Brownsville's graceless streets my Texas, which had begun at Red River with so exuberant a bang, went out at the Rio Grande not even with a whimper, only a half-hearted haggle. I was homesick already. Where was Ed's Café now? I asked myself rhetorically as I looked over the brown and sluggish river. Where did Brownsville's blue-bonnets nod? Where was the barber of Hico, where the post-mistress of Duffau? To whom would I turn in this unlovely town, if I left my keys in the trunk? So I gave my car in at the airport and took a ticket northwards once again, humming to myself as I boarded the aircraft a lyric I had lately grown to like, to the effect that good ol' boys is all we'll ever be.

PAUL THEROUX

SUBTERRANEAN

GOTHIC

Nick Maland

New Yorkers say some terrible things about the subway—that they hate it, or are scared stiff of it, or that it deserves to go broke. For tourists, it seems just another dangerous aspect of New York, though most don't know it exists. 'I haven't been down there in years,' is a common enough remark from a city dweller. Even people who ride it seem to agree that there is more Original Sin among subway passengers. And more desperation, too, making you think of choruses of 'O dark dark dark. They all go into the dark....'

'Subway' is not its name because, strictly-speaking, more than half of it is elevated. But which person who has ridden it lately is going to call it by its right name, 'The Rapid Transit'? It is also frightful-looking. It has paint and signatures all over its aged face. The graffiti is bad, violent and destructive, and is so extensive and so dreadful it is hard to believe that the perpetrators are not the recipients of some enormous foundation grant. The subway has been vandalized from end to end. It smells so hideous you want to put a clothes-pin on your nose, and it is so noisy the sound actually hurts. Is it dangerous? Ask anyone and he or she will tell you there are about two murders a day on the subway. It really is the pits, people say.

You have to ride it for a while to find out what it is and who takes it and who gets killed on it.

It is full of surprises. Three and a half million fares a day pass through it, and in the first nine months of last year the total number of murder victims on the subway amounted to six. This half-dozen does not include suicides (one a week), 'man-under' incidents (one a day), or 'space-cases'—people who get themselves jammed between the train and the platform. Certainly the subway is very ugly and extremely noisy, but it only *looks* like a death-trap. People ride it looking stunned and holding their breath. It's not at all like the BART system in San Francisco, where people are constantly chattering, saying, 'I'm going to my father's wedding,' or 'I'm looking after my mom's children,' or 'I've got a date with my fiancée's boyfriend.' In New York, the subway is a serious matter—the rackety train, the silent passengers, the occasional scream.

We were at Flushing Avenue, on the GG line, talking about rules for riding the subway. You need rules: the subway is like a complex—and diseased—circulatory system. Some people liken it to a sewer and others hunch their shoulders and mutter about being in the bowels of the earth. It is full of suspicious-looking people.

I said, 'Keep away from isolated cars, I suppose.'

And my friend, a police officer, said, 'Never display jewellery.'

Just then, a man walked by, and he had Chinese coins—the old ones with a hole through the middle—woven somehow into his hair. There were enough coins in that man's hair for a swell night out in old Shanghai, but robbing him would have involved scalping him. There was a woman at the station, too. She was clearly crazy, and she lived in the subway the way people live in railway stations in India, with stacks of dirty bags. The police in New York call such people 'skells' and are seldom harsh with them. 'Wolfman Jack' is a skell, living underground at Hoyt-Schermerhorn, also on the GG line; the police in that station give him food and clothes, and if you ask him how he is, he says, 'I'm getting some calls.' Term them colourful characters and they don't look so dangerous or pathetic.

This crazy old lady at Flushing Avenue was saying, 'I'm a member of the medical profession.' She had no teeth, and her plastic bags were taped around her feet. I glanced at her and made sure she kept her distance. The previous day, a crazy old lady just like her, came at me and shrieked, 'Ahm goon cut you up!' This was at Pelham Parkway, on the IRT-2 line in the Bronx. I left the car at the next stop, Bronx Park East, where the zoo is, though who could be blamed for thinking that in New York City, the zoo is everywhere?

Then a Muslim unflapped his prayer mat—while we were at Flushing Avenue, talking about rules—and spread it on the platform and knelt on it, just like that, and was soon on all fours, beseeching Allah and praising the Prophet Mohammed. This is not remarkable. You see people praying, or reading the Bible, or selling religion, on the subway all the time. 'Hallelujah, brothers and sisters,' the man with the leaflets says on the BMT-RR line at Prospect Avenue in Brooklyn. 'I love Jesus! I used to be a wino!' And Muslims beg and push their green plastic cups at passengers, and try to sell them copies of something called *Arabic Religious Classics*. It is December and Brooklyn, and the men are dressed for the Great Nafud Desert, or Jiddah or Medina—skullcap, gallabieh, sandals.

'And don't sit next to the door,' the second police officer said. We were still talking about rules. 'A lot of these snatchers like to play the doors.'

The first officer said, 'It's a good idea to keep near the conductor. He's got a telephone. So does the man in the token booth. At night, stick around the token booth until the train comes in.'

'Although…token booths,' the second officer said. 'A few years ago, some kids filled a fire extinguisher with gasoline and pumped it into a token booth at Broad Channel. There were two ladies inside, but before they could get out the kids set the gas on fire. The booth just exploded like a bomb, and the ladies died. It was a revenge thing. One of the kids had got a summons for Theft of Service—not paying his fare.'

Just below us, at Flushing Avenue, there was a stream running between the tracks. It gurgled and glugged down the whole length of the long platform. It gave the station the atmosphere of a sewer—dampness and a powerful smell. The water was flowing towards Myrtle and Willoughby. And there was a rat. It was only my third rat in a week of riding the subway, but this one was twice the size of rats I've seen elsewhere. I thought, *Rats as big as cats.*

'Stay with the crowds. Keep away from quiet stairways. The stairways at 41st and 43rd are usually quiet, but 42nd is always busy—that's the one to use.'

So many rules! It's not like taking a subway at all; it's like walking through the woods—through dangerous jungle, rather: Do this, Don't do that….

'It reminds me,' the first officer said. 'The burning of that token booth at Broad Channel. Last May, six guys attempted to murder someone at Forest Parkway, on the J line. It was a whole gang against this one guy. Then they tried to burn the station down with Molotov cocktails. We stopped that, too.'

The man who said this was six-feet four, and weighed about twenty stone. He carried a .38 in a shoulder holster and wore a bullet-proof vest. He had a radio, a can of Mace and a blackjack. He was a plain-clothes man.

The funny thing is that, one day, a boy—five-feet six, and about ten stone—tried to mug him. The boy slapped him across the face while the plain-clothes man was seated on a train. The boy said, 'Give me your money,' and then threatened the man in a vulgar way. The boy still punched at the man when the man stood up; he still said, 'Give me all your money!'

The plain-clothes man then took out his badge and his pistol and said, 'I'm a police officer and you're under arrest.'

'I was just kidding!' the boy said, but it was too late.

I laughed at the thought of someone trying to mug this well-armed giant.

'Rule one for the subway,' he said. 'Want to know what it is?' He looked up and down the Flushing Avenue platform, at the old lady and the Muslim and the running water and the vandalized signs. 'Rule one is—don't ride the subway if you don't have to.'

A lot of people say that. I did not believe it when he said it, and, after a week of riding the trains, I still didn't. The subway is New York City's best hope. The streets are impossible, the highways are a failure, there is nowhere to park. The private automobile has no future in this city whatsoever. This is plainest of all to the people who own and use cars in the city; they know, better than anyone, that the car is the last desperate old-fangled fling of a badly-planned transport system. What is amazing is that back in 1904 a group of businessmen solved New York's transport problems for centuries to come. What vision! What enterprise! What an engineering marvel they created in this underground railway! And how amazed they would be to see what it has become, how foul-seeming to the public mind.

The subway is a gift to any connoisseur of superlatives. It has the longest rides of any subway in the world, the biggest stations, the fastest trains, the most track, the most passengers, the most police officers. It also has the filthiest trains, the most bizarre graffiti, the noisiest wheels, the craziest passengers, the wildest crimes. Some New Yorkers have never set foot in the subway; other New Yorkers actually live there, moving from station to station, whining for money, eating yesterday's bagels and sleeping on benches. These 'skells' are not merely down-and-out. Many are insane, chucked out of New York hospitals in the early 1970s when it was decided that long-term care was doing them little good. 'They were resettled in rooms or hotels,' Ruth Cohen, a psychiatric social-worker at

Bellevue, told me. 'But many of them can't follow through. They get lost, they wander the streets. They're not violent, suicidal or dangerous enough for Bellevue—this is an acute-care hospital. But these people who wander the subway, once they're on their own they begin to de-compensate.'

Ahm goon cut you up: that woman who threatened to slash me was de-compensating. Here are a few more de-compensating—one is weeping on a wooden bench at Canal Street, another has wild hair and is spitting into a Coke can. One man who is de-compensating in a useful way, has a bundle of brooms and is setting forth to sweep the whole of the change area at Grand Central; another is scrubbing the stairs at 14th Street with scraps of paper. They drink, they scream, they gibber like monkeys. They sit on subway benches with their knees drawn up, just as they do in mental hospitals. A police officer told me, 'There are more serious things than people screaming on trains.' This is so, and yet the deranged person who sits next to you and begins howling at you seems at the time very serious indeed.

The subway, which is many things, is also a madhouse.

W hen people say the subway frightens them, they are not being silly or irrational. It is no good saying how cheap or how fast it is. The subway *is* frightening. It is also very easy to get lost on the subway, and the person who is lost in New York City has a serious problem. New Yorkers make it their business to avoid getting lost.

It is the stranger who gets lost. It is the stranger who follows people hurrying into the stair-well: subway entrances are just dark holes in the sidewalk—the stations are below ground. There is nearly always a bus-stop near the subway entrance. People waiting at a bus-stop have a special pitying gaze for people entering the subway. It is sometimes not pity, but fear, bewilderment, curiosity, or fatalism; often they look like miners' wives watching their menfolk going down the pit.

The stranger's sense of disorientation down below is immediate. The station is all tile and iron and dampness; it has bars and turnstiles and steel grates. It has the look of an old prison or a monkey cage.

Buying a token, the stranger may ask directions, but the token booth—reinforced, burglar-proof, bullet-proof—renders the reply incoherent. And subway directions are a special language: 'A-train…Downtown…Express to the Shuttle…Change at Ninety-sixth for the two…Uptown…The Lex…CC…LL…The Local…'

Most New Yorkers refer to the subway by the now-obsolete forms 'IND', 'IRT', 'BMT'. No one intentionally tries to confuse the stranger; it is just that, where the subway is concerned, precise directions are very hard to convey.

Verbal directions are incomprehensible, written ones are defaced. The signboards and subway maps are indiscernible beneath layers of graffiti. That Andy Warhol, the stylish philistine, has said, 'I love graffiti' is almost reason enough to hate it. One is warier still of Norman Mailer, who naively encouraged this public scrawling in his book *The Faith of Graffiti*. 'Misguided' seems about the kindest way of describing Mailer who, like Warhol, limps after the latest fashions in the hope of discovering youthfulness or celebrity in colourful outrage. That Mailer's judgement is appalling is clear from his bluster in the cause of the murderer and liar Jack Abbot, who brought about a brief, bloody New York run of *Mr Loveday's Little Outing*. Mailer admires graffiti.

Graffiti is destructive; it is anti-art; it is an act of violence, and it can be deeply menacing. It has displaced the subway signs and maps, blacked-out the windows of the trains and obliterated the instructions. *In case of emergency*—is cross-hatched with a felt-tip. *These seats are for the elderly and disabled*—a yard-long signature obscures it. *The subway tracks are very dangerous: if the train should stop, do not*—the rest is black and unreadable. The stranger cannot rely on printed instructions or warnings, and there are few cars out of the six thousand on the system in which the maps have not been torn out. Assuming the stranger has boarded the train, he or she can feel only panic when, searching for a clue to his route, he sees in the map-frame the message, *Guzmán—Ladrón, Maricón y Asesino*.

Panic: and so he gets off the train, and then his troubles really begin.

He may be in the South Bronx or the upper reaches of Broadway on the Number 1 line, or on any one of a dozen lines that traverse Brooklyn. He gets off the train, which is covered in graffiti, and steps on to a station platform which is covered in graffiti. It is possible (this is true of many stations) that none of the signs will be legible. Not only will the stranger not know where he is, but the stairways will be splotched and stinking—no *Uptown*, no *Downtown*, no *Exit*. It is also possible that not a single soul will be around, and the most dangerous stations—ask any police officer—are the emptiest. Of course, the passenger might just want to sit on a broken bench and, taking Mailer's word for it, contemplate the *macho* qualities of the graffiti; on the other hand, he is more likely to want to get the hell out of there.

This is the story that most people tell of subways fear. In every detail it is like a nightmare, complete with rats and mice and a tunnel and a low ceiling. It is manifest suffocation, straight out of Poe. Those who tell this story seldom have a crime to report. They have experienced fear. It is completely understandable—what is worse than being trapped underground?—but it has been a private horror. In most cases, the person will have come to no harm. He will, however, remember his fear on that empty station for the rest of his life.

When New Yorkers recount an experience like this they are invariably speaking of something that happened on another line, not their usual route. Their own line is fairly safe, they'll say; it's cleaner than the others; it's got a little charm, it's kind of dependable; they've been taking it for years. Your line has crazy people on it, but my line has 'characters'. This sense of loyalty to a regularly-used line is the most remarkable thing about the subway passenger in New York. It is, in fact, a jungle attitude.

In any jungle, the pathway is a priority. People move around New York in various ways, but the complexities of the subway have allowed the New Yorker to think of his own route as something personal, even *original*. No one uses maps on the subway—you seldom see any. Most subway passengers were shown how to ride it by parents or friends. Then habit turns it into instinct, just like a trot down a jungle path. The passenger knows where he is going because he never diverges from his usual route. But that is also why, unless you are getting off at precisely his stop, he cannot tell you how to get where you're going.

In general, people have a sense of pride in their personal route; they may be superstitious about it and even a bit secretive. Vaguely fearful of other routes, they may fantasize about them—these 'dangerous' lines that run through unknown districts. This provokes them to assign a specific character to the other lines. The IRT is the oldest line; for some people it is dependable, with patches of elegance (those beaver mosaics at Astor Place), and for others it is dangerous and dirty. One person praises the IND, another person damns it. 'I've got a soft spot for the BMT,' a woman told me, but found it hard to explain why. 'Take the A train,' I was told. 'That's the best one, like the song.' But some of the worst stations are on the (very long) A line. The CC, 8th Avenue local, was described to me as 'scuzz'—disreputable—but this train, running from Bedford Park Boulevard, the Bronx, via Manhattan and Brooklyn, to Rockaway Park, Queens, covers a distance of some thirty-two miles. The fact is that for some of these miles it is pleasant and for others it is not. There is part of one line that is indisputably bad; that is the stretch of the 2 line (IRT) from Nostrand to New Lots Avenue. It is dangerous and ugly and when you get to New Lots Avenue you cannot imagine why you went. The police call this line 'The Beast'.

But people in the know—the police, the Transit Authority, the people who travel throughout the system—say that one line is pretty much like another.

No line is entirely good or bad, crime-ridden or crime-free. The trains carry crime with them, picking it up in one area and bringing it to another. They pass through a district and take on the characteristics of that place. The South Bronx is regarded as a high risk area, but seven lines pass through it, taking vandals and thieves all over the system. There is a species of vandalism that was once peculiar to the South Bronx: boys would swing on the stanchions—those chrome poles in the centre of the car—and, raising themselves sideways until they were parallel with the floor, they would kick hard against a window and break it. Now this South Bronx window-breaking technique operates throughout the system. This business about one line being dependable and another being charming and a third being dangerous is just jungle talk.

The most-mugged man in New York must be the white-haired creaky-looking fellow in Bedford-Stuyvesant who has had as many as thirty mugging attempts made on him in a single year. And he still rides the subway trains. He's not as crazy as he looks: he's a cop in the Transit Police, a plain-clothes man who works with the Mobile Task Force in the district designated 'Brooklyn North'. This man is frequently a decoy. In the weeks before Christmas he rode the J and the GG and the 2 lines looking like a pathetic senior citizen, with two gaily-wrapped parcels in his shopping bag. He was repeatedly ambushed by unsuspecting muggers, and then he pulled out his badge and handcuffs and arrested his attackers.

Muggers are not always compliant. Then the Transit Police Officer unholsters his pistol, but not before jamming a coloured headband over his head to alert any nearby uniformed officer. Before the advent of headbands many plain-clothes men were shot by their colleagues in uniform.

'And then we rush in,' says Sergeant Donnery of the Mobile Task Force. 'Ninety per cent of the guys out there can kick my ass, one on one. You've got to come on yelling and screaming. "You so-and-so! You so-and-so! I'm going to kill you!" Unless the suspect is deranged and has a knife or something. In that case you might have to talk quietly. But if the guy's tough and you go in meek you get sized up very fast.'

The Transit Police has three thousand officers and thirteen dogs. It is one of the biggest police forces in the United States and is altogether independent from the New York City Police, though the pay and training are exactly the same. It is so independent the men cannot speak to each other on their radios, which many Transit Police find inconvenient when chasing a suspect up the subway stairs into the street.

What about the dogs? 'Dogs command respect,' I was told at Transit Police Headquarters. 'Think of them as a tool, like a gun or a nightstick. At the moment it's just a test programme for high-crime stations, late-night hours, that kind of thing.'

I wondered aloud whether it would work, and the reply was, 'A crime is unlikely to be committed anywhere near one of these dogs.'

The Canine Squad is housed with a branch of the Mobile Task Force at the underground junction of the LL and GG lines: Lorimer Street—Metropolitan Avenue. The bulletin board on the plain-clothes men's side is plastered with unit citations and merit awards, and Sgt Donnery of the Task Force was recently made 'Cop of the Month' for a particularly clever set of arrests. Sgt Donnery is in charge of thirty-two plain-clothes men and two detectives. Their motto is 'Soar with the Eagles.' A sheaf of admiring newspaper clippings testifies to their effectiveness. As we talked, the second shift was preparing to set out for the day.

'Morale seems very high,' I said. The men were joking, watching the old-man decoy spraying his hair and beard white.

'Sure, morale is high,' Sgt Donnery said. 'We feel we're getting something accomplished. It isn't easy. Sometimes you have to hide in a porter's room with a mop for four days before you get your man. We dress up as porters, conductors, motormen, track-workers. If there are a lot of robberies and track-workers in the same station, we dress up as track-workers. We've got all the uniforms.'

'Plain-clothes men' is something of a misnomer for the Task Force that has enough of a theatrical wardrobe to mount a production of *Subways are for Sleeping*.

And yet, looking at Howard Haag and Joseph Minucci standing on the platform at Nassau Avenue on the GG line, you would probably take them for a pair of physical-education teachers on the way to the school gym. They look tough, but not aggressively so; they are healthy and well-built—but some of that is padding: they both wear bullet-proof vests. Underneath the ordinary clothes the men are well armed. Each man carries a .38, a blackjack and a can of Mace. Minucci has a two-way radio.

Haag has been on the force for seventeen years, Minucci for almost seven. Neither has in that time ever fired his gun, though each has an excellent arrest-record and a pride in detection. They are funny, alert and indefatigable, and together they make Starsky and Hutch look like a pair of hysterical cream-puffs. Their job is also much harder than any City cop's. I had been told repeatedly that the average City cop would refuse to work in the conditions that the Transit Police endure every day. At Nassau Avenue, Minucci told me why.

'Look at the stations! They're dirty, they're cold, they're noisy. If you fire your gun you'll kill about ten innocent people—you're trapped here. You stand here some days and the cold and the dampness creep into your bones and you start shivering. And that smell ‹—smell it?›—it's like that all the time, and you've got to stand there and breathe it in. Bergen Street Station, the snow comes through the bars and you freeze. They call it "The Ice-Box". Then some days, kids recognize you—they've seen you make a collar—and they swear at you, call you names, try to get you to react, smoke pot right under your nose. "Here come the DT's"—that's what they call us. It's the conditions. They're awful. You have to take so much crap from these schoolkids. And your feet are killing you. So you sit down, read a newspaper, drink coffee, and then you get a rip from a shoofly—'

Minucci wasn't angry; he said all this in a smiling, ironical way. Like Howie Haag, he enjoys his work and takes it seriously. A 'shoofly', he explained, is a police-inspector who rides the subway looking for officers who are goldbricking—though having a coffee on a cold day hardly seemed to me like goldbricking. 'We're not supposed to drink coffee,' Minucci said, and he went on to define other words in the Transit Police vocabulary: 'lushworker' (a person who robs drunks or sleeping passengers); and 'Flop Squad' (decoys who pretend to be asleep, in order to attract lushworkers).

Just then, as we were talking at Nassau, the station filled up with shouting boys—big ones, aged anywhere from fifteen to eighteen. There were hundreds of them and, with them, came the unmistakable odour of smouldering marijuana. They were boys from Automotive High School, heading south on the GG. They stood on the platform howling and screaming and sucking smoke out of their fingers, and when the train pulled in they began fighting towards the doors.

'You might see one of these kids being a pain in the neck, writing graffiti or smoking dope or something,' Howie Haag said. 'And you might wonder why we don't do anything. The reason is we're looking for something serious—robbers, snatchers, assault, stuff like that.'

Minucci said, 'The Vandalism Squad deals with window-kickers and graffiti. Normally we don't.'

Once on the train the crowd of yelling boys thinned out. I had seen this sort of activity before: boys get on the subway train and immediately bang through the connecting doors and walk from car to car. I asked Minucci why this was so.

'They're marking the people. See them? They're looking for an old lady near a door or something they can snatch, or a pocket they can pick. They're sizing up the situation. They're also heading for the last car. That's where they hang out on this train.'

223

Howie said, 'They want to see if we'll follow them. If we do, they'll mark us as cops.'

Minucci and Haag did not follow, though at each stop they took cautious looks out of the train, using the reflections in mirrors and windows.

'They play the doors when it's crowded,' Minucci said.

Howie said, 'School-kids can take over a train.'

'Look at that old lady,' Minucci said. 'She's doing everything wrong.'

The woman, in her late sixties, was sitting next to the door. Her wristwatch was exposed and her handbag dangled from the arm closest to the door. Minucci explained that one of the commonest subway crimes was inspired by this posture. The snatcher reached through the door from the platform and, just before the doors shut, he grabbed the bag or watch, or both; and then he was off, and the train was pulling out, with the victim trapped on board.

I wondered whether the plain-clothes men would warn her. They didn't. But they watched her closely, and when she got off they escorted her in an anonymous way. The old woman never knew how well protected she was and how any person making a move to rob her would have been hammered flat to the platform by the combined weight of Officers Minucci and Haag.

There were men on the train drinking wine out of bottles sheathed in paper bags. Such men are everywhere in New York, propped against walls, with bottle and bag. A few hours earlier, at Myrtle-Willoughby, I had counted forty-six men hanging around outside a housing project, drinking this way. I had found their idleness and their stares and their drunken slouching a little sinister.

Minucci said, 'The winos don't cause much trouble. It's the kids coming home from school. They're the majority of snatchers and robbers.'

Minucci went on, 'On the LL line, on Grant Street, there's much more crime than before, because Eastern District High School relocated there. It's mostly larceny and bag snatches.'

It was a salutary experience for me, riding through Brooklyn with Officers Minucci and Haag. Who, except a man flanked by two armed plain-clothes men, would travel from one end of Brooklyn to the other, walking through housing projects and derelict areas, and waiting for hours at subway stations? It was a perverse hope of mine that we would happen upon a crime, or even be the victims of a mugging-attempt. We were left alone, things were quiet, there were no arrests; but for the first time in my life I was travelling the hinterland of New York City with my head up, looking people in the eye with curiosity and lingering scrutiny and no fear. It is a shocking experience. I felt at first, because of my bodyguards, like Haile Selassie; and then I seemed to be looking at an alien land—I had never had the courage to gaze at it so steadily. It was a land impossible to glamourize and hard to describe. I had the feeling I was looking at the future.

'It's not the train that's dangerous—it's the area it passes through.'

The speaker was a uniformed Transit Police Officer named John Burgois. He was in his mid-thirties and described himself as 'of Hispanic origin'. He had four citations. Normally he worked with the Strike Force out of Midtown Manhattan in areas considered difficult: 34th and 7th, 34th and 8th, and Times Square. Officer Burgois told me that the job of the uniformed cop is to reassure people by being an obvious presence that someone in trouble can turn to. The Transit cop in uniform also deals with loiterers and fare evaders, assists injured people and lost souls, keeps a watch on public toilets ('toilets attract a lot of crime') and as for drunks, 'We ask drunks to remove themselves.'

I asked Officer Burgois whether he considered his job dangerous. 'Once or twice a year I get bitten,' he said. 'Bites are bad. You always need a tetanus shot for human bites.'

One of the largest and busiest change-areas on the subway is at Times Square. It is the junction of four lines, including the Shuttle, which operates with wonderful efficiency between Times Square and Grand Central. This, for the Christmas season, was John Burgois's beat. I followed him and for an hour I made notes, keeping track of how he was working.

4.21—Smoker warned (smoking is forbidden in the subway, even on ramps and stairs).

4.24—Panicky shout from another cop. There's a woman with a gun downstairs on the platform. Officer Burgois gives chase, finds the

225

woman. She is drunk and has a toy pistol. Woman warned.

4.26—'Which way to the Flushing Line?'

4.29—'How do I transfer here?'

4.30—'Is this the way to 23rd street?'

4.37—'Donde esta Quins Plaza?'

4.34—'Where is the A train?' As Officer Burgois answers this question, a group of people gathers around him. There are four more requests for directions. It occurs to me that, as all maps have been vandalized, the lost souls need very detailed directions.

4.59—*Radio call:* there is an injured passenger at a certain token booth—a gash on her ankle. Officer Burgois lets another cop attend to it.

5.02—'Where ees the Shuffle?' asks a boy carrying an open can of beer. 'Over there,' Officer Burgois says, 'and dispose of that can. I'm watching you.'

5.10—*Radio call:* a man whose wallet has been stolen is at the Transit Police cubicle on the Times Square concourse. Officer Burgois steps in to observe.

Man: What am I going to do?

Officer: The officer-in-charge will take down the information.

Man: Are you going to catch him?

Officer: We'll prosecute if you can identify him.

Man: I only saw his back.

Officer: That's too bad.

Man: He was tall, thin, and black. I had twenty-two dollars in that wallet.

Officer: You can kiss your money goodbye. Even if we caught him he'd say, 'This is my money.'

Man: This is the first time anything like this has ever happened to me.

5.17—Seeing Officer Burgois, a member of the public says, 'There's two kids on the train downstairs snatching bags—go get them!' Officer Burgois runs and finds the boys hanging over the gate between trains, the favourite spot for snatching bags from passengers on the platform. Officer Burgois apprehends them. The boys, named Troy and Sam, are from the Bronx. They can't remember when they were born; they seem to be about fourteen or fifteen. They deny they were snatching bags. Each boy has about thirty-five dollars in his pocket. They are sullen but not at all afraid. Officer Burgois gives them a YD form and says, 'If I catch you again, your mother's going to pick you up from the station....'

5.28—'Hey, Officer, how do I get to...?'

At this point I stopped writing. I could see that it would be repetitious—and so it was, dreary questions, petty crime and obstinate sneaks. But no one-bit officer Burgois. He has been doing this every hour of every working day for twelve and a half years, and will go on doing it, or something very much like it, for the rest of his working life.

It costs twenty-five dollars or more to go by taxi from Midtown to Kennedy Airport. For five dollars it is possible to go by subway, on 'The JFK Express' and the forty minutes it takes is the same or less than a taxi. But it is rumoured that this service will soon be withdrawn, because so few people use it. If that happens, there is another option—the express on the A line to Howard Beach, which takes under an hour and costs seventy-five cents.

There are ducks at Howard Beach, and herons farther on at Jamaica Bay, and odd watery vistas all the way from Broad Channel to Far Rockaway. The train travels on a causeway past sleepy fishing villages and woodframe houses, and it's all ducks and geese until the train reaches the far side of the bay, where the dingier bungalows and the housing projects begin. Then, roughly at Frank Avenue station, the Atlantic Ocean pounds past jetties of black rocks, not far from the tracks; and at Mott Avenue is the sprawling two-storey town of Far Rockaway, with its main street and its slap-happy architecture and its ruins. It looks like its sister-cities in Ohio and Rhode Island, with just enough trees to hide its dullness, and though part of it is in a state of decay, it looks small enough to save.

That was a pleasant afternoon, when I took the train to the Rockaways. I had spent the whole week doing little else except riding the subway. Each morning I decided on a general direction, and then I set off, sometimes sprinting to the end of the line and making my way back slowly; or else stopping along the way and varying my route back. I went from Midtown to Jamaica Estates in Queens, and returned via Coney Island. There are white Beluga whales at the

Aquarium at Coney Island, and Amazonian electric eels that produce six hundred and fifty volts (the Congo River electric catfish is punier at three hundred and fifty volts), and the African lungfish which drowns if held underwater but can live four years out of water. There are drunks and transvestites and troglodytes in the rest of out-of-season Coney, and the whole place looks as if it has been insured and burned. Though it is on Rockaway Inlet, it is a world away from Rockaway Park. It is also the terminus for six lines.

Never mind the dirt, ignore the graffiti—you can get anywhere you want in New York this way. There are two hundred and thirty route miles on the system—twice as many as the Paris Métro. The trains run all night—in London they shut down at midnight. New York's one-price token system is the fairest and most sensible in the world; London's multi-fare structure is clumsy, ridiculous and a wasteful sop to the unions; Japan's, while just as complicated, is run by computers which spit tickets at you and then belch out your change. The Moscow Metro has grandiose chandeliers to light some stations, but the New York subway has hopeful signs, like the one at 96th and 7th Ave: 'New Tunnel lighting is being installed at this area as part of a Major Rehabilitation Programme. Completion is expected in the summer of 1980.' They are over a year late in finishing, but at least they know there's a problem. In most of the world's subway trains, the driver's cab occupies the whole of the front of the first car. But on the New York system you can stand at the front of the train and watch the rats hurrying aside as the train careers towards the black tilting tunnel and the gleaming tracks.

The trains are always the same, but the stations differ, usually reflecting what is above ground: Spring Street is raffish, Forest Hills smacks of refinement, Livonia Avenue on the LL looks bombed. People aspire to Bay Ridge and say they wouldn't be caught dead in East Harlem—though others are. Fort Hamilton turns into the amazing Verrazano-Narrows Bridge and the 1 into a ferry landing. By the time I had reached 241st Street on the 2, I thought I had got to somewhere near Buffalo, but returning on the 5 and dropping slowly through the Bronx to Lexington Avenue and then to Lower Manhattan and across on the 4 to Flatbush, I had a sense of unrelieved desolation.

No one speaks on the subway except to the person on his

immediate right or left, and only then if they are very old friends or else married. Avoiding the stranger's gaze is what the subway passenger does best: there is not much eye-contact below ground. Most passengers sit bolt upright, with fixed expressions, ready for anything. A look of alertness prevails. As a New York City subway passenger you are J. Alfred Prufrock—you 'prepare a face to meet the faces that you meet.' Few people look relaxed or off-guard. Those new to the subway have the strangest expressions, like my English friend, who told me there was only one way to survive the subway: 'You have to look as if you're the one with the meat cleaver. You have to go in with your eyes flashing.'

In order to appear inconspicuous on the subway, many people read. Usually they read *The Daily News*—and a few read—*Nowy Dziennik,* which is the same thing; the *Times* is less popular, because it takes two hands to read it. But the Bible is very popular, along with religious tracts and the Holy Koran and Spanish copies of *The Watchtower*; lots of boys study for their Bar-Mitzvah on the F line in Queens. I saw *The Bragg Toxic-less Diet* on the B and *La Pratique du Français Parlé* on the RR. All over the system riders read lawbooks—*The Interpretation of Contracts, The Law of Torts, Maritime Law.* The study of law is a subway preoccupation, and it is especially odd to see all these lawbooks in this lawless atmosphere—the law student sitting on the vandalized train. The police officers on the vandalized trains create the same impression of incongruity. When I first saw them, they looked mournful to me, but after I got to know them I realized that most of them are not mournful at all, just dead-tired and overworked and doing a thankless job.

Not long ago, *The Daily News* ran a series about the subway called 'The Doomsday Express'. It was about all the spectacular catastrophes that are possible on the New York system—crashes and nuclear disasters and floods with heavy casualties. 'Doomsday' has a curious appeal to a proud and vaguely religious ego. One of the conceits of modern man is his thinking that the world will end with a big bang. It is a kind of hopeful boast, really, the idea that it will take destruction on a vast scale for us to be wiped out.

It is easy to frighten people with catastrophes; much harder to

Paul Theroux

convince them that decay and trivial-seeming deterioration can be inexorable. The New York subway system is wearing out, and parts of it are worn out; all of it looks threadbare. No city can survive without people to run it, and the class divisions which have distinct geographical centres in New York make the subway all the more necessary.

There is a strong political commitment to the subway, particularly among down-market Democrats. But only money can save it. To this end there is a plan afoot called 'The Five-Year Capital Programme' of $7.2 billion dollars. It remains to be seen whether this programme is instituted. If it isn't, New York will come even closer to looking like dear old Calcutta. There will be no big bang.

Anyway, I am a supporter of the whimper theory—the more so after my experience of the subway.

The subway is buried and unspectacular-looking. Its worst aspects are not its crime or its dangers, but the cloudy fears it inspires, and its dirt and delay. It ought to be fixed, and very soon.

HUGH BRODY

JIM'S JOURNEY

There is no coming to conclusions in England. Unless you fly young into unknown winds, you neither leave nor stay. I left in order to stay, went off to collect my thoughts in other continents only to retell stories (deceivingly, too, as if they were my own) at home.

On journeys, in strange landscapes, in other cultures, England can fade. Yet distances never seem quite great enough; and some moral imperative dictates engagements on local fields of battle.

When the ships were trumpeted to Port Stanley, the wish to leave pressed with new strength against the need to stay. People seemed to re-live old styles of war. But as this mad nostalgia was turned to electoral credit, I thought: It is time to talk and think about what happens here, to write entirely from within this country. Travel encourages unchallenging descriptions. Simply to evoke England is to lose the argument. The sound of a fanfare, of a cricket bat striking the ball, of rivet guns in a shipyard, and too many minds fill with a sense of special Englishness. The images, even attacks upon ourselves, somehow bind us tight to our proper places.

I sharpen pencils, stare at the paper . . . and escape, to the Nass Valley, to a memory of Jim Murray. His childhood could have been edited from dreams. My mind slips out of here, to his story.

Jim Murray's father taught geography in a one-room school in Wales. He was a tall, very thin man who spent his summer evenings exploring and fishing tight fertile valleys, and housebound winter evenings staring at maps of Canada. His eyes searched the dark green, shades of brown, white: a steep and folding land, ice-capped mountain ranges. Jim's father discovered in the far northwest, on his maps, a series of huge rivers flowing into the Pacific. The rivers drained the western Rockies and—he could tell from the blues and browns—poured through coastal ranges. Their feeder streams and tributaries showed on the map as the size of the Wye or Severn; their rapids must boil through hundreds of miles; at their esturaries they would have turned against tides, banks strewn with boulders and great trees torn out of the distant interior. He imagined the salmon—he had read that not one but five species leaped their way to spawning creeks and lakes far inland. He had heard that in winter

233

these rivers of life became corridors of ice. Even their names pulled at him: Skeena, Nass, Iskut, Stikhine. . . .

The young teacher seemed too solitary. He was so quiet, so lost in reverie, as to appear ineffectual. In 1920, in mid-Wales, no one sneered behind their hands that he cared too much for little boys and girls. But even if he had a gentle sympathy for pupils, teacher Murray hated every day at the blackboard.

Then an English farmer bought part of a river and much of a valley near the school. At first this made little difference to Jim's father's life, other than to stir an old but slow resentment of intruding landowners. But the farmer hired a water bailiff to enforce the privacy of his salmon pools. Jim's father found notices to warn trespassers where before he had believed he was free to roam. And he received a note from the farmer that accused him of poaching.

The teacher surprised his neighbours by visiting the would-be squire. He gained entrance to the imposing drawing room, and denounced the man for his high-handedness. The farmer responded with an aloof request that Murray leave the house, and with a sharp little warning that as the largest of the region's landowners he had influence over more than the fish in his rivers. But the farmer's daughter, who had been a silent witness of the exchange, was delighted by the visitor.

This daughter contrived to meet Jim's father outside the school one afternoon; he, only in part from a wish to show disdain for any convention that might forbid it, urged her to come in for tea. They became friends.

Yearning for revenge against England, and outraged by an understanding of her father's way of life in it, the farmer's daughter joined the thin, shy young man in battle. They met at the schoolhouse whenever they could, and at weekends took long walks together. At first they shared a furious dream of breaking the landlord's grip; later they shared fantasies of escape.

After four turbulent months the parish seniors who ran the school summoned Murray to a meeting, and told him he would do well to find another job, in a town perhaps. His ideas, he was assured, would fit better in more crowded places. A week later he and the farmer's daughter eloped: the relief maps of Canada had done their work; those valleys beyond the Rockies were no longer to be resisted.

They shipped to Montreal, then travelled on the Canadian Pacific Railway to Vancouver. In the train across the country, the two of them watched the eastern woodlands give way to prairies, to mountains, then to the coast—a train day or more in each immense landscape. At Vancouver they found passage on a steamship that took them up the northern British Columbia coastline. They arrived at Prince Rupert.

They did not travel light. The Welsh teacher, an immediate eccentric in this land, regarded a library as an essential part of every life, even a new one. Trunks filled with books were hauled along docksides, railways stations and eventually in wagons that took them inland from Prince Rupert. In the end the books were piled along the walls of the first log cabin that the Murrays could find— insulation, she used to say, against every kind of chill wind. This was 1923: leathery sets of complete works, individual volumes of Romantic poets, and much that was new.

This first log cabin was in the valley of a tributary of the River Nass. No other Europeans lived so far into the interior; the young couple were beyond the white man's frontier. As Jim tells it, his mother's passion for escape had been soon spent. Two weeks in Vancouver and Victoria searching for a boat to go north had been her best times. These new and old towns, small but bursting with energy, heartlands of immigration, were mecca enough: here she was free of a genteel background, free to live for the first time, in a vigorous but unexacting society. For her, the journey onwards, northwards, was frightening and pointless. She felt no need for solitudes, and had no compulsion to battle with a nature made elemental, as she saw it, by newcomers' ignorance. Anyway, battles were won by society, she always said, from within society: she denied (though with a diffidence that saw her to the cabin on the Nass) any understanding of her husband's determination to keep travelling until they were beached beyond any known tide line. Victoria and Vancouver continued to pull at her: arranging and rearranging rows of books against the tired joins of poorly chinked logs was how she remembered the two years she stayed. Though in fact her time was spent carting and carrying and digging and cooking and clearing and, at the end of the two years, giving birth to Jim. Then she left— not in a fury, not in defiance, but quietly and decisively: she told her husband she was taking the baby to Victoria for a while. He suspected she would never return, but did not oppose her. The land had already closed in on him; he contemplated a greater solitude with, as she saw it, a grim equanimity.

Once he had been left, he moved further up the valley, deeper into the forest, to become a full-time trapper and fur trader. This was how he had begun to live anyway. Nothing seemed more obvious than to be higher in the hills, nearer the territories of Tlingit and Tsimshean Indians with whom he planned to trade and to whom (schoolteacher still) he had a keen but, as it turned out, dying belief in carrying the joys of literacy.

Trader Murray hit a frontier jackpot. In the 1920s, while the rest of the economic universe staggered, fur prices boomed. Indians brought in their lynx and beaver and marten and mink, and Murray paid them in guns, ammunition, flour, sugar, tea and tobacco. Then he took accumulations of furs to Vancouver, where they sold for fortunes. More and more supplies were hauled to the remotest trading post in the territory. Other white men, refugees from poverty and joblessness, roamed into the forests and mountains of the far northwest, but none ever reached Murray's hidden centre. He became a myth, a legend of a wild woodsman. He was thirty-five.

On trips to Vancouver he visited his wife and son. He spent enough time there for them to have two more children—a girl, then another boy. He invited but did not urge his wife to return with him. He even managed to joke about the draught-stopping books: they now had a windproof library. She'd be snug as a Welsh afternoon, he said, for he'd been adding shelves. But she was satisfied to hear his few stories—fewer and fewer, for as the years went by he became taciturn.

She was not unhappy when he proposed that Jim go back with him to the Nass. At eight Jim was a noisy and difficult child who seemed to be at odds with his mother: the two new children enraged him, and he had begun to whine and demand that his father take him 'home'. Perhaps father, mother and eight-year-old Jim all believed that this division of the family would be insupportable, that the heart of life could not be split, and that father plus firstborn would be a renewed northern family, a pole to which natural forces would drive them all in the end.

Jim's memory begins with his return north. The Welsh school, gentleman's daughter, the journeys, his mother taking him to Victoria, their life there—all this was told to him in bits and pieces, as prehistory, the episodes through which he tunnelled an egress to the self he could remember. Jim insists that he cannot even find a glimmer of the Victoria he must have known, not the school he attended there for a year, or even his father's fur-selling visits. The early years are closed. Exclusion of the boy from his parents' struggle seems to have caused a total ignorance. But when Jim tells those parts of the story, he finds passion and detail that are absent from his own recollections. The unremembered events have challenged him to discover or create places, appearances, decisive moments, feelings. While events he remembers are imbued with a matter of factness that is at once bewildering and astounding. Even growing up in such a wild fastness, the occasional longing for his mother, the relentlessness of his father's activity—all these are given as stubborn, unmoulded facts, goods arranged according to some self-evident principle: packages on a grocer's shelf. In the end, and therefore in retrospect, Jim's Nass valley life was what he knew, expected and never thought to alter. (Jim's story is too evocative for me to leave it in Jim's packaging: I cannot, try as I might, retell it in his idiom.)

Jim remembers sitting at a quayside in Victoria. His father was overseeing an immense heap of supplies being loaded onto the boat. He could not think what these crates and barrels and sacks contained, except that they would support them for the coming year. Had someone asked Jim what it all was, he would have replied: turnips, what keep a person alive. It was his father's favourite saying, and one Jim must have heard when listening to his father and mother talk—with edges to their voices, he later realized, of accumulated but unadmitted rancour.

In fact, most of the supplies were trade goods: guns by the dozen, flour by the hundredweight, the stuff to be turned into furs.

Jim's memory of the journey up the coast is a picture of his father sorting slips of paper and counting—always counting. Close to the ship's rails were the steep and forested edges of islands and fjords, the ragged overgrown precipice where North America has fallen crazily into the North Pacific. Jim watched the passageways through which the ships steered a sheltered route northwards, but he saw only his father's blind counting.

At Prince Rupert they loaded the supplies from ship to wagons, and began the long haul inland. It was autumn. The air was heavy with mists, and smelling of mosses. By the time they had travelled ten days along the valley, the distant hills were white-capped. Within a week of arriving at the log house they were snowbound.

That first winter, says Jim, he learned to walk—the walking of people who live in snow and beside mountains, and use forest trails: on snowshoes, always with a sense of orientation, and without tiring. His father dourly urged him to read; and joyously encouraged him to learn outdoor skills. The library was a dark, unhappy part of their home. Outside, the boy thrived. But they were not as alone as he had expected: his father had never spoken about the Indian families that lived within a few miles of the trading post, still less of the family that lived alongside, if not in it. The Welshman had not battled beyond society, but had created his own new one—for which purpose he had taken more than furs from the Indians. There was one Indian who helped with carrying and carting and, most important of all, buying and selling in the local languages. This post-servant had expertise that came to be grafted deep into the new-comer's life. To Jim he seemed to be an old man, but fifteen years later seemed no older.

Then there was a woman who 'helped about the place.' She had two younger sisters and a small child of her own. No one ever discussed the woman's place in his father's house, nor was much said about the young daughter for whom Jim's father showed special affection. Jim understood that these were, in effect, his stepmother and stepsister. Here was Jim's home, a vast terrain which he soon knew and understood and took for granted. His father needed to spend some time with his old books, and kept adding to the library. And he needed to tell Jim about Wales, Europe, travel, their arrival in Canada . . . . All this Jim processed into stories, vivid and unfathomably important. But the new place itself was his, completely.

Jim tells one story. It was his third northern winter. He likes to tell it, he says, because no one believes it.

That year the snow came early and stayed late. In spring a

false thaw took place: the show melted, there was some rain, then it froze harder than ever. The whole surface of the earth was glazed with ice. Deer and moose and rabbits could not break through to their browse: they moved away or died. The Indians were dependent on supplies of smoked fish, or on the trader. This was the year Jim's father established his surest grip on the region's people: every trapper was in debt to him.

After the false thaw, Jim's father stayed at home. He neither hunted, nor checked his traps, nor went visiting the Indians. He spent whole days with his books. And he insisted that Jim also spent time in the library. One night they sat there at a table, crouched at an oil lamp. It was the coldest of nights: the air itself seemed to be frozen into stillness. Jim's father had moved the table near to the stove, well away from the chill that radiated from a window in the opposite wall. Behind them, on the floor between table and window, was a patterned rug that Jim's father had bought from Asian dealers in Victoria. He always referred to it as his civilization mat, and was proud of its lustrous, alien design.

Jim's father was reading aloud. The log walls, the stove's heat, the smell of woodsmoke and the man's unmodulating voice dulled Jim's thoughts. He may as well have been asleep; his father was lost to duty and nostalgia.

Then there was an explosion in the window behind them, and the sound of glass falling, and freezing air stabbing into the room. Jim's father lurched out of his chair; Jim remembers being unable to move, daring only to turn his head and stare.

Half through the window, impaled on a broken toothline of glass, sprawled a cougar, a mountain lion. The animal was panting, bleeding and clawing the inside wall under the window frame (the marks were there for years afterwards—the house's most fabulous feature). The cougar had sprung with all its strength, hurling itself into the room. The blow of unseen glass had stunned it into helplessness: its movements as it sprawled there, ripped open, were only half wild.

Jim's father reached for a kindling axe by the stove, walked to within striking distance, and smashed the blade into the animal's skull.

Cold air met the room's warmth and condensed: icy white

clouds rolled through the window. Jim later imagined he had seen a mixture of lion's soul and breath. His father stood prepared to strike the crushed skull again, and began to examine the body. Without turning to his son: 'Starving, gone mad, I reckon.' And with a chuckle: 'Almost made it to civilization.'

The cougar's rather mangy skin hung around the house for a long time, and Jim often dreamed of its death at the window. In these dreams the animal leaps, but passes through glass, and lands on the Asian rug; there it lies, stretched out and comfortable, a part of the exotic pattern. In waking dreams, the story became folklore: the starving animal is not weakened but maddened by hunger; the axe blow to its head comes after a battle between cougar and father who protects his lion's dinner of a son. The story was fed by some of Jim's father's opinions: in defiance of other local lore, he liked to insist that no animal need be feared—not even the killer whale and grizzly bear. So the killing of a mountain lion became part of the story. . . .

In some unexplained way Jim was expected to live up to the image of his father. This may be why the cougar at the window was a form of *rite de passage*, Jim's initiation. He was not supposed to follow his father's steps by way of any absurd derring-do, but by knowing how to look after himself. If he had to find a horse that had strayed up the valley, no one would suggest that he should take care, or be sure to have a companion on the trail. And he was never spared the tough tasks. As the fur trading post began to turn into a ranch, it was Jim who cut posts, cleared roots, and broke new horses. He herded stock, bringing reluctant groups of cattle along thirty or more miles of wagon trail. By the time he was sixteen, Jim spent nights rolled in a blanket alongside a fire, fearing only that straying stock would fall prey to wolves. He laughs at the notion he might have been in danger himself. When he was in his late teens, Jim also walked to the cluster of homesteads and posts that was the nucleus of a new town: sixty miles of trails to go to dance or visit—sometimes walking alone, sometimes with one or other of his step-mother's relatives.

As Jim grew older, fur trading ceased to bring great profits: prices tumbled and the paradoxical riches of the twenties and thirties were no longer to be had. For a while

Jim and his father continued to go each year to Victoria and Vancouver, but they no longer hauled immense loads back north with
them. The difficulties of these years were added to, even symbolized by, unexpected and furious disputes between Jim's mother
and father. They openly blamed one another for some undescribed,
almost unacknowledged but terrible loss. To each the other seemed
to have caused a barrenness, a failure of existence. And to each the
other represented the easy option: to Jim's father, his wife had
shirked the real task, while to her, he (and the son) had taken a
senseless and immoral flight into boyscoutland. To him, she had
broken the contract they had jointly made with adventure. To her,
the young teacher had hated then fled the landlord class only to set
up his own fiefdom. The man sneered at the woman's softness; the
woman despised the man's vainglory.

At first Jim had longed to tell his mother about his adventures.
As he unwound a rabbit from a snare or dragged a salmon onto the
bank, he had taken a special if sad pleasure in imagining telling the
story. And during the first summer visits, she had listened . . . .
Then the disputes grew, and the silences among them all began to be
insurmountable. In 1942, when Jim was seventeen, they made their
last trip to Victoria. Jim's father, who supposed his son would begin
to feel the need for escape, was afraid the young man would be
tempted to join the Canadian army. This was the reason he gave
much later for no longer leaving the Nass. In fact, Jim's father had
ceased to need these journeys: supplies were now easily moved, and
purchases made, by agents, shipping companies, and dealers. The
world was changing; the frontier was being opened wide. And Jim's
father's response was to allow the Nass Valley to close forever on his
life.

He survived the depression in fur prices, and turned towards
farming. The two men, father and son, worked a subsistence holding, supplementing their livelihoods by continuing to trade with
Indians. They bought some furs, but offered simple provisions for
money. They became shopkeeper-farmers. In mid-winter and
spring Jim's father went off for short periods to work his old trapline, and came home with his own furs. But these expeditions were
re-enactments of an old need to create distance between himself and
the world: as his economic life narrowed to a limited acreage, as
trapping territory gave way to hay fields, he found space in the bush

241

and the library. Jim was left to his own devices.

His father appeared to need the boy's company less and less. In August 1945, on the day they heard over a new radio that the war in the Pacific was over, Jim's father relaxed. His son would not be running to the army. A month later Jim announced that he had decided to become a fisherman, and moved the the coast.

Jim told me this story, or some of this story, for the first time in 1969. We met on the west shore of Vancouver Island. He lived then in a wooden A-frame house about half a mile from a jetty where his boat was moored. The house stood among others, in the shelter of high cedars and firs. Beyond this shelter, outside the harbour inlet, the open sea boiled onto mile upon mile of steep and rocky shoreline. He was a salmon fisherman, selling his catches to a cannery along the coast. He lived among fishermen. His neighbours were from the island, and nearly all Indians. Jim's life in the interior, son of a white trader, was strange to them, too. But Jim had the rare facility of showing, in his matter-of-fact accounts of life on the Nass, just who he was. He melted into reminiscences, and left no suspicions about himself. Everyone appeared to trust and admire him. During bitter strikes against cannery prices in the 1960s, Jim became the local organizer.

Jim was among fishermen, and with his own family. I imagined him as an epitome of sturdy health. Yet his father's literacy was with him: turns of phrase, points of entry into events, sudden and startling consideration of other worlds would now and then surface, the result of dark afternoons and the library table. Still, Jim had come to live at a great distance from his origins. His mother had visited him once, when his own first child was born. But she had hurried away. Any journey north of Victoria represented a broken promise to herself: she had vowed never to take another step in the direction of the Nass. Jim saw her often enough in her beloved Victoria, but there was no peace between them: her life was built around her other children. And Jim's father stayed in his valley, in his log house, near his trapline. Jim enjoyed occasional visits there—not so much for the silences he could share with the aging Welshman, but for the pleasure of walking favourite trails, fishing in favourite salmon pools, being at home with the people of his boy-

hood. But he never stayed long. He had established what he saw as
real life on the coast, in his small trolling boat, on the sea, and within
a vibrant but settled little community. His wife was from the coast;
her people lived near; their children belonged there. He had no wish
to oppose this with his father's dreams. At home, by the sea, the
interior was far away and, even to Jim, fantastic.

The day I left the village where Jim and his family now lived,
and stood trying to say some adequate and cheery good-bye, Jim
caught my arm and said, 'Know something? You'll be taking me to
the old Wales they came from. When there's the money.'

Twelve years later there was the money. In 1982, in spring, Jim
travelled to Europe to see, he said, his father's Wales. We went
together to find that the schoolhouse was now a smart country
home: the teacherage and schoolroom knocked into one residence.
No one was there: it was not a weekend. We walked along a path to
the side of the building, and on up the hill behind. Jim was by habit
a quick, decisive walker. But as we climbed to wider views of the
valley, he stopped again and again, turned and stared—as if hoping
at each slight shift in our elevation to find that something essential
to this visit, some trace of his father and mother, would be visible at
last. And then with an odd shrug and a grunt strode on.

We didn't talk much. We came to a stone-wall that wound
across the hill, dividing meadows from a clump of ash trees. The
wall was decayed, and we sat on a pile of its fallen stones. We looked
down on the old school and its little valley. I asked Jim what had
become of his parents. His mother, he told me, had died in 1971, in
Victoria. She had been ill for a while, and at the end he and his
family had all gone to stay with her. There had been no reconcilia-
tion. She refused to speak about her husband; and never asked to
see him. For his part, though told of her illness and then her death,
he stayed in the north. By then, said Jim, his father had severed
connections with almost every part of his life. He had become
marooned even in his forest community: the Indian homes had
emptied, the people moving (or being moved) to larger villages
where government services and schools had taken control of their
lives. His servant-interpreter had died; and Jim's step-family had
left to live in Prince Rupert. Occasional trappers had come and
gone. But old trader Murray remained on his island. The last time

Jim saw him was Christmas, 1975. The next February a visiting trapper found him dead in his library chair.

And what had happened to the house, trading post, ranch?

Jim said that the forest had regrown over much of it even before his father's death. Since then just about everything must have disappeared. I remember Jim smiled as he told me this, and explained the smile: the frontier couldn't reach him.

As we walked through the edge of the trees and along the rim of the valley, Jim spoke of his father with unusual harshness. He had been a tough dealer. He had used the wildness of his surroundings —wildness in the eye only of the immigrant, of course—to justify ruthlessness in all things. Yes, the books and his odd jokes and his gentle if sombre dealings with his son had made him seem eccentric and learned. But in the end he had profited and domineered whenever he could: survival of the fittest he would have called it. Here, in his old Wales, he had wanted to fight, or so they had claimed, an opposite kind of battle. That's the trouble with travel, said Jim, with emigrating. . . . His mother's voice, his own fisherman's voice, was loud. . . .

We looped round the fields to get back to the school. Jim had fallen silent and resumed his usual walk. I was lost in my own thoughts. Jim's visit had not been easy. He arrived a day after the English Armada had been launched on its way to the South Atlantic. I had been in the grip of furious preoccupations: the country's leaders at their most instinctively opportunistic and poisonous, and ugly, futile little war was being made inevitable. It was hard to talk of anything else. Jim endured my repetitive harangues, and wondered—out loud—why I did not return to Vancouver Island. I would find good work over there, could fish with him. He had long believed that summer trolling for spring salmon would be best further to the south: as far as Seattle, San Francisco, even: we could try it out. . . . What was there here?

We stood for a while outside the empty schoolhouse, trying to see through its windows, imagining Jim's father and mother, their impassioned romance, the old maps of Canada. I could lfeel the young teacher's resolve to fight, then to go. . . . I watched Jim's absorption in the old building and I thought, peer and imagine as he might, he did not have the anger to know why his father could have ever thought of staying, or why I could neither stay nor leave.

Gollancz Fiction

Sylvia Murphy
THE COMPLETE KNOWLEDGE OF SALLY FRY

'It's a joy to find a new original comic writer...
Tremendous fun' —
Susan Hill, *Good Housekeeping*   £7.95

M. John Harrison
THE ICE MONKEY

'Stylish, accomplished, evocative short
stories...most beautifully written' —
Angela Carter   £8.95

Ian Cochrane
THE SLIPSTREAM

'A serious comic novelist if ever there was one' —
Norman Shrapnel, *Guardian*   £7.95

Robert Silverberg
LORD OF DARKNESS

An imaginative tour-de-force set in
16th-century Africa.
'Silverberg's invention is prodigious' —
TLS on *Lord Valentine's Castle*   £9.95

Gollancz

NOTES FROM ABROAD

Notes from Italy
William Weaver

When I first came to Rome, as a student, in the autumn of 1947, it was a small city. Italy seemed small. The war had divided the country; its end had then shrunk it. And there was movement everywhere: tourists were still few, but the railroad stations were crammed with Italians ready to try their luck in a new place. Devastation was visible. One day, for instance, going to San Lorenzo station to collect a package, I saw the rubble from the 1943 air-raid that was described in Elsa Morante's *History* many years later; it had been only slightly disturbed, and plaster-dust swirled in the air. But you felt the excitement of freedom and renewal, and everyone I met seemed to be writing a book or directing a play or making a movie.

It was easy to meet people, especially if you were a wide-eyed American and spoke Italian. The literary world was particularly accessible, for all the intellectuals wanted to know about the States; grave professors, beetle-browed critics, questioned me closely, as if I were a personal friend of Hemingway, Louis Armstrong, Rita Hayworth, and Harry Truman. Before I had been in Rome a month, I had been invited to a party at the hospitable apartment of Morante and Alberto Moravia, just off the Piazza del Popolo; soon I was a regular guest, and there I met other writers: Carlo Levi (whose *Christ Stopped at Eboli* had been my introduction to contemporary Italian writing), and Vitaliano Brancati, and somewhat later, the young schoolteacher Pier Paolo Pasolini who had, at that time, published only a few poems, most of them in the (to me) exotic Friulan dialect.

At the other end of the Corso, in Via della Botteghe oscure there was Palazzo Caetani, where the American-born Princess Marguerite Caetani had just founded her eclectic, rich international magazine, named after her address. She also welcomed writers, famous and unknown—Italians like Giorgio Bassani (her managing editor) and the taciturn Ignazio Silone (and his beautfiul, ebullient Irish wife)—foreign residents like the Irish consul, Denis Devlin, and distinguished visitors: Ponge, T.S. Eliot, Spender, and Dylan Thomas, who had contributed the first version of *Under Milk Wood* to her magazine. The favourites were invited to Sunday luncheon parties at Ninfa, the Caetani villa south of the city, where the gardens—created largely by the Principessa and her daughter, Lelia—were a subtly-organized jungle of foliage and colour and perfumes. I soon became a favourite because I had volunteered as proof-reader for the magazine.

There was also the famous Bellonci salon, but by the time I got there the 'Sunday friends', as its regulars were called, had become so numerous that you could hardly move, much less talk or listen. Also on Sunday afternoons, there were more intimate tea-parties at the house of the critic, Emilio Cecchi. There, I was introduced to the legendary Sibilla Aleramo, though I had no idea who the handsome elderly lady was or that she had been an enthusiastic, scandalous practitioner of what an older generation would have called 'free love', leaving a trail of men across the Italian literary world of the early decades of the century.

Looking back, I remember all those parties, but I don't remember what we ate or drank (funny, because eating was a major concern in my straitened days); it can't have been much. Correction: I *do* remember a sumptuous risotto at a huge New Year's Eve buffet supper at Luchino Visconti's; but I remember it chiefly because, as I ate it, sitting on the staircase in the hall, on a lower step Anna Magnani was eating it, too. She was surrounded by admiring friends, and every now and then she would throw back the famous unruly black locks and laugh the famous throaty laugh. And every time she did it, my breath would stop for a second.

I lived in Rome (with a couple of extended absences in America) until the 1960s. I saw *Botteghe oscure* peter out and cease publication. Moravia and Morante separated, and the parties stopped. Some writers died; others moved away. And in the last years there, I found myself—through a gradual, unconscious process—spending more and more time with the Anglo-American colony. Jennie Cross, Iris Tree, John and Virginia Becker were giving the parties, entertaining the writers. But then they too died or, like me, moved away.

Now I live in the country, and when I leave my retreat and go to Rome, I ask my Italian writer-friends where the parties are; and they answer: there aren't any. I don't really miss the parties in themselves, but I miss the stimulation, the novelty. One young critic I spoke with recently suggested that this lack of a social-literary focus was what has driven several writers into Parliament (Alberto Arbasino, for instance, is a member for the Republicans; Natalia Ginzburg for the Communists). There's plenty of company in the Chamber and the Senate.

*P*arliament may have replaced the salons; and another possible replacement is The Institution of the Convegno, 'the Conference'. In Italy, these are not like academic meetings elsewhere—the MLA Conference, for instance, held in the States—days of dull professional talk in the ballroom of a Sheraton or a Hilton, an arid gathering of specialists. The Italian Convegno is almost always held at some seaside resort or spa or beauty-spot, Capri or Venice or Stresa; and it need not be on anything terribly specialized. Not long ago there was a Conference on Dreams in Venice (the novelist Luigi Malerba and the critic Guido Almansi were participants); and in Reggio Emilia—not exactly a resort, more a gastronomic capital—there was a well-attended and much-praised conference on pork.

More predictable Convegni are devoted to individual writers, usually with the idea of fostering a revival. There was an attempt (with Convegno on Capri) to elevate the late (by me unlamented) Curzio Malaparte to the rank of Great Neglected Writer; it seems to have failed. The Florentines then tried the operation with Giovanni Papini, and a fascinating photo exhibition, which I saw, suggested that the venture was more deserving of success. As a rule, the driving force behind such a conference is a critic who wants to write a study of the to-be-revived author or has provided a preface for some reprint. He can usually enlist financial support from the tourist bureau in the author's home town, and the invitations are sent out. If the swimming is good, or the food sounds promising, the invitations are likely to be accepted.

Besides the parties, I miss the magazines, *Botteghe oscure* in particular. Italy has magazines, of course (like *Alfabeto*, dominated by the protean Umberto Eco, or *La Gola*, for which intellectuals write, occasionally pompously, about food), but most Italian magazines these days are produced by a coterie, which also represents their readership. The general literary magazine probably no longer has a reason to exist here, because the better daily papers have greatly expanded their intellectual coverage and content. In *La Repubblica* you can regularly read stories by Calvino, Malerba, and others, as well as reportages by Arbasino, Attilio Bertolucci, and (generally boring, I fear) Gabriel García Márquez. The 'third page' (i.e. the cultural page) of the *Corriere della sera* still operates, despite the vicissitudes of the firm of Rizzoli, the owners. Years ago, on this page, Moravia published all of his *Racconti romani*; now he contributes annual accounts of his journeys in Africa, some of his most perceptive writing.

Italo Calvino, for some of his newspaper pieces, first in the *Corriere* and now in the *Repubblica*, has invented an alter ego, Signor Palomar, whose quirkish reflections—on a mis-mated pair of slippers, on giraffes at the zoo, on the shape of waves—are glints of the complex mind that invented, most recently, the multi-novel *If on a Winter's Night a Traveller*.... Since its best-selling success, Calvino has come in for some sniping. He and, with him, Umberto Eco, whose *The Name of the Rose*, has had an even more phenomenal international sale, have been accused of inventing a 'formula' to seduce the general public. This kind of critical backlash is a permanent feature of Italian literary life. As soon as an author achieves popularity (and, worse, popularity abroad), the smart thing is to deprecate him. When I arrived in Rome in the late forties, Moravia's fiction—*Two Adolescents, The Woman of Rome*—was just beginning to be acclaimed in the States. At the parties, several well-meaning littérateurs took me aside to inform me that Moravia wrote very bad Italian (the same thing had been said of Svevo, and no doubt, in another century, of Manzoni).

When accused of writing a best-seller by formula, Eco said, in an interview: 'Oh yes, if the big audience likes a lot of Latin, little sex, many philosophical discussions, then I have a great smell, because I understand the real wishes of the average audience.'

Little (indeed, no) sex and considerable philosophical discussion describe a current best-selling work of fiction, *Il Natale del 1833*, by the Neapolitan novelist and scholar Mario Pomilio. The book has won this year's Strega Prize. On Christmas day of 1833, Alessandro Manzoni's beloved first wife died, and in the course of the following year his favourite daughter followed her to the grave. With imaginative compassion, Pomilio reconstructs the moral and intellectual struggle of the devoutly Catholic Manzoni to come to terms with his bereavement. More than a novel, Pomilio's book is a complex speculation on suffering and loss; and the success of the book is as curious and unpredictable as that of Eco's novel (perhaps I should declare an interest at this point, as Eco's translator). Manzoni, however, seems to maintain a special popularity. A recent survey revealed that *I promessi sposi* is the second most-stolen book from Italian bookshops (the number one is the great Artusi cook-book, *L'arte di mangiar bene*).

Another highly successful volume this past year was Natalia Ginzburg's *La famiglia Manzoni*, a kind of documentary biography, a mosaic family history pieced together from letters and other documents. The picture that emerges is a touching mixture of the ordinary and the extraordinary, of the usual family quarrels and losses, all under the shadow of a genius. Ginzburg and Pomilio complement each other: the left-wing novelist's undisguised lack of sympathy for Manzoni's religiosity is balanced by the insight of the Catholic writer from Naples.

The past year has also been marked—scarred, I would almost say—by the Mussolini centenary. When I first lived in Italy, it was against the law to publish anything that might be considered 'apologia for Fascism'. The law was broken, but furtively. I remember shabby little publications, smudgily printed on cheap grey paper: reminiscences of die-hard Fascist generals, shoddy magazines with articles like 'I was the Duce's chauffeur'. For the hundredth anniversary of his birth, they are all back again. No doubt, the law is still on the statute books; but nobody bothers now. So the silly reminiscences appear in glossy weeklies, and respectable firms bring out pop biographies of Donna Rachele Mussolini.

There have also been a number of serious books on Mussolini, of course. The most successful, indeed a non-fiction best-seller, is the journalist Giorgio Bocca's essay, *Mussolini Social–fascista*. In Italy, the fashionable thing to say about best-sellers is 'Oh, I bought it, but I couldn't get through it.' I'm afraid that's the case with me and Bocca's essay. He has an interesting point—that Italian communism, socialism, and fascism came from the same social matrix, had similar goals and methods, and other common characteristics—but he makes the point early, then belabours it for another hundred pages or so. Needless to say, that theme has enraged the left-wing intellectuals, and the ensuing polemics have enlived an otherwise dull season.

From time to time I make a dutiful stab at reading the novels of the younger generation. Recently, I had a look at two by the thirty-year-old Andrea De Carlo, who is something of a protégé of Calvino. The better of the two novels, *Treno di panna* (*Whipped-cream Train*), is about a young Italian who goes to seek his fortune in a near-mythical America: Los Angeles, Hollywood. Again, I was reminded of a young aspiring writer of thirty or more years ago, for whom America was the obsessive myth. He was the first Italian, I believe, to wear blue jeans and the even more eccentric seersucker jacket. De Carlo's autobiographical protagonist has some of the same engaging enthusiasm. Perhaps things haven't changed as much as I think since the late 1940s. Perhaps if I conducted a thorough search for things past I might even find a literary party....

FREYA STARK
PATRICK LEIGH FERMOR
DERVLA MURPHY
JOHN KEAY

are among the authors who continue the long established tradition of the house of John Murray for travel literature. They follow such writers as Arthur Grimble, Axel Munthe, Edward Whymper and Robin Fedden. Recent publications also include guides to the West Coast of the USA and to the art museums and historic buildings of Russia — guides whose predecessors were the famous Murray Handbooks. Only one of the latter is still in print, and the Handbook to India, Pakistan, Nepal, Bangladesh and Sri Lanka is now in its 22nd Edition.

Included in our current list are:

Eight Feet in the Andes

The eight feet belonged to DERVLA MURPHY, her nine-year-old daughter Rachel and Juana, their staunch and beloved mule. In spite of daily (and nightly) hazards Dervla and Rachel revelled in the unpredictability of their journey and the challenging grandeur of their wild surroundings.
Illustrated £9.95

Eccentric Travellers

'JOHN KEAY does not merely deliver routine potted biographies of his chosen seven, rehashed from previously published full-length studies... he packs a remarkable amount of fascinating incidental material into each essay.' *Irish Times*   Illustrated £9.50

Trespassers on the Roof of the World
The Race for Lhasa
'A rich harvest of harrowing adventures which PETER HOPKIRK recounts in fascinating and well researched detail...(the) book makes an ideal introduction to the Tibetan background.' *Daily Telegraph*
Illustrated £9.75

For full details about all our current and forthcoming travel books, please write to John Murray, 50 Albemarle Street, London W1X 4BD

Notes on Contributors

Gabriel García Márquez's last contribution to *Granta* was 'The Solitude of Latin America', published in issue 9. He has recently returned to Columbia where he is founding a newspaper. **Todd McEwen's** first novel, *Fisher's Hornpipe,* was published last year by Harvill Press. 'Evensong', a short story, was published in *Granta* 8. **Russell Hoban's** last novel was *Pilgermann.* He is a regular contributor to *Granta.* **Jonathan Raban** is the author of a number of books, including *Arabia through the Looking-Glass, Soft City,* and *Old Glory.* 'Sea-Room' is from a work-in-progress that, when completed, will be published by Collins. He is currently living on the Isle of Man. **James Fenton** was born in Lincoln in 1949. From 1973 to 1975, he was a freelance correspondent in Southeast Asia, and he currently reviews theatre for the *Sunday Times.* Penguin has just published *The Memory of War and Children in Exile,* a collection of his poetry written since 1968. James Fenton and **Redmond O'Hanlon** were in Borneo from February to April of last year. Redmond O'Hanlon is on the staff of the *TLS*; later this year, the Salamander Press will publish his first book, *Joseph Conrad and Charles Darwin: Scientific Thought in Lord Jim.* **Colin Thubron** is the author of five books of travel, the most recent of which is *Among the Russians.* **Martha Gellhorn** is a novelist, short-story writer and journalist. Her most recent book, a collection of travel-pieces entitled *Travels with Myself and Another,* has just been published in paperback by Eland Books. **Bruce Chatwin** is the author of *In Patagonia, On the Black Hill,* and *The Viceroy of Ouidah.* He was in Benin in 1977. **Richard Holmes** is the author of *Shelley: the Pursuit*; he has also translated a selection of Gautier's supernatural short stories in a book entitled *Gautier: My Fantoms.* 'In Stevenson's Footsteps' is the first part of a work-in-progress that, when completed, will be published by Hodder and Stoughton. **Norman Lewis** is the author of a number of books including *A Dragon Apparent* and *Naples '44,* both of which have been recently re-issued by Eland Books. 'Village of Cats' is the beginning of a longer work on the time he spent in Spain. **Saul Bellow** won the Nobel Prize for Literature in 1976. He is completing a collection of stories to be published this spring. The beginning of **Patrick**

Marnham's journey into El Salvador is described in 'Border Country', published in *Granta* 9. He is the author of a number of books, including *Fantastic Invasion: Dispatches from Africa.* **Jan Morris** publishes two books this year: *Portrait of an Imaginary City* (Allen Lane) and *Journeys* (OUP), a collection of travel pieces that will also include 'Interstate 281'. **Paul Theroux's** most recent book is *The Kingdom by the Sea.* He lives in London and on Long Island in New York. **Hugh Brody** has lived extensively in the High Arctic, where he studied the Inuit. He is the author of a number of books including *Indians on Skid Row, Gola: Life and Last Days of an Island Community,* and *Maps and Dreams.* **William Weaver** has translated from Italian the work of Italo Calvino, Alberto Moravia, Umberto Eco, and many, many others. He lives outside Florence.

Photo credits: 'Portsmouth Harbour Inn Sign' by Georg Gerster (John Hillelson); 'Buddhist Monk' (J. Allan Cash); 'Fenton Afloat' by Redmond O'Hanlon; 'Fenton Sinking' by Redmond O'Hanlon; 'B–52 Round the Clock Alert' (Popper-foto); 'Black Women' by Marc Riboud (John Hillelson); 'Revolution in Africa' by Ian Berry (John Hillelson); 'Cafe, Paris' (J. Allan Cash); 'Trotsky' (Illustrated London News); 'Texas' by Georg Gerster (John Hillelson); 'USA Indian' by Georg Gerster (John Hillelson).

Maps by Reginald Piggott. Subway illustration by Nick Maland. Maps of the High Cevennes and the Verlay by Noel Rooke from Robert Louis Stevenson, *Travels with a Donkey,* Chatto & Windus (1909).

Note: Chatto & Windus publish Antonio Lobo Antunes, *South of Nowhere,* an account of the war in Angola, and, in March, will publish Manlio Argueta, *A Day of Life,* based on the war in El Salvador. Pluto Press have recently published Ariel Dorfman, *The Empire's Old Clothes: What the Lone Ranger, Babar, and other Innocent Heroes do to our Minds.* Collins publish Raymond Carver, *Cathedral,* a collection of stories. Parts from each of these books originally appeared in *Granta.*